th
sun

John Grisham is th
one work of non-
and a novel for young readers. He is on the Board
of Directors of the Innocence Project in New
York and is the Chairman of the Board of Directors
of the Mississippi Innocence Project at the
University of Mississippi School of Law. He lives
in Virginia and Mississippi.

john
grisham
the
summons

arrow books

Reissued in the United Kingdom by Arrow Books in 2011

19 20 18

First published in the United Kingdom in 2002 by Century
First published in paperback in 2002 by Arrow books

Arrow Books
The Random House Group Limited
20 Vauxhall Bridge Road, London, SW1V 2SA

www.randomhouse.co.uk

Addresses for companies within The Random House Group Limited can
be found at: www.randomhouse.co.uk/offices.htm

The Random House Group Limited Reg. No. 954009

A CIP catalogue record for this book
is available from the British Library

ISBN 9780099406136

The Random House Group Limited supports The Forest Stewardship Council
(FSC®), the leading international forest certification organisation. Our books
carrying the FSC label are printed on FSC® certified paper. FSC is the only
forest certification scheme endorsed by the leading environmental organisations,
including Greenpeace. Our paper procurement policy can be found at
www.randomhouse.co.uk/environment

Printed and bound by
CPI Group (UK) Ltd, Croydon, CR0 4YY

The Summons

Chapter 1

It came by mail, regular postage, the old-fashioned way since the Judge was almost eighty and distrusted modern devices. Forget e-mail and even faxes. He didn't use an answering machine and had never been fond of the telephone. He pecked out his letters with both index fingers, one feeble key at a time, hunched over his old Underwood manual on a rolltop desk under the portrait of Nathan Bedford Forrest. The Judge's grandfather had fought with Forrest at Shiloh and throughout the Deep South, and to him no figure in history was more revered. For thirty-two years, the Judge had quietly refused to hold court on July 13, Forrest's birthday.

It came with another letter, a magazine, and two invoices, and was routinely placed in the law school mailbox of Professor Ray Atlee. He recognized it immediately since such envelopes had been a part of his life for as long as he could remember. It was from his father, a man he too called the Judge.

Professor Atlee studied the envelope, uncertain whether he should open it right there or wait a moment. Good news or bad, he never knew with the Judge, though the old man was dying and good news had been rare. It was thin and appeared to contain only one sheet of paper; nothing unusual about that. The Judge was frugal with the written word, though he'd once been known for his windy lectures from the bench.

It was a business letter, that much was certain. The Judge was not one for small talk, hated gossip and idle chitchat, whether written or spoken. Ice tea with him on the porch would be a refighting of the Civil War, probably at Shiloh, where he would once again lay all blame for the Confederate defeat at the shiny, untouched boots of General Pierre G. T. Beauregard, a man he would hate even in heaven, if by chance they met there.

He'd be dead soon. Seventy-nine years old with cancer in his stomach. He was overweight, a diabetic, a heavy pipe smoker, had a bad heart that had survived three attacks, and a host of lesser ailments that had tormented him for twenty years and were now finally closing in for the kill. The pain was constant. During their last phone call three weeks earlier, a call initiated by Ray because the Judge thought long distance was a rip-off, the old man sounded weak and strained. They had talked for less than two minutes.

2

The return address was gold-embossed: Chancellor Reuben V. Atlee, 25th Chancery District, Ford County Courthouse, Clanton, Mississippi. Ray slid the envelope into the magazine and began walking. Judge Atlee no longer held the office of chancellor. The voters had retired him nine years earlier, a bitter defeat from which he would never recover. Thirty-two years of diligent service to his people, and they tossed him out in favor of a younger man with radio and television ads. The Judge had refused to campaign. He claimed he had too much work to do, and, more important, the people knew him well and if they wanted to reelect him then they would do so. His strategy had seemed arrogant to many. He carried Ford County but got shellacked in the other five.

It took three years to get him out of the courthouse. His office on the second floor had survived a fire and had missed two renovations. The Judge had not allowed them to touch it with paint or hammers. When the county supervisors finally convinced him that he had to leave or be evicted, he boxed up three decades' worth of useless files and notes and dusty old books and took them home and stacked them in his study. When the study was full, he lined them down the hallways into the dining room and even the foyer.

Ray nodded to a student who was seated in the hall. Outside his office, he spoke to a colleague. Inside, he locked the door behind him and placed the mail in the center of his desk. He took off his jacket, hung it on the back of the door, stepped over a stack of thick law books he'd been stepping over for half a year, and then to himself uttered his daily vow to organize the place.

The room was twelve by fifteen, with a small desk and a small sofa, both covered with enough work to make Ray seem like a very busy man. He was not. For the spring semester he was teaching one section of antitrust. And he was supposed to be writing a book, another drab, tedious volume on monopolies that would be read by no one but would add handsomely to his pedigree. He had tenure, but like all serious professors he was ruled by the 'publish or perish' dictum of academic life.

He sat at his desk and shoved papers out of the way.

The envelope was addressed to Professor N. Ray Atlee, University of Virginia School of Law, Charlottesville, Virginia. The *e*'s and *o*'s were smudged together. A new ribbon had been needed for a decade. The Judge didn't believe in zip codes either.

The N was for Nathan, after the general, but few people knew it. One of their uglier fights had been over the son's decision to drop Nathan altogether and plow through life simply as Ray.

The Judge's letters were always sent to the law school, never to his son's apartment in downtown Charlottesville. The Judge liked titles and important addresses, and he wanted folks in Clanton, even the postal workers, to know that his son was a professor of law. It was unnecessary. Ray had been teaching (and writing) for thirteen years, and those who mattered in Ford County knew it.

He opened the envelope and unfolded a single sheet of paper. It too was grandly embossed with the Judge's name and former title and address, again minus the zip code. The old man probably had an unlimited supply of the stationery.

It was addressed to both Ray and his younger brother, Forrest, the only two offspring of a bad marriage that had ended in 1969 with the death of their mother. As always, the message was brief:

> Please make arrangements to appear in my study on Sunday, May 7, at 5 P.M., to discuss the administration of my estate.
> Sincerely, Reuben V. Atlee.

The distinctive signature had shrunk and looked unsteady. For years it had been emblazoned across orders and decrees that had changed countless lives. Decrees of divorce, child custody, termination of parental rights, adoptions. Orders settling will contests, election contests, land disputes, annexation fights. The Judge's autograph had been authoritative and well known; now it was the vaguely familiar scrawl of a very sick old man.

Sick or not, though, Ray knew that he would be present in his father's study at the appointed time. He had just been summoned, and as irritating as it was, he had no doubt that he and his brother would drag themselves before His Honor for one more lecture. It was typical of the Judge to pick a day that was convenient for him without consulting anybody else.

It was the nature of the Judge, and perhaps most judges for that matter, to set dates for hearings and deadlines with little regard for the convenience of others. Such heavy-handedness was learned and even required when dealing with crowded dockets, reluctant litigants, busy lawyers, lazy lawyers. But the Judge had run his family in pretty much the same manner as he'd run his courtroom, and that was the principal reason Ray Atlee was teaching law in Virginia and not practicing it in Mississippi.

He read the summons again, then put it away, on top of the pile of current matters to deal with. He walked to the window and looked out at the courtyard where everything was in bloom. He wasn't angry or bitter, just frustrated that his father could once again dictate so much. But the old man was dying, he told himself. Give him a break. There wouldn't be many more trips home.

The Judge's estate was cloaked with mystery. The principal asset was the house – an antebellum hand-me-down from the same Atlee who'd fought with General Forrest. On a shady street in old Atlanta it would be worth over a million dollars, but not in Clanton. It sat in the middle of five neglected acres three blocks off the town square. The floors sagged, the roof leaked, paint had not touched the walls in Ray's lifetime. He and his brother could sell it for perhaps a hundred thousand dollars, but the buyer would need twice that to make it livable. Neither would ever live there; in fact, Forrest had not set foot in the house in many years.

The house was called Maple Run, as if it were some grand estate with a staff and a social calendar. The last worker had been Irene the maid. She'd died four years earlier and since then no one had vacuumed the floors or touched the furniture with polish. The Judge paid a local felon twenty dollars a week to cut the grass, and he did so with great reluctance. Eighty dollars a month was robbery, in his learned opinion.

When Ray was a child, his mother referred to their home as Maple Run. They never had dinners at their home, but rather at Maple Run. Their address was not the Atlees on Fourth Street, but instead it was Maple Run on Fourth Street. Few other folks in Clanton had names for their homes.

She died from an aneurysm and they laid her on a table in the front parlor. For two days the town stopped by and paraded across the front porch, through the foyer, through the parlor for last respects, then to the dining room for punch and cookies. Ray and Forrest hid in the attic and

7

cursed their father for tolerating such a spectacle. That was their mother lying down there, a pretty young woman now pale and stiff in an open coffin.

Forrest had always called it Maple Ruin. The red and yellow maples that once lined the street had died of some unknown disease. Their rotted stumps had never been cleared. Four huge oaks shaded the front lawn. They shed leaves by the ton, far too many for anyone to rake and gather. And at least twice a year the oaks would lose a branch that would fall and crash somewhere onto the house, where it might or might not get removed. The house stood there year after year, decade after decade, taking punches but never falling.

It was still a handsome house, a Georgian with columns, once a monument to those who'd built it, and now a sad reminder of a declining family. Ray wanted nothing to do with it. For him the house was filled with unpleasant memories and each trip back depressed him. He certainly couldn't afford the financial black hole of maintaining an estate that ought to be bulldozed. Forrest would burn it before he owned it.

The Judge, however, wanted Ray to take the house and keep it in the family. This had been discussed in vague terms over the past few years. Ray had never mustered the courage to ask, 'What family?' He had no children. There was an ex-wife but no prospect of a current one.

Same for Forrest, except he had a dizzying collection of ex-girlfriends and a current housing arrangement with Ellie, a three-hundred-pound painter and potter twelve years his senior.

It was a biological miracle that Forrest had produced no children, but so far none had been discovered.

The Atlee bloodline was thinning to a sad and inevitable halt, which didn't bother Ray at all. He was living life for himself, not for the benefit of his father or the family's glorious past. He returned to Clanton only for funerals.

The Judge's other assets had never been discussed. The Atlee family had once been wealthy, but long before Ray. There had been land and cotton and slaves and railroads and banks and politics, the usual Confederate portfolio of holdings that, in terms of cash, meant nothing in the late twentieth century. It did, however, bestow upon the Atlees the status of 'family money.'

By the time Ray was ten he knew his family had money. His father was a judge and his home had a name, and in rural Mississippi this meant he was indeed a rich kid. Before she died his mother did her best to convince Ray and Forrest that they were better than most folks. They lived in a mansion. They were Presbyterians. They vacationed in Florida, every third year. They occasionally went to the Peabody Hotel in Memphis for dinner. Their clothes were nicer.

Then Ray was accepted at Stanford. His

bubble burst when the Judge said bluntly, 'I can't afford it.'

'What do you mean?' Ray had asked.

'I mean what I said. I can't afford Stanford.'

'But I don't understand.'

'Then I'll make it plain. Go to any college you want. But if you go to Sewanee, then I'll pay for it.'

Ray went to Sewanee, without the baggage of family money, and was supported by his father, who provided an allowance that barely covered tuition, books, board, and fraternity dues. Law school was at Tulane, where Ray survived by waiting tables at an oyster bar in the French Quarter.

For thirty-two years, the Judge had earned a chancellor's salary, which was among the lowest in the country. While at Tulane Ray read a report on judicial compensation, and he was saddened to learn that Mississippi judges were earning fifty-two thousand dollars a year when the national average was ninety-five thousand.

The Judge lived alone, spent little on the house, had no bad habits except for his pipe, and he preferred cheap tobacco. He drove an old Lincoln, ate bad food but lots of it, and wore the same black suits he'd been wearing since the fifties. His vice was charity. He saved his money, then he gave it away.

No one knew how much money the Judge donated annually. An automatic ten percent went to the Presbyterian Church. Sewanee got two thousand dollars a year, same for the Sons of Confederate Veterans. Those three gifts were carved in granite. The rest were not.

Judge Atlee gave to anyone who would ask. A crippled child in need of crutches. An all-star team traveling to a state tournament. A drive by the Rotary Club to vaccinate babies in the Congo. A shelter for stray dogs and cats in Ford County. A new roof for Clanton's only museum.

The list was endless, and all that was necessary to receive a check was to write a short letter and ask for it. Judge Atlee always sent money and had been doing so ever since Ray and Forrest left home.

Ray could see him now, lost in the clutter and dust of his rolltop, pecking out short notes on his Underwood and sticking them in his chancellor's envelopes with scarcely readable checks drawn on the First National Bank of Clanton – fifty dollars here, a hundred dollars there, a little for everyone until it was all gone.

The estate would not be complicated because there would be so little to inventory. The ancient law books, threadbare furniture, painful family photos and mementos, long forgotten files and papers – all a bunch of rubbish that would make an impressive bonfire. He and Forrest would sell the house for whatever it might bring and be quite happy to salvage anything from the last of the Atlee family money.

He should call Forrest, but those calls were

always easy to put off. Forrest was a different set of issues and problems, much more complicated than a dying, reclusive old father hell-bent on giving away his money. Forrest was a living, walking disaster, a boy of thirty-six whose mind had been deadened by every legal and illegal substance known to American culture.

What a family, Ray mumbled to himself.

He posted a cancellation for his eleven o'clock class, and went for therapy.

Chapter 2

Spring in the Piedmont, calm clear skies, the foothills growing greener by the day, the Shenandoah Valley changing as the farmers crossed and recrossed their perfect rows. Rain was forecast for tomorrow, though no forecast could be trusted in central Virginia.

With almost three hundred hours under his belt, Ray began each day with an eye on the sky as he jogged five miles. The running he could do come rain or shine, the flying he could not. He had promised himself (and his insurance company) that he would not fly at night and would not venture into clouds. Ninety-five percent of all small plane crashes happened either in weather or in darkness, and after nearly three years of flying Ray was still determined to be a coward. 'There are old pilots and bold pilots,' the adage went, 'but no old bold pilots.' He believed it, and with conviction.

Besides, central Virginia was too beautiful to buzz over in clouds. He waited for perfect weather – no wind to push him around and make landings complicated, no haze to dim the horizon and get him lost, no threat of storms or moisture. Clear skies during his jog usually determined the rest of his day. He could move lunch up or back, cancel a class, postpone his research to a rainy day, or a rainy week for that matter. The right forecast, and Ray was off to the airport.

It was north of town, a fifteen-minute drive from the law school. At Docker's Flight School he was given the normal rude welcome by Dick Docker, Charlie Yates, and Fog Newton, the three retired Marine pilots who owned the place and had trained most of the private aviators in the area. They held court each day in the Cockpit, a row of old theater chairs in the front office of the flight school, and from there they drank coffee by the gallon and told flying tales and lies that grew by the hour. Each customer and student got the same load of verbal abuse, like it or not, take it or leave it, they didn't care. They were drawing nice pensions.

The sight of Ray prompted the latest round of lawyer jokes, none of which were particularly funny, all of which drew howls at the punch lines.

'No wonder you don't have any students,' Ray said as he did the paperwork.

'Where you going?' demanded Docker.

'Just punching a few holes in the sky.'

'We'll alert air traffic control.'

'You're much too busy for that.'

Ten minutes of insults and rental forms, and Ray was free to go. For eighty bucks an hour he could rent a Cessna that would take him a mile above the earth, away from people, phones, traffic, students, research, and, on this day, even farther from his dying father, his crazy brother, and the inevitable mess facing him back home.

There were tie-downs for thirty light aircraft at the general aviation ramp. Most were small Cessnas with high wings and fixed landing gears, still the safest airplanes ever built. But there were some fancier rigs. Next to his rented Cessna was a Beech Bonanza, a single-engine, two-hundred-horsepower beauty that Ray could handle in a month with a little training. It flew almost seventy knots faster than the Cessna, with enough gadgets and avionics to make any pilot drool. Even worse, the Bonanza was for sale – $450,000 – off the charts, of course, but not that far off. The owner built shopping centers and wanted a King Air, according to the latest analysis from the Cockpit.

Ray stepped away from the Bonanza and concentrated on the little Cessna sitting next to it. Like all new pilots, he carefully inspected his plane with a checklist. Fog Newton, his instructor, had begun each lesson with a gruesome tale of fire and death caused by pilots too hurried or lazy to use checklists.

When he was certain all outside parts and

surfaces were perfect, he opened the door and strapped himself inside. The engine started smoothly, the radios sparked to life. He finished a pre-takeoff list and called the tower. A commuter flight was ahead of him, and ten minutes after he locked his doors he was cleared for takeoff. He lifted off smoothly and turned west, toward the Shenandoah Valley.

At four thousand feet, he crossed Afton Mountain, not far below him. A few seconds of mountain turbulence bounced the Cessna, but it was nothing out of the ordinary. When he was past the foothills and over the farmlands, the air became still and quiet. Visibility was officially twenty miles, though at this altitude he could see much farther. No ceiling, not a cloud anywhere. At five thousand feet, the peaks of West Virginia rose slowly on the horizon. Ray completed an in-flight checklist, leaned his fuel mixture for normal cruise, and relaxed for the first time since taxiing into position for takeoff.

Radio chatter disappeared, and it wouldn't pick up again until he switched to the Roanoke tower, forty miles to the south. He decided to avoid Roanoke and stay in uncontrolled airspace.

Ray knew from personal experience that psychiatrists worked for two hundred dollars an hour in the Charlottesville area. Flying was a bargain, and much more effective, though it was a very fine shrink who'd suggested he pick up a new hobby, and quickly. He was seeing the fellow because he had to see someone. Exactly a month after the former Mrs. Atlee filed for divorce, quit her job, and walked out of their townhouse with only her clothes and jewelry, all done with ruthless efficiency in less than six hours, Ray left the psychiatrist for the last time, drove to the airport, stumbled into the Cockpit, and took his first insult from either Dick Docker or Fog Newton, he couldn't remember which.

The insult felt good, someone cared. More followed, and Ray, wounded and confused as he was, had found a home. For three years now he had crossed the clear, solitary skies of the Blue Ridge Mountains and the Shenandoah Valley, soothing his anger, shedding a few tears, hashing out his troubled life to an empty seat beside him. She's gone, the empty seat kept saying.

Some women leave and come back eventually. Others leave and endure a painful reconsideration. Still others leave with such boldness they never look back. Vicki's departure from his life was so well planned and her execution of it was so cold-blooded that Ray's lawyer's first comment was, 'Give it up, pal.'

She'd found a better deal, like an athlete swapping teams at the trading deadline. Here's the new uniform, smile for the cameras, forget the old arena. While Ray was at work one fine morning, she left in a limousine. Behind it was a van with her things. Twenty minutes later, she walked into her new place, a mansion on a horse farm east of town where Lew the Liquidator was waiting with open arms and a prenuptial agreement. Lew was a corporate vulture whose raids had netted him a half a billion or so, according to Ray's research, and at the age of sixty-four he'd cashed in his chips, left Wall Street, and for some reason picked Charlottesville as his new nest.

Somewhere along the way he'd bumped into Vicki, offered her a deal, gotten her pregnant with the children Ray was supposed to father, and now with a trophy wife and another family he wanted to be taken seriously as the new Big Fish.

Enough of this, Ray said aloud. He talked loudly at five thousand feet, and no one talked back.

He was assuming, and hoping, that Forrest was clean and sober, though such assumptions were usually wrong and such hopes were often misguided. After twenty years of rehab and relapse, it was doubtful if his brother would ever overcome his addictions. And Ray was certain that Forrest would be broke, a condition that went hand in hand with his habits. And being broke, he'd be looking for money, as in his father's estate.

What money the Judge had not given away to charities and sick children, he had poured down the black hole of Forrest's detoxification. So much money had been wasted there, along with so many years, that the Judge, as only he could do, had basically excommunicated Forrest from their father-son relationship. For thirty-two years he had terminated marriages, taken children away from parents, given children to foster homes, sent mentally ill people away forever, ordered delinquent fathers to jail – all manner of drastic and far-reaching decrees that were accomplished merely by signing his name. When he first went on the bench, his authority had been granted by the State of Mississippi, but late in his career he took his orders only from God.

If anyone could expel a son, it was Chancellor Reuben V. Atlee.

Forrest pretended to be unbothered by his banishment. He fancied himself as a free spirit and claimed he had not set foot inside the house at Maple Run in nine years. He had visited the Judge once in the hospital, after a heart attack when the doctors rounded up the family. Surprisingly, he'd been sober then. 'Fifty-two days, Bro,' he'd whispered proudly to Ray as they huddled in the ICU corridor. He was a walking scoreboard when rehab was working.

If the Judge had plans to include Forrest in his estate, no one would have been more surprised than Forrest. But with the chance that money or assets were about to change hands, Forrest would be there looking for crumbs and leftovers.

Over the New River Gorge near Beckley, West Virginia, Ray turned around and headed back. Though flying cost less than professional therapy, it wasn't cheap. The meter was ticking.

If he won the lottery, he would buy the Bonanza and fly everywhere. He was due a sabbatical in a couple of years, a respite from the rigors of academic life. He'd be expected to finish his eight-hundred-page brick on monopolies, and there was an even chance that that might happen. His dream, though, was to lease a Bonanza and disappear into the skies.

Twelve miles west of the airport, he called the tower and was directed to enter the traffic pattern. The wind was light and variable, the landing would be a cinch. On final approach, with the runway a mile away and fifteen hundred feet down, and Ray and his little Cessna gliding at a perfect descent, another pilot came on the radio. He checked in with the controller as 'Challenger-two-four-four-delta-mike,' and he was fifteen miles to the north. The tower cleared him to land, number two behind Cessna traffic.

Ray pushed aside thoughts of the other aircraft long enough to make a textbook landing, then turned off the runway and began taxiing to the ramp.

A Challenger is a Canadian-built private jet that seats eight to fifteen, depending on the configuration. It will fly from New York to Paris, nonstop, in splendid style, with its own flight attendant serving drinks and meals. A new one sells for somewhere around twenty-five million dollars, depending on the endless list of options.

The 244DM was owned by Lew the Liquidator, who'd pinched it out of one of the many hapless companies he'd raided and fleeced. Ray watched it land behind him, and for a second he hoped it would crash and burn right there on the runway, so he could enjoy the show. It did not, and as it sped along the taxiway toward the private terminal, Ray was suddenly in a tight spot.

He'd seen Vicki twice in the years since their divorce, and he certainly didn't want to see her now, not with him in a twenty-year-old Cessna while she bounded down the stairway of her gold-plated jet. Maybe she wasn't on board. Maybe it was just Lew Rodowski returning from yet another raid.

Ray cut the fuel mixture, the engine died, and as the Challenger moved closer to him he began to sink as low as possible in his captain's seat.

By the time it rolled to a stop, less than a hundred feet from where Ray was hiding, a shiny black Suburban had wheeled out onto the ramp, a little too fast, lights on, as if royalty had arrived in Charlottesville. Two young men in matching green shirts and khaki shorts jumped out, ready to receive the Liquidator and whoever else might be on board. The Challenger's door opened, the steps came down, and Ray, peeking above his instrument deck with a complete view, watched with fascination as one of the pilots came down first, carrying two large shopping bags.

Then Vicki, with the twins. They were two years old now, Simmons and Ripley, poor children given genderless last names as first names because their mother was an idiot and their father had already sired nine others before them and probably didn't care what they were called. They were boys, Ray knew that much for sure because he'd watched the vitals in the local paper – births, deaths, burglaries, etc. They were born at Martha Jefferson Hospital seven weeks and three days after the Atlees' no-fault divorce became final, and seven weeks and two days after a very pregnant Vicki married Lew Rodowski, his fourth trip down the aisle, or whatever they used that day at the horse farm.

Clutching the boys' hands, Vicki carefully descended the steps. A half a billion dollars was looking good on her – tight designer jeans on her long legs, legs that had become noticeably thinner since she had joined the jet set. In fact, Vicki appeared to be superbly starved – bone-thin arms, small flat ass, gaunt cheeks. He couldn't see her eyes because they were well hidden behind black wrap-arounds, the latest style from either Hollywood or Paris, take your pick.

The Liquidator had not been starving. He waited impatiently behind his current wife and current litter. He claimed he ran marathons, but then so little of what he said in print turned out to be true. He was stocky, with a thick belly. Half his hair was gone and the other half was gray with age. She was forty-one and could pass for thirty. He was sixty-four and looked seventy, or at least Ray thought so, with great satisfaction.

They finally made it into the Suburban while the two pilots and two drivers loaded and reloaded luggage and large bags from Saks and Bergdorf. Just a quick shopping jaunt up to Manhattan, forty-five minutes away on your Challenger.

The Suburban sped off, the show was over, and Ray sat up in the Cessna.

If he hadn't hated her so much, he would have sat there a long time reliving their marriage.

There had been no warnings, no fights, no change in temperature. She'd simply stumbled upon a better deal.

He opened the door so he could breathe and realized his collar was wet with sweat. He wiped his eyebrows and got out of the plane.

For the first time in memory, he wished he'd stayed away from the airport.

Chapter 3

The law school was next to the business school, and both were at the northern edge of a campus that had expanded greatly from the quaint academic village Thomas Jefferson designed and built.

To a university that so revered the architecture of its founder, the law school was just another modern campus building, square and flat, brick and glass, as bland and unimaginative as many others built in the seventies. But recent money had renovated and landscaped things nicely. It was ranked in the Top Ten, as everybody who worked and studied there knew so well. A few of the Ivys were ranked above it, but no other public school. It attracted a thousand top students and a very bright faculty.

Ray had been content teaching securities law at Northeastern in Boston. Some of his writings caught the attention of a search committee, one thing led to another, and the chance to move South to a better school became attractive. Vicki was from Florida, and though she thrived in the city life of Boston, she could never adjust to the winters. They quickly adapted to the slower pace of Charlottesville. He was awarded tenure, she earned a doctorate in romance languages. They were discussing children when the Liquidator wormed his way into the picture.

Another man gets your wife pregnant, then takes her, and you'd like to ask him some questions. And perhaps have a few for her. In the days right after her exit he couldn't sleep for all the questions, but as time passed he realized he would never confront her. The questions faded, but seeing her at the airport brought them back. Ray was cross-examining her again as he parked in the law school lot and returned to his office.

He kept office hours late in the afternoon, no appointment was necessary. His door was open and any student was welcome. It was early May, though, and the days were warm. Student visits had become rare. He reread the directive from his father, and again became irked at the usual heavy-handedness.

At five o'clock he locked his office, left the law school, and walked down the street to an intramural sports complex where the third-year students were playing the faculty in the second of a three-game softball series. The professors had lost the first game in a slaughter. Games two and three were not really necessary to determine the better team.

Smelling blood, first- and second-year students filled the small bleachers and hung on the fence along the first-base line, where the faculty team was huddled for a useless pregame pep talk. Out in left field some first-years of dubious reputation were bunched around two large coolers, the beer already flowing.

There's no better place to be in the springtime than on a college campus, Ray thought to himself as he approached the field and looked for a pleasant spot to watch the game. Girls in shorts, a cooler always close by, festive moods, impromptu parties, summer approaching. He was forty-three years old, single, and he wanted to be a student again. Teaching keeps you young, they all said, perhaps energetic and mentally sharp, but what Ray wanted was to sit on a cooler out there with the hell-raisers and hit on the girls.

A small group of his colleagues loitered behind the backstop, smiling gamely as the faculty took the field with a most unimpressive lineup. Several were limping. Half wore some manner of knee brace. He spotted Carl Mirk, an associate dean and his closest friend, leaning on a fence, tie undone, jacket slung over his shoulder.

'Sad-looking crew out there,' Ray said.

'Wait till you see them play,' Mirk said. Carl was from a small town in Ohio where his father was a local judge, a local saint, everybody's grandfather. Carl, too, had fled and vowed never to return.

'I missed the first game,' Ray said.

'It was a hoot. Seventeen to nothing after two innings.'

The leadoff hitter for the students ripped the first pitch into the left-field gap, a routine double, but by the time the left fielder and center fielder hobbled over, corralled the ball, kicked it a couple of times, fought over it, then flung it toward the infield, the runner walked home and the shutout was blown. The rowdies in left field were hysterical. The students in the bleachers yelled for more errors.

'It'll get worse,' Mirk said.

Indeed it did. After a few more fielding disasters, Ray had seen enough. 'I'll be out of town early next week,' he said between batters. 'I've been called home.'

'I can tell you're excited,' Mirk said. 'Another funeral?'

'Not yet. My father is convening a family summit to discuss his estate.'

'I'm sorry.'

'Don't be. There's not much to discuss, nothing to fight over, so it'll probably be ugly.'

'Your brother?'

'I don't know who'll cause more trouble, brother or father.'

'I'll be thinking of you.'

'Thanks. I'll notify my students and give them assignments. Everything should be covered.'

'Leaving when?'

'Saturday, should be back Tuesday or Wednesday, but who knows.'

'We'll be here,' Mirk said. 'And hopefully this series will be over.'

A soft ground ball rolled untouched between the legs of the pitcher.

'I think it's over now,' Ray said.

Nothing soured Ray's mood like thoughts of going home. He hadn't been there in over a year, and if he never went back it would still be too soon.

He bought a burrito from a Mexican takeout and ate at a sidewalk café near the ice rink where the usual gang of black-haired Goths gathered and spooked the normal folks. The old Main Street was a pedestrian mall – a very nice one with cafés and antique stores and book dealers – and if the weather was pleasant, as it usually was, the restaurants spread outdoors for long evening meals.

When he'd suddenly become single again, Ray unloaded the quaint townhouse and moved downtown, where most of the old buildings had been renovated for more urban-style housing. His six-room apartment was above a Persian rug dealer. It had a small balcony over the mall, and at least once a month Ray had his students over for wine and lasagne.

It was almost dark when he unlocked the door on the sidewalk and trudged up the noisy steps to his place. He was very much alone – no mate, no dog, no cat, no goldfish. In the past few years he'd met two women he'd found attractive and had dated neither. He was much too frightened for romance. A saucy third-year student named Kaley was making advances, but his defences were in place. His sex drive was so dormant he had considered counseling, or perhaps wonder drugs. He flipped on lights and checked the phone.

Forrest had called, a rare event indeed, but not completely unexpected. Typical of Forrest, he had simply checked in, without leaving a number. Ray fixed tea with no caffeine and put on some jazz, trying to stall as he prepped himself for the call. Odd that a phone chat with his only sibling should take so much effort, but chatting with Forrest was always depressing. They had no wives, no children, nothing in common but a name and a father.

Ray punched in the number to Ellie's house in Memphis. It rang for a long time before she answered. 'Hello, Ellie, this is Ray Atlee,' he said pleasantly.

'Oh,' she grunted, as if he'd called eight times already. 'He's not here.'

Doing swell, Ellie, and you? Fine, thanks for asking. Great to hear your voice. How's the weather down there?

'I'm returning his call,' Ray said.

'Like I said, he's not here.'

'I heard you. Is there a different number?'

29

'For what?'

'For Forrest. Is this still the best number to reach him?'

'I guess. He stays here most of the time.'

'Please tell him I called.'

They met in detox, she for booze, Forrest for an entire menu of banned substances. At the time she weighed ninety-eight pounds and claimed she'd lived on nothing but vodka for most of her adult life. She kicked it, walked away clean, tripled her body weight, and somehow got Forrest in the deal too. More mother than girlfriend, she now had him a room in the basement of her ancestral home, an eerie old Victorian in midtown Memphis.

Ray was still holding the phone when it rang. 'Hey, Bro,' Forrest called out. 'You rang?'

'Returning yours. How's it going?'

'Well, I was doing fairly well until I got a letter from the old man. You get one too?'

'It arrived today.'

'He thinks he's still a judge and we're a couple of delinquent fathers, don't you think?'

'He'll always be the Judge, Forrest. Have you talked to him?'

A snort, then a pause. 'I haven't talked to him on the phone in two years, and I haven't set foot in the house in more years than I can remember. And I'm not sure I'll be there Sunday.'

'You'll be there.'

'Have you talked to him?'

'Three weeks ago. I called, he didn't. He

sounded very sick, Forrest, I don't think he'll be around much longer. I think you should seriously consider –'

'Don't start, Ray. I'm not listening to a lecture.'

There was a gap, a heavy stillness in which both of them took a breath. Being an addict from a prominent family, Forrest had been lectured to and preached at and burdened with unsolicited advice for as long as he could remember.

'Sorry,' Ray said. 'I'll be there. What about you?'

'I suppose so.'

'Are you clean?' It was such a personal question, but one that was as routine as How's the weather? With Forrest the answer was always straight and true.

'A hundred and thirty-nine days, Bro.'

'That's great.'

It was, and it wasn't. Every sober day was a relief, but to still be counting after twenty years was disheartening.

'And I'm working too,' he said proudly.

'Wonderful. What kind of work?'

'I'm running cases for some local ambulance chasers, a bunch of sleazy bastards who advertise on cable and hang around hospitals. I sign 'em up and get a cut.'

It was difficult to appreciate such a seedy job, but with Forrest any employment was good news. He'd been a bail bondsman, process

31

server, collection agent, security guard, investigator, and at one time or another had tried virtually every job at the lesser levels of the legal profession.

'Not bad,' Ray said.

Forrest started a tale, this one involving a shoving match in a hospital emergency room, and Ray began to drift. His brother had also worked as a bouncer in a strip bar, a calling that was short-lived when he was beaten up twice in one night. He'd spent one full year touring Mexico on a new Harley-Davidson; the trip's funding had never been clear. He had tried leg-breaking for a Memphis loan shark, but again proved deficient when it came to violence.

Honest employment had never appealed to Forrest, though, in all fairness, interviewers were generally turned off by his criminal record. Two felonies, drug-related, both before he turned twenty but permanent blotches nonetheless.

'Are you gonna talk to the old man?' he was asking.

'No, I'll see him Sunday,' Ray answered.

'What time will you get to Clanton?'

'I don't know. Sometime around five, I guess. You?'

'God said five o'clock, didn't he?'

'Yes, he did.'

'Then I'll be there sometime after five. See you, Bro.'

Ray circled the phone for the next hour, deciding yes, he would call his father and just say hello, then deciding no, that anything to be said now could be said later, and in person. The Judge detested phones, especially those that rang at night and disrupted his solitude. More often than not he would simply refuse to answer. And if he picked up he was usually so rude and gruff that the caller was sorry for the effort.

He would be wearing black trousers and a white shirt, one with tiny cinder holes from the pipe ashes, and the shirt would be heavily starched because the Judge had always worn them that way. For him a white cotton dress shirt lasted a decade, regardless of the number of stains and cinder holes, and it got laundered and starched every week at Mabe's Cleaners on the square. His tie would be as old as his shirt and the design would be some drab print with little color. Navy blue suspenders, always.

And he would be busy at his desk in his study, under the portrait of General Forrest, not sitting on the porch waiting for his sons to come home. He would want them to think he had work to do, even on a Sunday afternoon, and that their arrivals were not that important.

Chapter 4

The drive to Clanton took fifteen hours, more or less, if you went with the truckers on the busy four-lanes and fought the bottlenecks around the cities, and it could be done in one day if you were in a hurry. Ray was not.

He packed a few things in the trunk of his Audi TT roadster, a two-seat convertible he'd owned for less than a week, and said farewell to no one because no one really cared when he came or went, and left Charlottesville. He would not exceed the speed limits and he would not drive on a four-lane, if he could possibly avoid it. That was his challenge – a trip without sprawl. On the leather seat next to him he had maps, a thermos of strong coffee, three Cuban cigars, and a bottle of water.

A few minutes west of town he turned left on the Blue Ridge Parkway and began snaking his way south on the tops of the foothills. The TT was a 2000 model, just a year or two off the

drawing board. Ray had read Audi's announce-
ment of a brand-new sports car about eighteen
months earlier, and he'd rushed to order the first
one in town. He had yet to see another one,
though the dealer assured him they would
become popular.

At an overlook, he put the top down, lit a
Cuban, and sipped coffee, then took off again at
the maximum speed of forty-five. Even at that
pace Clanton was looming

Four hours later, in search of gas, Ray found
himself sitting at a stoplight on Main Street in a
small town in North Carolina. Three lawyers
walked in front of him, all talking at once, all
carrying old briefcases that were scuffed and
worn almost as badly as their shoes. He looked
to his left and noticed a courthouse. He looked
to his right and watched as they disappeared
into a diner. He was suddenly hungry, both for
food and for sounds of people.

They were in a booth near the front window,
still talking as they stirred their coffee. Ray sat at
a table not too far away and ordered a club
sandwich from an elderly waitress who'd been
serving them for decades. One glass of ice tea,
one sandwich, and she wrote it all down in great
detail. Chef's probably older, he thought.

The lawyers had been in court all morning
haggling over a piece of land up in the mountains. The land was sold, a lawsuit followed,
etc., etc., and now they were having the trial.
They had called witnesses, quoted precedents to

the judge, disputed everything the others had said, and in general had gotten themselves heated up to the point of needing a break.

And this is what my father wanted me to do, Ray almost said aloud. He was hiding behind the local paper, pretending to read but listening to the lawyers.

Judge Reuben Atlee's dream had been for his sons to finish law school and return to Clanton. He would retire from the bench, and together they would open an office on the square. There, they would follow an honorable calling and he would teach them how to be lawyers – gentleman lawyers, country lawyers.

Broke lawyers was the way Ray had figured things. Like all small towns in the South, Clanton was brimming with lawyers. They were packed in the office buildings opposite the courthouse square. They ran the politics and banks and civic clubs and school boards, even the churches and Little Leagues. Where, exactly, around the square was he supposed to fit in?

During summer breaks from college and law school, Ray had clerked for his father. For no salary, of course. He knew all the lawyers in Clanton. As a whole, they were not bad people. There were just too many of them.

Forrest's turn for the worse came early in life and put even more pressure on Ray to follow the old man into a life of genteel poverty. The pressure was resisted, though, and by the time

Ray had finished one year of law school he had promised himself he would not remain in Clanton. It took another year to find the courage to tell his father, who went eight months without speaking to him. When Ray graduated from law school, Forrest was in prison. Judge Atlee arrived late for the commencement, sat in the back row, left early, and said nothing to Ray. It took the first heart attack to reunite them.

But money wasn't the primary reason Ray fled Clanton. Atlee & Atlee never got off the ground because the junior partner wanted to escape the shadow of the senior.

Judge Atlee was a huge man in a small town.

Ray found gas at the edge of town, and was soon back in the hills, on the parkway, driving forty-five miles an hour. Sometimes forty. He stopped at the overlooks and admired the scenery. He avoided the cities and studied his maps. All roads led, sooner or later, to Mississippi.

Near the North Carolina state line, he found an old motel that advertised air conditioning, cable TV, and clean rooms for $29.99, though the sign was crooked and rusted around the edges. Inflation had arrived with the cable because the room was now $40. Next door was an all-night café where Ray choked down dumplings, the nightly special. After dinner he sat on a bench in front of the motel, smoked another cigar, and watched the occasional car go by.

Across the road and down a hundred yards

was an abandoned drive-in movie theater. The marquee had fallen and was covered with vines and weeds. The big screen and the fences around the perimeter had been crumbling for many years.

Clanton had once had such a drive-in, just off the main highway entering town. It was owned by a chain from up North and provided the locals with the typical lineup of beach romps, horror flicks, kung-fu action, movies that attracted the younger set and gave the preachers something to whine about. In 1970, the powers up North decided to pollute the South once again by sending down dirty movies.

Like most things good and bad, pornography arrived late in Mississippi. When the marquee listed *The Cheerleaders* it went unnoticed by the passing traffic. When *XXX* was added the next day, traffic stopped and tempers rose in the coffee shops around the square. It opened on a Monday night to a small, curious, and somewhat enthusiastic crowd. The reviews at school were favorable, and by Tuesday packs of young teenagers were hiding in the woods, many with binoculars, watching in disbelief. After Wednesday night prayer meeting, the preachers got things organized and launched a counterattack, one that relied more on bullying than on shrewd tactics.

Taking a lesson from the civil rights protectors, a group they had had absolutely no sympathy for, they led their flocks to the highway in front of the drive-in, where they carried posters and prayed and sang hymns and hurriedly scribbled down the license plate numbers of those cars trying to enter.

Business was cut off like a faucet. The corporate guys up North filed a quick lawsuit, seeking injunctive relief. The preachers put together one of their own, and it was no surprise that all of this landed in the courtroom of the Honorable Reuben V. Atlee, a lifelong member of the First Presbyterian Church, a descendant of the Atlees who'd built the original sanctuary, and for the past thirty years the teacher of a Sunday School class of old goats who met in the church's basement kitchen.

The hearings lasted for three days. Since no Clanton lawyer would defend *The Cheerleaders,* the owners were represented by a big firm from Jackson. A dozen locals argued against the movie and on behalf of the preachers.

Ten years later, when he was in law school at Tulane, Ray studied his father's opinion in the case. Following the most current federal cases, Judge Atlee's ruling protected the rights of the protestors, with certain restrictions. And, citing a recent obscenity case ruling by the U.S. Supreme Court, he allowed the show to go on.

Judicially, the opinion could not have been more perfect. Politically, it could not have been uglier. No one was pleased. The phone rang at night with anonymous threats. The preachers denounced Reuben Atlee as a traitor. Wait till the next election, they promised from their pulpits.

Letters flooded the *Clanton Chronicle* and *The Ford County Times,* all castigating Judge Atlee for allowing such filth in their unblemished community. When the Judge was finally fed up with the criticism, he decided to speak. He chose a Sunday at the First Presbyterian Church as his time and place, and word spread quickly, as it always did in Clanton. Before a packed house, Judge Atlee strode confidently down the aisle, up the carpeted steps and to the pulpit. He was over six feet tall and thick, and his black suit gave him an aura of dominance. 'A Judge who counts votes before the trial should burn his robe and run for the county line,' he began sternly.

Ray and Forrest were sitting as far away as possible, in a corner of the balcony, both near tears. They had begged their father to allow them to skip the service, but missing church was not permissible under any circumstances.

He explained to the less informed that legal precedents have to be followed, regardless of personal views or opinions, and that good judges follow the law. Weak judges follow the crowd. Weak judges play for the votes and then cry foul when their cowardly rulings are appealed to higher courts.

'Call me what you want,' he said to a silent crowd, 'but I am no coward.'

Ray could still hear the words, still see his

father down there in the distance, standing alone like a giant.

After a week or so the protestors grew weary, and the porno ran its course. Kung-fu returned with a vengeance and everybody was happy. Two years later, Judge Atlee received his usual eighty percent of the vote in Ford County.

Ray flipped the cigar into a shrub and walked to his room. The night was cool so he opened a window and listened to the cars as they left town and faded over the hills.

Chapter 5

Every street had a story, every building a memory. Those blessed with wonderful childhoods can drive the streets of their hometowns and happily roll back the years. The rest are pulled home by duty and leave as soon as possible. After Ray had been in Clanton for fifteen minutes he was anxious to get out.

The town had changed, but then it hadn't. On the highways leading in, the cheap metal buildings and mobile homes were gathering as tightly as possible next to the roads for maximum visibility. Ford County had no zoning whatsoever. A landowner could build anything with no permit, no inspection, no code, no notice to adjoining landowners, nothing. Only hog farms and nuclear reactors required approvals and paperwork. The result was a slash-and-build clutter that got uglier by the year.

But in the older sections, nearer the square, the town had not changed at all. The long shaded streets were as clean and neat as when

Ray had roamed them on his bike. Most of the houses were still owned by people he knew, or if those folks had passed on the new owners kept the lawns clipped and the shutters painted. Only a few were being neglected. A handful had been abandoned.

This deep in Bible country, it was still an unwritten rule that little was done on Sundays except go to church, sit on porches, visit neighbors, rest and relax the way God intended.

It was cloudy, quite cool for May, and as he toured his old turf, killing time until the appointed hour, he tried to dwell on the good memories from Clanton. There was Dizzy Dean Park where he had played Little League for the Pirates, and there was the public pool he'd swum in every summer except 1969 when the city closed it rather than admit black children. There were the churches – Baptist, Methodist, and Presbyterian – facing each other at the intersection of Second and Elm like wary sentries, their steeples competing for height. They were empty now, but in an hour or so the more faithful would gather for evening services.

The square was as lifeless as the streets leading to it. With eight thousand people, Clanton was just large enough to have attracted the discount stores that had wiped out so many small towns. But here the people had been faithful to their downtown merchants, and there wasn't a single empty or boarded-up building around the square – no small miracle. The retail

43

shops were mixed in with the banks and law offices and cafés, all closed for the Sabbath.

He inched through the cemetery and surveyed the Atlee section in the old part, where the tombstones were grander. Some of his ancestors had built monuments for their dead. Ray had always assumed that the family money he'd never seen must have been buried in those graves. He parked and walked to his mother's grave, something he hadn't done in years. She was buried among the Atlees, at the far edge of the family plot because she had barely belonged.

Soon, in less than an hour, he would be sitting in the Judge's study, sipping bad instant tea and receiving instructions on exactly how his father would be laid to rest. Many orders were about to be given, many decrees and directions, because the Judge was a great man and cared deeply about how he was to be remembered.

Moving again, Ray passed the water tower he'd climbed twice, the second time with the police waiting below. He grimaced at his old high school, a place he'd never visited since he'd left it. Behind it was the football field where Forrest Atlee had romped over opponents and almost became famous before getting bounced off the team.

It was twenty minutes before five, Sunday, May 7. Time for the family meeting.

There was no sign of life at Maple Run. The front lawn had been cut within the past few days, and the Judge's old black Lincoln was parked in the rear, but other than those two pieces of evidence there was no sign that anyone had lived there for many years.

The front of the house was dominated by four large round columns under a portico, and when Ray had lived there these columns were painted white. Now they were green with vines and ivy. The wisteria was running wildly along the tops of the columns and onto the roof. Weeds choked everything – flower beds, shrubs, walkways.

Memories hit hard, as they always did when he pulled slowly into the drive and shook his head at the condition of a once fine home. And there was always the same wave of guilt. He should've stayed, should've gone in with the old man and founded the house of Atlee & Atlee, should've married a local girl and sired a half-dozen descendants who would live at Maple Run, where they would adore the Judge and make him happy in his old age.

He slammed his door as loudly as possible, hoping to alert anyone who might need to be alerted, but the noise fell softly on Maple Run. The house next door to the east was another relic occupied by a family of spinsters who'd been dying off for decades. It was also an antebellum but without the vines and weeds, and it was completely shadowed by five of the largest oak trees in Clanton.

The front steps and the front porch had been swept recently. A broom was leaning near the door, which was open slightly. The Judge refused to lock the house, and since he also refused to use air conditioning he left windows and doors open around the clock.

Ray took a deep breath and pushed the door open until it hit the doorstop and made noise. He stepped inside and waited for the odor to hit, whatever it might be this time. For years the Judge kept an old cat, one with bad habits, and the house bore the results. But the cat was gone now, and the smell was not unpleasant at all. The air was warm and dusty and filled with the heavy scent of pipe tobacco.

'Anybody home?' he said, but not too loudly. No answer.

The foyer, like the rest of the house, was being used to store the boxes of ancient files and papers the Judge clung to as if they were important. They had been there since the county evicted him from the courthouse. Ray glanced to his right, to the dining room where nothing had changed in forty years, and he stepped around the corner to the hallway that was also cluttered with boxes. A few soft steps and he peeked into his father's study.

The Judge was napping on the sofa.

Ray backed away quickly and walked to the kitchen, where, surprisingly, there were no dirty dishes in the sink and the counters were clean. The kitchen was usually a mess, but not today. He found a diet soda in the refrigerator and sat at the table trying to decide whether to wake his father or to postpone the inevitable. The old man was ill and needed his rest, so Ray sipped his drink and watched the clock above the stove move slowly toward 5 P.M.

Forrest would show up, he was certain. The meeting was too important to blow off. He'd never been on time in his life. He refused to wear a watch and claimed he never knew what day it was, and most folks believed him.

At exactly five, Ray decided he was tired of waiting. He had traveled a long way for this moment, and he wanted to take care of business. He walked into the study, noticed his father hadn't moved, and for a long minute or two was frozen there, not wanting to wake him, but at the same time feeling like a trespasser.

The Judge wore the same black pants and the same white starched shirt he'd worn as long as Ray could remember. Navy suspenders, no tie, black socks, and black wing tips. He'd lost weight and his clothes swallowed him. His face was gaunt and pale, his hair thin and slicked back. His hands were crossed at his waist and were almost as white as the shirt.

Next to his hands, attached to his belt on the right side, was a small white plastic container. Ray took a step closer, a silent step, for a better look. It was a morphine pack.

Ray closed his eyes, then opened them and glanced around the room. The rolltop desk under General Forrest had not changed in his lifetime. The ancient Underwood typewriter still sat there, a pile of papers beside it. A few feet away was the large mahogany desk left behind by the Atlee who'd fought with Forrest.

Under the stern gaze of General Nathan Bedford Forrest, and standing there in the center of a room that was timeless, Ray began to realize that his father was not breathing. He comprehended this slowly. He coughed, and there was not the slightest response. Then he leaned down and touched the Judge's left wrist. There was no pulse.

Judge Reuben V. Atlee was dead.

Chapter 6

There was an antique wicker chair with a torn cushion and a frayed quilt over the back. No one had ever used it but the cat. Ray backed into it because it was the nearest place to sit, and for a long time he sat there across from the sofa, waiting for his father to start breathing, to wake up, sit up, take charge of matters, and say, 'Where is Forrest?'

But the Judge was motionless. The only breathing at Maple Run was Ray's rather labored efforts to get control of himself. The house was silent, the still air even heavier. He stared at the pallid hands resting peacefully, and waited for them to rise just slightly. Up and down, very slowly as the blood began pumping again and the lungs filled and emptied. But nothing happened. His father was straight as a board, with hands and feet together, chin on chest, as if he knew when he lay down that this last nap would be eternal. His lips were together with a hint of a smile. The powerful drug had stopped the pain.

As the shock began to fade, the questions took over. How long had he been dead? Did the cancer get him or did the old man just crank up the morphine? What was the difference? Was this staged for his sons? Where the hell was Forrest? Not that he would be of any help.

Alone with his father for the last time, Ray fought back tears and fought back all the usual tormenting questions of why didn't I come earlier, and more often, and why didn't I write and call and the list could go on if he allowed it.

Instead, he finally moved. He knelt quietly beside the sofa, put his head on the Judge's chest, whispered, 'I love you, Dad,' then said a short prayer. When he stood he had tears in his eyes, and that was not what he wanted. Younger brother would arrive in a moment, and Ray was determined to handle the situation with no emotion.

On the mahogany desk he found the ashtray with two pipes. One was empty. The bowl of the other was full of tobacco that had recently been smoked. It was slightly warm, at least Ray thought so, though he was not certain. He could see the Judge having a smoke while he tidied up the papers on his desk, didn't want the boys to see too much of a mess, then when the pain hit he stretched out on the sofa, a touch of morphine for a little relief, then he drifted away.

Next to the Underwood was one of the

Judge's official envelopes, and across the front he had typed, 'Last Will and Testament of Reuben V. Atlee.' Under it was yesterday's date, May 6, 2000. Ray took it and left the room. He found another diet soda in the refrigerator and walked to the front porch, where he sat on the swing and waited for Forrest.

Should he call the funeral home and have his father moved before Forrest arrived? He debated this with a fury for a while, then he read the will. It was a simple, one-page document with no surprises.

He decided he would wait until precisely 6 P.M., and if Forrest hadn't arrived he would call the funeral home.

The Judge was still dead when Ray returned to his study, and that was not a complete surprise. He replaced the envelope next to the typewriter, shuffled through some more papers, and at first felt odd doing so. But he would be executor of his father's estate, and would soon be in charge of all the paperwork. He would inventory the assets, pay the bills, help lead the last remnants of the Atlee family money through probate, and finally put it to rest. The will split everything between the two sons, so the estate would be clean and relatively simple.

As he watched the time and waited for his brother, Ray poked around the study, each step watched carefully by General Forrest. Ray was quiet, still not wanting to disturb his father. The drawers to the rolltop were filled with stationery.

There was a pile of current mail on the mahogany desk.

Behind the sofa was a wall of bookshelves crammed with law treatises that appeared to have been neglected for decades. The shelves were made of walnut and had been built as a gift by a murderer freed from prison by the Judge's grandfather late in the last century, according to family lore, which as a rule went unquestioned, until Forrest came along. The shelves rested on a long walnut cabinet that was no more than three feet high. The cabinet had six small doors and was used for storage. Ray had never looked inside. The sofa was in front of the cabinet, almost entirely blocking it from view.

One of the cabinet doors was open. Inside, Ray could see an orderly stack of dark green Blake & Son stationer's boxes, the same ones he'd seen as long as he could remember. Blake & Son was an ancient printing company in Memphis. Virtually every lawyer and judge in the state bought letterheads and envelopes from Blake & Son, and had been doing so forever. He crouched low and moved behind the sofa for a better look. The storage spaces were tight and dark.

A box of envelopes without a top had been left sitting in the open door, just a few inches above the floor. There were no envelopes, however. The box was filled with cash – one-hundred-dollar bills. Hundreds of them packed neatly in a box that was twelve inches across, eighteen inches long, and maybe five inches deep. He lifted the box, and it was heavy. There were dozens more tucked away in the depths of the cabinet.

Ray pulled another one from the collection. It too was filled with one-hundred-dollar bills. Same for the third. In the fourth box, the bills were wrapped with yellow paper bands with '$2,000' printed on them. He quickly counted fifty-three bands.

One hundred and six thousand dollars.

Crawling on all fours along the back of the sofa, and careful not to touch it and disturb anybody, Ray opened the other five doors of the cabinet. There were at least twenty dark green Blake & Son boxes.

He stood and walked to the door of the study, then through the foyer onto the front porch for fresh air. He was dizzy, and when he sat on the top step a large drop of sweat rolled down the bridge of his nose and fell onto his pants.

Though clear thinking was not entirely possible, Ray was able to do some quick math. Assuming there were twenty boxes and that each held at least a hundred thousand dollars, then the stash greatly exceeded whatever the Judge had grossed in thirty-two years on the bench. His office of chancellor had been full time, nothing on the side, and not much since his defeat nine years earlier.

He didn't gamble, and to Ray's knowledge, had never bought a single share of stock.

A car approached from down the street. Ray froze, instantly fearful that it was Forrest. The car passed, and Ray jumped to his feet and ran to the study. He lifted one end of the sofa and moved it six inches away from the bookshelves, then the same for the other end. He dropped to his knees and began withdrawing the Blake & Son boxes. When he had a stack of five, he carried them through the kitchen to a small room behind the pantry where Irene the maid had always kept her brooms and mops. The same brooms and mops were still there, evidently untouched since Irene's death. Ray swatted away spiderwebs, then set the boxes on the floor.

The broom closet had no window and could not be seen from the kitchen.

From the dining room, he surveyed the front driveway, saw nothing, then raced back to the study where he balanced seven Blake & Son boxes in one stack and took them to the broom closet. Back to the dining room window, nobody out there, back to the study where the Judge was growing colder by the moment. Two more trips to the broom closet and the job was finished. Twenty-seven boxes in total, all safely stored where no one would find them.

It was almost 6 P.M. when Ray went to his car and removed his overnight bag. He needed a dry shirt and clean pants. The house was filled with dust and dirt and everything he touched left a smudge. He washed and dried himself with a towel in the only downstairs bathroom. Then he tidied up the study, moved the sofa back in place, and went from room to room looking for more cabinets.

He was on the second floor, in the Judge's bedroom with the windows up, going through his closets, when he heard a car in the street. He ran downstairs and managed to slip into the swing on the porch just as Forrest parked behind his Audi. Ray took deep breaths and tried to calm himself.

The shock of a dead father was enough for one day. The shock of the money had left him shaking.

Forrest crept up the steps, as slowly as possible, hands stuck deep in his white painter's pants. Shiny black combat boots with bright green laces. Always different.

'Forrest,' Ray said softly, and his brother turned to see him.

'Hey, Bro.'

'He's dead.'

Forrest stopped and for a moment studied him, then he gazed at the street. He was wearing an old brown blazer over a red tee shirt, an ensemble no one but Forrest would attempt to pull off. And no one but Forrest could get by with it. As Clanton's first self-proclaimed free spirit, he had always worked to be cool, offbeat, avant-garde, hip.

He was a little heavier and was carrying the weight well. His long sandy hair was turning gray much quicker than Ray's. He wore a battered Cubs baseball cap.

'Where is he?' Forrest asked.

'In there.'

Forrest pulled open the screen and Ray followed him inside. He stopped in the door of the study and seemed uncertain as to what to do next. As Forrest stared at his father his head fell slightly to one side, and Ray thought for a second he might collapse. As tough as he tried to act, Forrest's emotions were always just under the surface. He mumbled, 'Oh my God,' then moved awkwardly to the wicker chair where he sat and looked in disbelief at the Judge.

'Is he really dead?' he managed to say with his jaws clenched.

'Yes, Forrest.'

He swallowed hard and fought back tears and finally said, 'When did you get here?'

Ray sat on a stool and turned it to face his brother. 'About five, I guess. I walked in, thought he was napping, then realized he was dead.'

'I'm sorry you had to find him,' Forrest said, wiping the corners of his eyes.

'Somebody had to.'

'What do we do now?'

'Call the funeral home.'

Forrest nodded as if he knew that was exactly what you're supposed to do. He stood slowly and unsteadily and walked to the sofa. He touched his father's hands. 'How long has he been dead?' he mumbled. His voice was hoarse and strained.

'I don't know. Couple of hours.'

'What's that?'

'A morphine pack.'

'You think he cranked it up a little too much?'

'I hope so,' Ray said.

'I guess we should've been here.'

'Let's not start that.'

Forrest looked around the room as if he'd never been there before. He walked to the rolltop and looked at the typewriter. 'I guess he won't need a new ribbon after all,' he said.

'I guess not,' Ray said, glancing at the cabinet behind the sofa. 'There's a will there if you want to read it. Signed yesterday.'

'What does it say?'

'We split everything. I'm the executor.'

'Of course you're the executor.' He walked behind the mahogany desk and gave a quick look at the piles of papers covering it. 'Nine years since I set foot in this house. Hard to believe, isn't it?'

'It is.'

'I stopped by a few days after the election, told him how sorry I was that the voters had turned him out, then I asked him for money. We had words.'

'Come on, Forrest, not now.'

Stories of the war between Forrest and the Judge could be told forever.

'Never did get that money,' he mumbled as he opened a desk drawer. 'I guess we'll need to go through everything, won't we?'

'Yes, but not now.'

'You do it, Ray. You're the executor. You handle the dirty work.'

'We need to call the funeral home.'

'I need a drink.'

'No, Forrest, please.'

'Lay off, Ray. I'll have a drink anytime I want a drink.'

'That's been proven a thousand times. Come on, I'll call the funeral home and we'll wait on the porch.'

A policeman arrived first, a young man with a shaved head who looked as though someone had interrupted his Sunday nap and called him into action. He asked questions on the front porch, then viewed the body. Paperwork had to be done, and as they went through it Ray fixed a pitcher of instant tea with heavy sugar.

'Cause of death?' the policeman asked.

'Cancer, heart disease, diabetes, old age,' Ray said. He and Forrest were rocking gently in the swing.

'Is that enough?' Forrest asked, like a true smart-ass. Any respect he might've once had for cops had long since been abandoned.

'Will you request an autopsy?'

'No,' they said in unison.

He finished the forms and took signatures from both Ray and Forrest. As he drove away, Ray said, 'Word will spread like wildfire now.'

'Not in our lovely little town.'

'Hard to believe, isn't it? Folks actually gossip around here.'

'I've kept them busy for twenty years.'

'Indeed you have.'

They were shoulder to shoulder, both holding empty glasses. 'So what's in the estate?' Forrest finally asked.

'You want to see the will?'

'No, just tell me.'

'He listed his assets – the house, furniture, car, books, six thousand dollars in the bank.'

'Is that all?'

'That's all he mentioned,' Ray said, avoiding the lie.

'Surely, there's more money than that around here,' Forrest said, ready to start looking.

'I guess he gave it all away,' Ray said calmly.

'What about his state retirement?'

'He cashed out when he lost the election, a huge blunder. Cost him tens of thousands of dollars. I'm assuming he gave everything else away.'

'You're not going to screw me, are you, Ray?'

'Come on, Forrest, there's nothing to fight over.'

'Any debts?'

'He said he had none.'

59

'Nothing else?'

'You can read the will if you want.'

'Not now.'

'He signed it yesterday.'

'You think he planned everything?'

'Sure looks like it.'

A black hearse from Magargel's Funeral Home rolled to a stop in front of Maple Run, then turned slowly into the drive.

Forrest leaned forward, elbows on knees, face in hand, and began crying.

Chapter 7

Behind the hearse was the county coroner,
Thurber Foreman, in the same red Dodge
pickup he'd been driving since Ray was in
college, and behind Thurber was Reverend Silas
Palmer of the First Presbyterian Church, an
ageless little Scot who'd baptized both Atlee
sons. Forrest slipped away and hid in the
backyard while Ray met the party on the front
porch. Sympathies were exchanged. Mr. B. J.
Magargel from the funeral home and Reverend
Palmer appeared to be near tears. Thurber had
seen countless dead bodies. He had no financial
interest in this one, however, and appeared to be
indifferent, at least for the moment.

Ray led them to the study where they respect-
fully viewed Judge Atlee long enough for
Thurber to officially decide he was dead. He did
this without words, but simply nodded at Mr.
Magargel with a somber, bureaucratic dip of the
chin that said, 'He's dead. You can take him

now.' Mr. Magargel nodded, too, thus completing a silent ritual they'd gone through many times together.

Thurber produced a single sheet of paper and asked the basics. The Judge's full name, date of birth, place of birth, next of kin. For the second time, Ray said no to an autopsy.

Ray and Reverend Palmer stepped away and took a seat at the dining room table. The minister was much more emotional than the son. He adored the Judge and claimed him as a close friend.

A service befitting a man of Reuben Atlee's stature would draw many friends and admirers and should be well planned. 'Reuben and I talked about it not long ago,' Palmer said, his voice low and raspy, ready to choke up at any moment.

'That's good,' Ray said.

'He picked out the hymns and scriptures, and he made a list of the pallbearers.'

Ray hadn't yet thought of such details. Perhaps they would've come to mind had he not stumbled upon a couple of million in cash. His overworked brain listened to Palmer and caught most of his words, then it would switch to the broom closet and start swirling again. He was suddenly nervous that Thurber and Magargel were alone with the Judge in the study. Relax, he kept telling himself.

'Thank you,' he said, genuinely relieved that

the details had been taken care of. Mr. Magargel's assistant rolled a gurney through the front door, through the foyer, and struggled to get it turned into the Judge's study.

'And he wanted a wake,' the reverend said. Wakes were traditional, a necessary prelude to a proper burial, especially among the older folks.

Ray nodded.

'Here in the house.'

'No,' Ray said instantly. 'Not here.'

As soon as he was alone, he wanted to inspect every inch of the house in search of more loot. And he was very concerned with the stash already in the broom closet. How much was there? How long would it take to count it? Was it real or counterfeit? Where did it come from? What to do with it? Where to take it? Who to tell? He needed time alone to think, to sort things out and develop a plan.

'Your father was very plain about this,' Palmer said.

'I'm sorry, Reverend. We will have a wake, but not here.'

'May I ask why not?'

'My mother.'

He smiled and nodded and said, 'I remember your mother.'

'They laid her on the table over there in the front parlor, and for two days the entire town paraded by. My brother and I hid upstairs and cursed my father for such a spectacle.' Ray's voice was firm, his eyes hot. 'We will not have a wake in this house, Reverend.'

Ray was utterly sincere. He was also concerned about securing the premises. A wake would require a thorough scouring of the house by a cleaning service, and the preparation of food by a caterer, and flowers hauled in by a florist. And all of this activity would begin in the morning.

'I understand,' the reverend said.

The assistant backed out first, pulling the gurney, which was being pushed gently by Mr. Magargel. The Judge was covered from head to foot by a starched white sheet that was tucked neatly under him. With Thurber following behind, they rolled him out, across the front porch and down the steps, the last Atlee to live at Maple Run.

Half an hour later, Forrest materialized from somewhere in the back of the house. He was holding a tall clear glass that was filled with a suspicious-looking brown liquid, and it wasn't ice tea. 'They gone?' he asked, looking at the driveway.

'Yes,' Ray said. He was sitting on the front steps, smoking a cigar. When Forrest sat down next to him, the aroma of sour mash followed quickly.

'Where'd you find that?' Ray asked.

'He had a hiding place in his bathroom. Want some?'

64

'No. How long have you known that?'

'Thirty years.'

A dozen lectures leapt forward, but Ray fought them off. They'd been delivered many times before, and evidently they had failed because here was Forrest sipping bourbon after 141 days of sobriety.

'How's Ellie?' Ray asked after a long puff.

'Crazy as hell, the same.'

'Will I see her at the funeral?'

'No, she's up to three hundred pounds. One-fifty is her limit. Under one-fifty and she'll leave the house. Over one-fifty, and she locks herself up.'

'When was she under one-fifty?'

'Three or four years ago. She found some wacko doctor who gave her pills. Got all the way down to a hundred pounds. Doctor went to jail and she gained another two hundred. Three hundred is her max, though. She weighs every day and freaks out if the big needle goes beyond three.'

'I told Reverend Palmer that we would have a wake, but not here, not in the house.'

'You're the executor.'

'You agree?'

'Sure.'

A long pull on the bourbon, another long puff on the cigar.

'What about that hosebag who ditched you? What's her name?'

'Vicki.'

'Yeah, Vicki, I hated that bitch even at your wedding.'

'I wish I had.'

'She still around?'

'Yep, saw her last week, at the airport, getting off her private jet.'

'She married that old fart, right, some crook from Wall Street?'

'That's him. Let's talk about something else.'

'You brought up women.'

'Always a big mistake.'

Forrest slugged another drink, then said, 'Let's talk about money. Where is it?'

Ray flinched slightly and his heart stopped, but Forrest was gazing at the front lawn and didn't notice. What money are you talking about, dear brother? 'He gave it away.'

'But why?'

'It was his money, not ours.'

'Why not leave some for us?'

Not too many years earlier, the Judge had confided to Ray that over a fifteen-year period he had spent more than ninety thousand dollars on legal fees, court fines, and rehab for Forrest. He could leave the money for Forrest to drink and snort, or he could give it away to charities and needy families during his lifetime. Ray had a profession and could take care of himself.

'He left us the house,' Ray said.

'What happens to it?'

'We'll sell it if you want. The money goes in a

pot with everything else. Fifty percent will go for estate taxes. Probate will take a year.'

'Gimme the bottom line.'

'We'll be lucky to split fifty thousand a year from now.'

Of course there were other assets. The loot was sitting innocently in the broom closet, but Ray needed time to evaluate it. Was it dirty money? Should it be included in the estate? If so, it would cause terrible problems. First, it would have to be explained. Second, at least half would get burned in taxes. Third, Forrest would have his pockets filled with cash and would probably kill himself with it.

'So I'll get twenty-five thousand bucks in a year?' Forrest said.

Ray couldn't tell if he was anxious or disgusted. 'Something like that.'

'Do you want the house?'

'No, do you?'

'Hell no. I'll never go back in there.'

'Come on, Forrest.'

'He kicked me out, you know, told me I'd disgraced this family long enough. Told me to never set foot on this soil again.'

'And he apologized.'

A quick sip. 'Yes, he did. But this place depresses me. You're the executor, you deal with it. Just mail me a check when probate is over.'

'We should at least go through his things together.'

'I'm not touching them,' he said and got to his

feet. 'I want a beer. It's been five months, and I want a beer.' He was walking toward his car as he talked. 'You want one?'

'No.'

'You wanna ride with me?'

Ray wanted to go so he could protect his brother, but he felt a stronger urge to sit tight and protect the Atlee family assets. The Judge never locked the house. Where were the keys? 'I'll wait here,' he said.

'Whatever.'

The next visitor was no surprise. Ray was in the kitchen digging through drawers, looking for keys, when he heard a loud voice bellowing at the front door. Though he hadn't heard it in years, there was no doubt it belonged to Harry Rex Vonner.

They embraced, a bear hug from Harry Rex, a retreating squeeze from Ray. 'I'm so sorry,' Harry Rex said several times. He was tall with a large chest and stomach, a big messy bear of a man who worshiped Judge Atlee and would do anything for his boys. He was a brilliant lawyer trapped in a small town, and it was to Harry Rex that Judge Atlee had always turned during Forrest's legal problems.

'When did you get here?' he asked.

'Around five. I found him in his study.'

'I've been in trial for two weeks, hadn't talked to him. Where's Forrest?'

'Gone to buy beer.'

68

They both digested the gravity of this. They sat in the rocking chairs near the swing. 'It's good to see you, Ray.'

'And you too, Harry Rex.'

'I can't believe he's dead.'

'Nor can I. I thought he'd always be here.'

Harry Rex wiped his eyes with the back of a sleeve. 'I'm so sorry,' he mumbled. 'I just can't believe it. I saw him two weeks ago, I guess it was. He was movin' around, sharp as a tack, in pain but not complainin'.'

'They gave him a year, and that was about twelve months ago. I thought he'd hang on, though.'

'Me too. Such a tough old fart.'

'You want some tea?'

'That'd be nice.'

Ray went to the kitchen and poured two glasses of instant ice tea. He took them back to the porch and said, 'This stuff isn't very good.'

Harry Rex took a drink and concurred. 'At least it's cold.'

'We need to have a wake, Harry Rex, and we're not doing it here. Any ideas?'

He pondered this only for a second, then leaned in with a big smile. 'Let's put him in the courthouse, first floor in the rotunda, lay him in state like a king or somethin'.'

'You're serious?'

'Why not. He'd love it. The whole town could parade by and pay their respects.'

'I like it.'

'It's brilliant, trust me. I'll talk to the sheriff and get it approved. Ever'body'll love it. When's the funeral?'

'Tuesday.'

'Then we'll have us a wake tomorrow afternoon. You want me to say a few words?'

'Of course. Why don't you just organize the whole thing?'

'Done. Y'all picked out a casket?'

'We were going in the morning'

'Do oak, forget that bronze and copper crap. We buried Momma last year in oak and it was the prettiest damned thang I'd ever seen. Magargel can get one out of Tupelo in two hours. And forget the vault, too. They're just rip-offs. Ashes to ashes, dust to dust, bury 'em and let 'em rot is the only way to go. The Episcopalians do it right.'

Ray was a little dazed by the torrent of advice, but was thankful nonetheless. The Judge's will had not mentioned the casket but had specifically requested a vault. And he wanted a nice headstone. He was, after all, an Atlee, and he was to be buried among the other great ones.

If anyone knew anything about the Judge's business, it was Harry Rex. As they watched the shadows fall across the long front lawn of Maple Run, Ray said, as nonchalantly as possible, 'Looks like he gave all his money away.'

'I'm not surprised. Are you?'

'No.'

'There'll be a thousand folks at his funeral

who were touched by his generosity. Crippled children, sick folks with no insurance, black kids he sent to college, every volunteer fire department, civic club, all-star team, school group headed for Europe. Our church sent some doctors to Haiti and the Judge gave us a thousand bucks.'

'When did you start going to church?'

'Two years ago.'

'Why?'

'Got a new wife.'

'How many is that?'

'Four. I really like this one, though.'

'Lucky for her.'

'She's very lucky.'

'I like this courthouse wake, Harry Rex. All those folks you just mentioned can pay their respects in public. Plenty of parking, don't have to worry about seating.'

'It's brilliant.'

Forrest wheeled into the drive and slammed on his brakes, stopping inches behind Harry Rex's Cadillac. He crawled out and lumbered toward them in the semidarkness, carrying what appeared to be a whole case of beer.

Chapter 8

When he was alone, Ray sat in the wicker chair across from the empty sofa, and tried to convince himself that life without his father would not be greatly different than life apart from him. This day was long in coming, and he would simply take it in stride and go on with a small measure of mourning. Just go through the motions, he told himself, wrap things up in Mississippi and race back to Virginia.

The study was lit by one weak bulb under the shade of a dust-covered lamp on the rolltop, and the shadows were long and dark. Tomorrow he would sit at the desk and plunge into the paperwork, but not tonight.

Tonight he needed to think.

Forrest was gone, hauled away by Harry Rex, both of them drunk. Forrest, typically, became sullen and wanted to drive to Memphis. Ray suggested he simply stay there. 'Sleep on the porch if you don't want to sleep in the house,' he said, without pushing. Pushing would only cause a fight. Harry Rex said he would, under normal circumstances, invite Forrest to stay with him, but the new wife was a hard-ass and two drunks were probably too much.

'Just stay here,' Harry Rex said, but Forrest wouldn't budge. Bullheaded enough when he was cold sober, he was intractable after a few drinks. Ray had seen it more times than he cared to remember and sat quietly as Harry Rex argued with his brother.

The issue was settled when Forrest decided he would rent a room at the Deep Rock Motel north of town. 'I used to go there when I was seeing the mayor's wife, fifteen years ago,' he said.

'It's full of fleas,' Harry Rex said.

'I miss it already.'

'The mayor's wife?' Ray asked.

'You don't want to know,' Harry Rex said.

They left a few minutes after eleven, and the house had been growing quieter by the minute.

The front door had a latch and the patio door had a deadbolt. The kitchen door, the only one at the rear of the house, had a flimsy knob with a lock that was not working. The Judge could not operate a screwdriver and Ray had inherited this lack of mechanical skill. Every window had been closed and latched, and he was certain that the Atlee mansion had not been this secure in decades. If necessary, he would sleep in the kitchen where he could guard the broom closet.

He tried not to think about the money. Sitting

73

in his father's sanctuary, he mentally worked on an unofficial obituary.

Judge Atlee was elected to the bench of the 25th Chancery District in 1959 and was reelected by a landslide every four years until 1991. Thirty-two years of diligent service. As a jurist, his record was impeccable. Rarely did the Appellate Court reverse one of his decisions. Often he was asked by his colleagues to hear untouchable cases in their districts. He was a guest lecturer at the Ole Miss Law School. He wrote hundreds of articles on practice, procedure, and trends. Twice he turned down appointments to the Mississippi Supreme Court; he simply didn't want to leave the trial bench.

When he wasn't wearing a robe, Judge Atlee kept his finger in all local matters – politics, civic work, schools, and churches. Few things in Ford County were approved without his endorsement, and few things he opposed were ever attempted. At various times he served on every local board, council, conference, and ad hoc committee. He quietly selected candidates for local offices and he quietly helped defeat the ones who didn't get his blessing.

In his spare time, what little of it there had been, he studied history and the Bible and wrote articles on the law. Never once had he thrown a baseball with his sons, never once had he taken them fishing.

He was preceded in death by his wife, Margaret, who died suddenly of an aneurysm in 1969. He was survived by two sons.

And somewhere along the way he managed to siphon off a fortune in cash.

Maybe the mystery of the money would be solved over there on the desk, somewhere in the stacks of papers or perhaps hidden in the drawers. Surely his father had left a clue, if not an outright explanation. There had to be a trail. Ray couldn't think of a single person in Ford County with a net worth of two million dollars, and to hold that much in cash was unthinkable.

He needed to count it. He'd checked on it twice during the evening. Just counting the twenty-seven Blake & Son's boxes had made him anxious. He would wait until early morning, when there was plenty of light and before the town began moving. He'd cover the kitchen windows and take one box at a time.

Just before midnight, Ray found a small mattress in a downstairs bedroom and dragged it into the dining room, to a spot twenty feet from the broom closet, where he could see the front drive and the house next door. Upstairs he found the Judge's .38-caliber Smith & Wesson in the drawer of his night table. With a pillow that smelled of mildew and a wool blanket that smelled of mold, he tried in vain to sleep.

The rattling noise came from the other side of the house. It was a window, though it took Ray minutes to wake up, clear his head, realize where he was and what he was hearing. A pecking sound, then a more violent shaking, then silence. A long pause as he poised himself on the mattress and gripped the .38. The house was much darker than he wanted because almost all the lightbulbs had burned out and the Judge had been too cheap to replace them.

Too cheap. Twenty-seven boxes of cash.

Put lightbulbs on the list, first thing in the morning.

There was the noise again, too firm and too rapid to be leaves or limbs brushing in the wind. Tap, tap, tap, then a hard push or shove as someone tried again to pry it open.

There were two cars in the drive – Ray's and Forrest's. Any fool could see the house had people in it, so whoever this fool was he didn't care. He probably had a gun, too, and he certainly knew how to handle it better than Ray.

Ray slid across the foyer on his stomach, wiggling like a crab and breathing like a sprinter. He stopped in the dark hallway and listened to the silence. Lovely silence. Just go away, he kept saying to himself. Please go away.

Tap, tap, tap, and he was sliding again toward the rear bedroom with the pistol aimed in front of him. Was it loaded? he asked himself, much too late. Surely the Judge kept his bedside gun loaded. The noise was louder and coming from a small bedroom they had once used for guests, but for decades now it had been collecting boxes of junk. He slowly nudged the door open with his head and saw nothing but cardboard boxes. The door swung wider and hit a floor lamp, which pitched forward and crashed near the first of three dark windows.

Ray almost began firing, but he held his ammo, and his breath. He lay still on the sagging wooden floor for what seemed like an hour, sweating, listening, swatting spiders, hearing nothing. The shadows rose and fell. A light wind was hitting every branch out there, and somewhere up near the roof a limb was gently rubbing the house.

It was the wind after all. The wind and the old ghosts of Maple Run, a place of many spirits, according to his mother, because it was an old house where dozens had died. They had buried slaves in the basement, she said, and their ghosts grew restless and roamed about.

The Judge hated ghost stories and refuted them all.

When Ray finally sat up, his elbows and knees were numb. With time he stood and leaned on the door frame, watching the three windows with his gun ready. If there had actually been an intruder, the noise evidently spooked him. But the longer Ray stood there the more he convinced himself that the racket had been nothing but the wind.

Forrest had the better idea. As grungy as the Deep Rock was, it had to be more restful than this place.

Tap, tap, tap, and he hit the floor again, stricken with fear once more, except this was worse because the noise came from the kitchen. He made the tactical decision to crawl instead of slide, and by the time he got back to the foyer his knees were screaming. He stopped at the French doors that led to the dining room and waited. The floor was dark but a faint porch light slanted feebly through the blinds and shone along the upper walls and ceiling.

Not for the first time, he asked himself what, exactly, was he, a professor of law at a prestigious university, doing hiding in the darkness of his childhood home, armed, frightened out of his mind, ready to jump out of his skin, and all because he wanted desperately to protect a mysterious hoard of cash he had stumbled upon. 'Answer that one,' he mumbled to himself.

The kitchen door opened onto a small wooden deck. Someone was shuffling around out there, just beyond the door, footsteps on boards. Then the doorknob rattled, the flimsy one with the malfunctioning lock. Whoever he was, he had made the bold decision to walk straight through the door instead of sneaking through a window.

Ray was an Atlee, and this was his soil. This was also Mississippi, where guns were expected to be used for protection. No court in the state would frown on drastic action in this situation. He crouched beside the kitchen table, took aim at a spot high in the window above the sink, and began squeezing the trigger. One loud gunshot, cracking through the darkness, coming from inside and shattering a window, would no doubt terrify any burglar.

Just as the door rattled again, he squeezed harder, the hammer clicked, and nothing happened. The gun had no bullets. The chamber spun, he squeezed again, and there was no discharge. In a panic, Ray grabbed the empty pitcher of tea on the counter and hurled it at the door. To his great relief, it made more noise than any bullet could possibly have done. Scared out of his wits, he hit a light switch and went charging to the door, brandishing the gun and yelling, 'Get the hell outta here!' When he yanked it open and saw no one, he exhaled mightily and began breathing again.

For half an hour he swept glass, making as much noise as possible.

The cop's name was Andy, nephew of a guy Ray finished high school with. That relationship was established within the first thirty seconds of his arrival, and once they were linked they talked about football while the exterior of Maple Run was inspected. No sign of entry at any of the downstairs windows. Nothing at the kitchen door but broken glass. Upstairs, Ray looked for bullets while Andy went from room to room. Both searches produced nothing. Ray brewed coffee and they drank it on the porch, chatting quietly in the early morning hours. Andy was the only cop protecting Clanton at that time, and he confessed he wasn't really needed. 'Nothin' ever happens this early Monday morning,' he said. 'Folks are asleep, gettin' ready for work.' With a little prodding, he reviewed the crime scene in Ford County – stolen pickups, fights at the honky-tonks, drug activity in Lowtown, the colored section. Hadn't had a murder in four years, he said proudly. A branch bank got robbed two years ago. He prattled on and took a second cup. Ray would keep pouring it, and brewing it if necessary, until sunrise. He was comforted by the presence of a well-marked patrol car sitting out front.

Andy left at three-thirty. For an hour Ray lay on the mattress, staring holes in the ceiling, holding a gun that was useless. He fought sleep by plotting strategies to protect the money. Not investment schemes, those could wait. More pressing was a plan to get the money out of the broom closet, out of the house, and into a safe place somewhere. Would he be forced to haul it to Virginia? He certainly couldn't leave it in Clanton, could he? And when could he count it?

At some point, fatigue and the emotional drain of the day overcame him, and he drifted away. The tapping came back, but he did not hear it. The kitchen door, now secured by a jammed chair and a piece of rope, was rattled and pushed, but Ray slept through it all.

Chapter 9

At seven-thirty, sunlight woke him. The money was still there, untouched. The doors and windows had not been opened, as far as he could tell. He fixed a pot of coffee, and as he drank the first cup at the kitchen table he made an important decision. If someone was after the money, then he could not leave it, not for a moment.

But the twenty-seven Blake & Son boxes would not fit in the small trunk of his little Audi roadster.

The phone rang at eight. It was Harry Rex, reporting that Forrest had been delivered to the Deep Rock Motel, that the county would allow a ceremony in the rotunda of the courthouse that afternoon at four-thirty, that he had already lined up a soprano and a color guard. And he was working on a eulogy for his beloved friend.

'What about the casket?' he asked.

'We're meeting with Magargel at ten,' Ray answered.

'Good. Remember, go with the oak. The Judge would like that.'

They talked about Forrest for a few minutes, the same conversation they'd had many times. When he hung up, Ray began moving quickly. He opened windows and blinds so he could see and hear any visitors. Word was spreading through the coffee shops around the square that Judge Atlee had died, and visitors were certainly possible.

The house had too many doors and windows, and he couldn't stand guard around the clock. If someone was after the money, then that someone could get it. For a few million bucks, a bullet to Ray's head would be a solid investment.

The money had to be moved.

Working in front of the broom closet, he took the first box and dumped the cash into a black plastic garbage bag. Eight more boxes followed, and when he had about a million bucks in bag number one he carried it to the kitchen door and peeked outside. The empty boxes were returned to the cabinet under the bookshelves. Two more garbage bags were filled. He backed his car close to the deck, as close to the kitchen as possible, then surveyed the landscape in search of human eyes. There were none. The only neighbors were the spinsters next door, and they couldn't see the television in their own den. Darting from the door to the car, he loaded the fortune into the

82

trunk, shoved the bags this way and that, and when it looked as though the lid might not close he slammed it down anyway. It clicked and locked and Ray Atlee was quite relieved.

He wasn't sure how he would unload the loot in Virginia and carry it from a parking lot down the busy pedestrian mall to his apartment. He would worry about that later.

The Deep Rock had a diner, a hot cramped greasy place Ray had never visited, but it was the perfect spot to eat on the morning after Judge Atlee's death. The three coffee shops around the square would be busy with gossip and stories about the great man, and Ray preferred to stay away.

Forrest looked decent. Ray had certainly seen much him worse. He wore the same clothes and he hadn't showered, but with Forrest that was not unusual. His eyes were red but not swollen. He said he'd slept well, but needed grease. Both ordered bacon and eggs.

'You look tired,' Forrest said, gulping black coffee.

Ray indeed felt tired. 'I'm fine, couple of hours of rest and I'm ready to roll.' He glanced through the window at his Audi, which was parked as close to the diner as possible. He would sleep in the damned thing if necessary.

'It's weird,' Forrest said. 'When I'm clean, I sleep like a baby. Eight, nine hours a night, a hard sleep. But when I'm not clean, I'm lucky to get five hours. And it's not a deep sleep either.'

'Just curious – when you're clean, do you think about the next round of drinking?'

'Always. It builds up, like sex. You can do without it for a while, but the pressure's building and sooner or later you gotta have some relief. Booze, sex, drugs, they all get me eventually.'

'You were clean for a hundred and forty days.'

'A hundred and forty-one.'

'What's the record?'

'Fourteen months. I came out of rehab a few years back, this great detox center that the old man paid for, and I kicked ass for a long time. Then I crashed.'

'Why? What made you crash?'

'It's always the same. When you're an addict you can lose it any time, any place, for any reason. They haven't designed a wagon that can hold me. I'm an addict, Bro, plain and simple.'

'Still drugs?'

'Sure. Last night it was booze and beer, same tonight, same tomorrow. By the end of the week I'll be doing nastier stuff.'

'Do you want to?'

'No, but I know what happens.'

The waitress brought their food. Forrest quickly buttered a biscuit and took a large bite. When he could speak he said, 'The old man's dead, Ray, can you believe it?'

Ray was anxious to change the subject too. If they dwelt on Forrest's shortcomings they would be fighting soon enough. 'No, I thought I was ready for it, but I wasn't.'

'When was the last time you saw him?'

'November, when he had prostate surgery. You?'

Forrest sprinkled Tabasco sauce on his scrambled eggs and pondered the question. 'When was his heart attack?'

There had been so many ailments and surgeries that they were difficult to remember. 'He had three.'

'The one in Memphis.'

'That was the second one,' Ray said. 'Four years ago.'

'That's about right. I spent some time with him at the hospital. Hell, it wasn't six blocks away. I figured it was the least I could do.'

'What did you talk about?'

'Civil War. He still thought we'd won.'

They smiled at this and ate in silence for a few moments. The silence ended when Harry Rex found them. He helped himself to a biscuit while offering the latest details of the splendid ceremony he was planning for Judge Atlee.

'Everybody wants to come out to the house,' he said with a mouthful.

'It's off limits,' Ray said.

'That's what I'm tellin' them. Y'all want to receive guests tonight?'

'No,' said Forrest.

'Should we?' asked Ray.

'It's the proper thing to do, either at the house or at the funeral home. But if you don't, it's no big deal. Ain't like folks'll get pissed and refuse to speak to you.'

'We're doing the courthouse wake and a funeral, isn't that enough?' Ray asked.

'I think so.'

'I'm not sittin' around a funeral home all night huggin' old ladies who've been talkin' about me for twenty years,' Forrest said. 'You can if you want, but I will not be there.'

'Let's pass on it,' Ray said.

'Spoken like a true executor,' Forrest said with a sneer.

'Executor?' said Harry Rex.

'Yes, there was a will on his desk, dated Saturday. A simple, one-page, holographic will, leaving everything to the two of us, listing his assets, naming me as the executor. And he wants you to do the probate, Harry Rex.'

Harry Rex had stopped chewing. He rubbed the bridge of his nose with a chubby finger and gazed across the diner. 'That's odd,' he said, obviously puzzled by something.

'What?'

'I did a long will for him a month ago.'

All had stopped eating. Ray and Forrest exchanged looks that conveyed nothing because neither had a clue what the other was thinking.

'I guess he changed his mind,' Harry Rex said.

'What was in the other will?' Ray asked.

'I can't tell you. He was my client, so it's confidential.'

'I'm lost here, fellas,' Forrest said. 'Forgive me for not being a lawyer.'

'The only will that matters is the last one,' said Harry Rex. 'It revokes all prior wills, so whatever the Judge put in the will I prepared is irrelevant.'

'Why can't you tell us what's in the old will?' Forrest asked.

'Because I, as a lawyer, cannot discuss a client's will.'

'But the will you prepared is no good, right?'

'Right, but I still can't talk about it.'

'That sucks,' Forrest said, and glared at Harry Rex. All three took a deep breath, then a large bite.

Ray knew in an instant that he would have to see the other will and see it soon. If it mentioned the loot hidden in the cabinet, then Harry Rex knew about it. And if he knew, then the money would quickly be removed from the trunk of the little TT convertible and repackaged in Blake & Son boxes and put back where it came from. It would then be included in the estate, which was a public record.

'Won't there be a copy of your will in his office?' Forrest asked, in the general direction of Harry Rex.

'No.'

'Are you sure?'

'I'm reasonably sure,' Harry Rex said. 'When you make a new will you physically destroy the old one. You don't want someone finding the old one and probating it. Some folks change their wills every year, and as lawyers we know to burn the old ones. The Judge was a firm believer in destroying revoked wills because he spent thirty years refereeing will contests.'

The fact that their close friend knew something about their dead father, and that he was unwilling to share it, chilled the conversation. Ray decided to wait until he was alone with Harry Rex to grill him.

'Magargel's waiting,' he said to Forrest.

'Sounds like fun.'

They rolled the handsome oak casket down the east wing of the courthouse on a funeral gurney draped with purple velvet. Mr. Magargel led while an assistant pushed. Behind the casket were Ray and Forrest, and behind them was a Boy Scout color guard with flags and pressed khaki uniforms.

Because Reuben V. Atlee had fought for his country, his casket was covered with the Stars and Stripes. And because of this a contingent of Reservists from the local armory snapped to attention when Retired Captain Atlee was stopped in the center of the courthouse rotunda. Harry Rex was waiting there, dressed in a fine black suit, standing in front of a long row of floral arrangements.

88

Every other lawyer in the county was present, too, and, at Harry Rex's suggestion, they were cordoned off in a special section close to the casket. All city and county officials, courthouse clerks, cops, and deputies were present, and as Harry Rex stepped forward to begin the crowd pressed closer. Above, on the second and third levels of the courthouse, another crowd leaned on the iron railings and gawked downward.

Ray wore a brand-new navy suit he'd purchased just hours earlier at Pope's, the only men's clothier in town. At $310 it was the most expensive in the store, and slashed from that hefty price was a ten percent discount that Mr. Pope insisted on giving. Forrest's new suit was dark gray. It cost $280 before the discount, and it had also been paid for by Ray. Forrest had not worn a suit in twenty years and swore he would not wear one for the funeral. Only a tongue lashing by Harry Rex got him to Pope's.

The sons stood at one end of the casket, Harry Rex at the other, and near the center of it Billy Boone, the ageless courthouse janitor, had carefully placed a portrait of Judge Atlee. It had been painted ten years earlier by a local artist, for free, and everyone knew the Judge had not been particularly fond of it. He hung it in his chambers behind his courtroom, behind a door so no one could see it. After his defeat, the county fathers placed it in the main courtroom, high above the bench.

Programs had been printed for the 'Farewell

to Judge Reuben Atlee.' Ray studied his intently because he didn't wish to look around the gathering. All eyes were on him, and Forrest. Reverend Palmer delivered a windy prayer. Ray had insisted that the ceremony be brief. There was a funeral tomorrow.

The Boy Scouts stepped forward with the flag and led the congregation in the Pledge of Allegiance, then Sister Oleda Shumpert from the Holy Ghost Church of God in Christ stepped forward and sang a mournful rendition of 'Shall We Gather at the River,' a cappella because she certainly didn't need any support. The words and melody brought tears to the eyes of many, including Forrest, who stayed close to his brother's shoulder with his chin low.

Standing next to the casket, listening to her rich voice echo upward through the rotunda, Ray for the first time felt the burden of his father's death. He thought of all the things they could have done together, now that they were men, all the things they had not done when he and Forrest were just boys. But he had lived his life and the Judge had lived his, and this had suited them both.

It wasn't fair now to relive the past just because the old man was dead. He kept telling himself this. It was only natural at death to wish he'd done more, but the truth was that the Judge had carried a grudge for years after Ray left Clanton. And, sadly, he had become a recluse since leaving the bench.

A moment of weakness, and Ray stiffened his back. He would not beat himself up because he had chosen a path that was not the one his father wanted.

Harry Rex began what he promised would be a brief eulogy. 'Today we gather here to say good-bye to an old friend,' he began. 'We all knew this day was coming, and we all prayed it would never get here.' He hit the highlights of the Judge's career, then told of his first appearance in front of the great man, thirty years ago, when Harry Rex was fresh out of law school. He was handling an uncontested divorce, which he somehow managed to lose.

Every lawyer had heard the story a hundred times, but they still managed a good laugh at the appropriate time. Ray glanced at them, then began studying them as a group. How could one small town have so many lawyers? He knew about half of them. Many of the old ones he'd known as a child and as a student were either dead or retired. Many of the younger ones he'd never seen before.

Of course they all knew him. He was Judge Atlee's boy.

Ray was slowly realizing that his speedy exit from Clanton after the funeral would only be temporary. He would be forced to return very soon, to make a brief court appearance with Harry Rex and begin probate, to prepare an inventory and do a half-dozen other duties as executor of his father's estate. That would be easy and routine and take just a few days. But weeks and perhaps months were looming out there as he tried to solve the mystery of the money.

Did one of those lawyers over there know something? The money had to originate from a judicial setting, didn't it? The Judge had no life outside of the law. Looking at them, though, Ray could not imagine a source rich enough to generate the kind of money now hidden in the trunk of his little car. They were small-town ham-and-egg lawyers, all scrambling to pay their bills and outhustle the guy next door. There was no real money over there. The Sullivan firm had eight or nine lawyers who represented the banks and insurance companies, and they earned just enough to hang out with the doctors at the country club.

There wasn't a lawyer in the county with serious cash. Irv Chamberlain over there with the thick eyeglasses and bad hairpiece owned thousands of acres handed down through generations, but he couldn't sell it because there were no buyers. Plus, it was rumored he was spending time at the new casinos in Tunica.

As Harry Rex droned on, Ray dwelt on the lawyers. Someone shared the secret. Someone knew about the money. Could it be a distinguished member of the Ford County bar?

Harry Rex's voice began to break, and it was time to quit. He thanked them all for coming and announced that the Judge would lie in state in the courthouse until 10 P.M. He directed the procession to begin where Ray and Forrest were standing. The crowd moved obediently to the east wing and formed a line that snaked its way outside.

For an hour, Ray was forced to smile and shake hands and graciously thank everyone for coming. He listened to dozens of brief stories about his father and the lives the great man had touched. He pretended to remember the names of all those who knew him. He hugged old ladies he'd never met before. The procession moved slowly by Ray and Forrest, then to the casket, where each person would stop and gaze forlornly at the Judge's bad portrait, then to the west wing where registers were waiting. Harry Rex moved about, working the crowd like a politician.

At some point during the ordeal, Forrest disappeared. He mumbled something to Harry Rex about going home, to Memphis, and something about being tired of death.

Finally, Harry Rex whispered to Ray, 'There's a line around the courthouse. You could be here all night.'

'Get me out of here,' Ray whispered back.

'You need to go to the rest room?' Harry Rex asked, just loud enough for those next in line to hear.

'Yes,' Ray said, already stepping away. They eased back, whispering importantly, and ducked

93

into a narrow hallway. Seconds later they emerged behind the courthouse.

They drove away, in Ray's car of course, first circling the square and taking in the scene. The flag in front of the courthouse was at half-mast. A large crowd waited patiently to pay their respects to the Judge.

Chapter 10

Twenty-four hours in Clanton, and Ray was desperate to leave. After the wake, he ate dinner with Harry Rex at Claude's, the black diner on the south side of the square where the Monday special was barbecued chicken and baked beans so spicy they served ice tea by the half-gallon. Harry Rex was reveling in the success of his grand send-off for the Judge and after dinner was anxious to return to the courthouse and monitor the rest of the wake.

Forrest had evidently left town for the evening. Ray hoped he was in Memphis, at home with Ellie, behaving himself, but he knew better. How many times could he crash before he died? Harry Rex said there was a fifty-fifty chance Forrest would make it to the funeral tomorrow.

When Ray was alone he drove away, out of Clanton, headed west to no place in particular. There were new casinos along the river, seventy miles away, and with each trip back to Mississippi he heard more talk and gossip about the state's newest industry. Legalized gambling had arrived in the state with the lowest per capita income in the country.

An hour and a half from Clanton, he stopped for gas and as he pumped it he noticed a new motel across the highway. Everything was new in what had recently been cotton fields. New roads, new motels, fast-food restaurants, gas stations, billboards, all spillover from the casinos a mile away.

The motel had rooms on two levels, with doors that opened to face the parking lot. It appeared to be a slow night. He paid $39.99 for a double on the ground level, around back where there were no other cars or trucks. He parked the Audi as close as possible to his room, and within seconds had the three garbage bags inside.

The money covered one bed. He did not stop to admire it because he was convinced it was dirty. And it was probably marked in some way. Maybe it was counterfeit. Whatever it was, it was not his to keep.

All the bills were one-hundred-dollar notes, some brand new and never used, others passed around a little. None were worn badly, and none were dated before 1986 or after 1994. About half were banded together in two-thousand-dollar stacks, and Ray counted those first – one hundred thousand dollars in one-hundred-dollar bills was about fifteen inches high. He counted the money from one bed, then arranged it on the other in neat rows and sections. He was very deliberate, time was of no concern. As he touched the money, he rubbed it between his forefingers and thumbs and even smelled it to see if it was counterfeit. It certainly appeared to be real.

Thirty-one sections, plus a few leftovers – $3,118,000 to be exact. Retrieved like buried treasure from the crumbling home of a man who had earned less than half that during his lifetime.

It was impossible not to admire the fortune spread before him. How many times in his life would he gaze upon three million bucks? How many others ever got the chance? Ray sat in a chair with his face in his hands, staring at the tidy rows of cash, dizzy with thoughts of where it came from and where it was headed.

A slamming car door somewhere outside jolted him back. This would be an excellent place to get robbed. When you travel around with millions in cash everybody becomes a potential thief.

He rebagged it, stuffed it back into the trunk of his car, and drove to the nearest casino.

His involvement with gambling was limited to a weekend junket to Atlantic City with two other law professors, both of whom had read a book on successful crap shooting and were convinced they could beat the house. They did not. Ray had rarely played cards. He found a home at the five-dollar blackjack table, and after two miserable days in a noisy dungeon he cleared sixty dollars and vowed not to return. His colleagues' losses were never nailed down, but he learned that those who gamble quite often lie about their success.

For a Monday night, there was a respectable crowd at the Santa Fe Club, a hastily built box the size of a football field. A ten-floor tower attached to it housed the guests, mostly retirees from up North who had never dreamed of setting foot in Mississippi but were now lured by unlimited slots and free gin while they gambled.

In his pocket he had five bills taken from five different sections of the loot he'd counted in the motel room. He walked to an empty blackjack table where the dealer was half-asleep and placed the first bill on the table. 'Play it,' he said.

'Playing a hundred,' the dealer said over her shoulder, where no one was there to hear it. She picked up the bill, rubbed it with little interest, then put it in play.

It must be real, he thought, and relaxed a little. She sees them all day long. She shuffled one deck, dealt the cards, promptly hit twenty-four, then took the bill from Judge Atlee's buried treasure and put down two black chips. Ray played them both, two hundred dollars a bet, nerves of steel. She dealt the cards quickly, and with fifteen showing she hit a nine. Ray now had four black chips. In less than a minute he'd won three hundred dollars.

Rattling the four black chips in his pocket, he strolled through the casino, first through the slots where the crowd was older and subdued, almost brain-dead as they sat on their stools, pulling the arm down again and again, staring sadly at the screens. At the craps table, the dice were hot and a rowdy bunch of rednecks were hollering instructions that made no sense to him. He watched for a moment, completely bewildered by the dice and the bets and the chips changing hands.

At another empty blackjack table, he tossed down the second hundred-dollar bill, more like a seasoned gambler now. The dealer pulled it close to his face, held it up to the lights, rubbed it, and took it a few steps over to the pit boss, who was immediately distrustful of it. The pit boss produced a magnifying device that he stuck in his left eye and examined the bill like a surgeon. Just as Ray was about to break and bolt through the crowd, he heard one of them say, 'It's good.' He wasn't sure which one said it because he was looking wildly around the casino for armed guards. The dealer returned to the table and placed the suspicious money in front of Ray, who said, 'Play it.' Seconds later, the queen of hearts and the king of spades were staring at Ray, and he'd won his third hand in a row.

Since the dealer was wide awake and his supervisor had done a close inspection, Ray decided to settle the matter once and for all. He pulled the other three hundred-dollar bills from his pocket and laid them on the table. The dealer inspected each carefully, then shrugged and said, 'You want change?'

'No, play them.'

'Playing three hundred cash,' the dealer said loudly, and the pit boss loomed over his shoulder.

Ray stood on a ten and a six. The dealer hit on a ten and a four, and when he turned over the jack of diamonds, Ray won his fourth straight hand. The cash disappeared and was replaced with six black chips. Ray now had ten, a thousand dollars, and he also had the knowledge that the other thirty thousand bills stuffed into the back of his car were not counterfeit. He left one chip for the dealer and went to find a beer.

The sports bar was elevated a few feet, so that if you wanted you could have a drink and take in all the action on the floor. Or you could watch pro baseball or NASCAR reruns or bowling on any of the dozen screens. But you couldn't gamble on the games; it wasn't allowed yet.

He was aware of the risks the casino posed. Now that the money was real, the next question was whether it was marked in some way. The suspicions of the second dealer and his supervisor would probably be enough to get the bills examined by the boys upstairs. They had Ray on video, he was certain, same as everybody else. Casino surveillance was extensive; he knew that from his two bright pals who'd planned to break the bank at the craps table.

If the money set off alarms, they could easily find him. Couldn't they?

But where else could he get the money examined? Walk in the First National in Clanton and hand the teller a few of the bills? 'Mind taking a look at these, Mrs. Dempsey, see if they're real or not?' No teller in Clanton had ever seen counterfeit money, and by lunch the entire town would know Judge Atlee's boy was sneaking around with a pocketful of suspicious money.

He'd thought of waiting until he was back in Virginia. He would go to his lawyer who could find an expert to examine a sample of the money, all nice and confidential. But he couldn't wait that long. If the money was fake, he'd burn it. Otherwise, he wasn't sure what to do with it.

He drank his beer slowly, giving them time to send down a couple of goons in dark suits who would walk up and say, 'Gotta minute?' They couldn't work that fast, and Ray knew it. If the money was marked, it would take days to link it to wherever it came from.

Suppose he got caught with marked money. What was his crime? He had taken it from his deceased father's house, a place that had been willed to him and his brother. He was the executor of the estate, soon to be charged with the responsibility of protecting its assets. He had months to report it to both the probate court and the tax authorities. If the Judge had somehow accumulated the money by illegal means, then sorry, he's dead now. Ray had done nothing wrong, at least for the moment.

He took his winnings back to the first blackjack table and placed a five-hundred-dollar bet. The dealer got the attention of her supervisor, who ambled over with his knuckles to his mouth and one finger tapping an ear, smugly, as if five hundred dollars on one hand of blackjack happened all the time at the Santa Fe Club. He was dealt an ace and a king, and the dealer slid over seven hundred fifty dollars.

'Would you like something to drink?' asked the pit boss, all smiles and bad teeth.

'Beck's beer,' Ray said, and a cocktail waitress appeared from nowhere.

He bet a hundred dollars on the next hand and lost. Then quickly he slid three chips out for the next hand, which he won. He won eight of the next ten hands, alternating his bets from a hundred to five hundred dollars as if he knew precisely what he was doing. The pit boss lingered behind the dealer. They had a potential card counter on their hands, a professional blackjack player, one to be watched and filmed. The other casinos would be notified.

If they only knew.

He lost consecutive bets of two hundred dollars, then just for the hell of it pushed ten chips out for a bold and reckless wager of a thousand dollars. He had another three million in the trunk. This was chicken feed. When two queens landed next to his chips, he kept a perfect poker face as if he'd been winning like this for years.

'Would you like dinner, sir?' the pit boss asked.

'No,' Ray said.

'Can we get anything for you?'

'A room would be nice.'

'King or a suite?'

A jerk would've said, 'A suite, of course,' but Ray caught himself. 'Any room will be fine,' he said. He'd had no plans to stay there, but after two beers he thought it best not to drive. What if he got stopped by a rural deputy? And what would the deputy do if he searched the trunk?

'No problem, sir,' said the pit boss. 'I'll get you checked in.'

For the next hour he broke even. The cocktail waitress stopped by every five minutes, pushing beverages, trying to loosen him up, but Ray nursed the first beer. During a shuffle, he counted thirty-nine black chips.

At midnight he began yawning, and he remembered how little he'd slept the night before. The room key was in his pocket. The table had a thousand-dollar limit per hand; otherwise he would've played it all at one time and gone down in a blaze of glory. He placed ten black chips in the circle and with an audience hit blackjack. Another ten chips, and the dealer blew it with twenty-two. He gathered his chips, left four for the dealer, and went to the cashier. He'd been in the casino for three hours.

From his fifth-floor room he could see the parking lot, and because his sports car was within view he felt compelled to watch it. As tired as he was, he could not fall asleep. He pulled a chair to the window and tried to doze, but couldn't stop thinking.

Had the Judge discovered the casinos? Could gambling be the source of his fortune, a lucrative little vice that he'd kept to himself?

The more Ray told himself that the idea was too far-fetched, the more convinced he became that he'd found the source of the money. To his knowledge, the Judge had never played the stock market, and if he had, if he'd been another Warren Buffett, why would he take his profits in cash and hide it under the bookshelves? Plus, the paperwork would be thick.

If he'd lived the double life of a judge on the take, there wasn't three million dollars to steal on the court dockets in rural Mississippi. And taking bribes would involve too many other people.

It had to be gambling. It was a cash business. Ray had just won six thousand dollars in one night. Sure it was blind luck, but wasn't all gaming? Perhaps the old man had a knack for cards or dice. Maybe he hit one of the big jackpots in the slot machines. He lived alone and answered to no one.

He could've pulled it off.

But three million dollars over seven years?

Didn't the casinos require paperwork for substantial winnings? Tax forms and such?

And why hide it? Why not give it away like the rest of his money?

Shortly after three, Ray gave it up and left his complimentary room. He slept in his car until sunrise.

Chapter 11

The front door was slightly cracked, and at eight o'clock in the morning with no one living there it was indeed an ominous sign. Ray stared at it for a long minute, not certain if he wanted to step inside but knowing he had no choice. He shoved it wider, clenched his fists as if the thief just might still be in there, and took a very deep breath. It swung open, creaking every inch of the way, and when the light fell upon the stacks of boxes in the foyer Ray saw muddy footprints on the floor. The assailant had entered from the rear lawn where there was mud and for some reason had chosen to leave through the front door.

Ray slowly removed the pistol from his pocket.

The twenty-seven green Blake & Son boxes were scattered around the Judge's study. The sofa was overturned. The doors to the cabinet below the bookshelves were open. The rolltop appeared to be unmolested but the papers from the desk were scattered on the floor.

The intruder had removed the boxes, opened them, and finding them empty, had evidently stomped them and thrown them in a fit of rage. As still as things were, Ray felt the violence and it made him weak.

The money could get him killed.

When he was able to move he fixed the sofa and picked up the papers. He was gathering boxes when he heard something on the front porch. He peeked through the window and saw an old woman tapping on the front door.

Claudia Gates had known the Judge like no one else. She had been his court reporter, secretary, driver, and many other things, according to gossip that had been around since Ray was a small boy. For almost thirty years, she and the Judge had traveled the six counties of the 25th District together, often leaving Clanton at seven in the morning and returning long after dark. When they were not in court, they shared the Judge's office in the courthouse, where she typed the transcripts while he did his paperwork.

A lawyer named Turley had once caught them in a compromising position during lunch at the office, and he made the awful mistake of telling others about it. He lost every case in Chancery Court for a year and couldn't buy a client. It took four years for Judge Atlee to get him disbarred.

'Hello, Ray,' she said through the screen. 'May I come in?'

'Sure,' he said, and opened the door wider.

Ray and Claudia had never liked each other. He had always felt that she was getting the attention and affection that he and Forrest were not, and she viewed him as a threat as well. When it came to Judge Atlee, she viewed everyone as a threat.

She had few friends and even fewer admirers. She was rude and callous because she spent her life listening to trials. And she was arrogant because she whispered to the great man.

'I'm very sorry,' she said.

'So am I.'

As they walked by the study, Ray pulled the door closed and said, 'Don't go in there.' Claudia did not notice the intruder's footprints.

'Be nice to me, Ray,' she said.

'Why?'

They went to the kitchen, where he put up some coffee and they sat across from each other. 'Can I smoke?' she asked.

'I don't care,' he said. Smoke till you choke, old gal. His father's black suits had always carried the acrid smell of her cigarettes. He'd allowed her to smoke in the car, in chambers, in his office, probably in bed. Everywhere but the courtroom.

The raspy breath, the gravelly voice, the countless wrinkles clustered around the eyes, ah, the joys of tobacco.

She'd been crying, which was not an insignificant event in her life. When he was clerking for his father one summer, Ray had had the misfortune of sitting through a gut-wrenching child abuse case. The testimony had been so sad and pitiful that everyone, including the Judge and all the lawyers, were moved to tears. The only dry eyes in the courtroom belonged to old stone-faced Claudia.

'I can't believe he's dead,' she said, then blew a puff of smoke toward the ceiling.

'He's been dying for five years, Claudia. This is no surprise.'

'It's still sad.'

'It's very sad, but he was suffering at the end. Death was a blessing.'

'He wouldn't let me come see him.'

'We're not rehashing history, okay?'

The history, depending on which version you believed, had kept Clanton buzzing for almost two decades. A few years after Ray's mother died, Claudia divorced her husband for reasons that were never clear. One side of town believed the Judge had promised to marry her after her divorce. The other side of town believed the Judge, forever an Atlee, never intended to marry such a commoner as Claudia, and that she got a divorce because her husband caught her fooling around with yet another man. Years passed with the two enjoying the benefits of married life, except for the paperwork and actual cohabitation. She continued to press the Judge to get married, he continued to postpone things. Evidently, he was getting what he wanted.

Finally she put forth an ultimatum, which proved to be a bad strategy. Ultimatums did not impress Reuben Atlee. The year before he got booted from office, Claudia married a man nine years younger. The Judge promptly fired her, and the coffee shops and knitting clubs talked of nothing else. After a few rocky years, her younger man died. She was lonely, so was the Judge. But she had betrayed him by remarrying, and he never forgave her.

'Where's Forrest?' she asked.

'He should be here soon.'

'How is he?'

'He's Forrest.'

'Do you want me to leave?'

'It's up to you.'

'I'd rather talk to you, Ray. I need to talk to someone.'

'Don't you have friends?'

'No. Reuben was my only friend.'

He cringed when she called him Reuben. She stuck the cigarette between her gluey red lips, a pale red for mourning, not the bright red she was once known for. She was at least seventy, but wearing it well. Still straight and slim, and wearing a tight dress that no other seventy-year-old woman in Ford County would attempt. She had diamonds in her ears and one on her finger, though he couldn't tell if they were real. She was also wearing a pretty gold pendant and two gold bracelets.

She was an aging tart, but still an active volcano. He would ask Harry Rex whom she was seeing these days.

He poured more coffee and said, 'What would you like to talk about?'

'Reuben.'

'My father is dead. I don't like history.'

'Can't we be friends?'

'No. We've always despised each other. We're not going to kiss and hug now, over the casket. Why would we do that?'

'I'm an old woman, Ray.'

'And I live in Virginia. We'll get through the funeral today, then we'll never see each other again. How's that?'

She lit another one and cried some more. Ray was thinking about the mess in the study, and what he would say to Forrest if he barged in now and saw the footprints and scattered boxes. And if Forrest saw Claudia sitting at the table, he might go for her neck.

Though they had no proof, Ray and Forrest had long suspected that the Judge had paid her more than the going rate for court reporters. Something extra, in exchange for the extras she was providing. It was not difficult holding a grudge.

'I want something to remember, that's all,' she said.

'You want to remember me?'

'You are your father, Ray. I'm clinging here.'

'Are you looking for money?'

'No.'

'Are you broke?'

'I'm not set for life, no.'

'There's nothing here for you.'

'Do you have his will?'

'Yes, and your name is not mentioned.'

She cried again, and Ray began a slow burn.
She got the money twenty years ago when he
was waiting tables and living on peanut butter
and trying to survive another month of law
school without getting evicted from his cheap
apartment. She always had a new Cadillac when
he and Forrest were driving wrecks. They were
expected to live like impoverished gentry while
she had the wardrobe and the jewelry.

'He always promised to take care of me,' she
said.

'He broke it off years ago, Claudia. Give it
up.'

'I can't. I loved him too much.'

'It was sex and money, not love. I'd rather not
talk about it.'

'What's in the estate?'

'Nothing. He gave it all away.'

'He what?'

'You heard me. You know how he loved to
write checks. It got worse after you left the
picture.'

'What about his retirement?' She wasn't crying now, this was business. Her green eyes were dry and glowing.

'He cashed in the year after he left office. It was a terrible financial blunder, but he did it without my knowledge. He was mad and half-crazy. He took the money, lived on some of it, and gave the rest to the Boy Scouts, Girl Scouts, Lions Club, Sons of the Confederacy, Committee to Preserve Historic Battlefields, you name it.'

If his father had been a crooked judge, something Ray was not willing to believe, then Claudia would know about the money. It was obvious she did not. Ray never suspected she knew, because if she had then the money would not have remained hidden in the study. Let her have a rip at three million bucks and everybody in the county would know about it. If she had a dollar, you were going to see it. As pitiful as she looked across the table, Ray suspected she had very few dollars.

'I thought your second husband had some money,' he said, with a little too much cruelty.

'So did I,' she said and managed a smile. Ray chuckled a bit. Then they both laughed, and the ice thawed dramatically. She had always been known for her bluntness.

'Never found it, huh?'

'Not a dime. He was this nice-looking guy, nine years younger, you know –'

'I remember it well. A regular scandal.'

113

'He was fifty-one years old, a smooth talker, had a line about making money in oil. We drilled like crazy for four years and I came up with nothing.'

Ray laughed louder. He could not, at that moment, ever remember having a talk about sex and money with a seventy-year-old woman. He got the impression she had plenty of stories. Claudia's greatest hits.

'You're looking good, Claudia, you have time for another one.'

'I'm tired, Ray. Old and tired. I'd have to train him and all. It's not worth it.'

'What happened to number two?'

'He croaked with a heart attack and I didn't even find a thousand dollars,' she said.

'The Judge left six.'

'Is that all?' she asked in disbelief.

'No stocks, no bonds, nothing but an old house and six thousand dollars in the bank.'

She lowered her eyes, shook her head, and believed everything Ray was saying. She had no clue about the cash.

'What will you do with the house?'

'Forrest wants to burn it and collect the insurance.'

'Not a bad idea.'

'We'll sell it.'

There was noise on the porch, then a knock. Reverend Palmer was there to discuss the funeral service, which would begin in two hours. Claudia hugged Ray as they walked to her car.

She hugged him again and said good-bye. 'I'm sorry I wasn't nicer to you,' she whispered as he opened her car door.

'Good-bye, Claudia. I'll see you at the church.'

'He never forgave me, Ray.'

'I forgive you.'

'Do you really?'

'Yes. You're forgiven. We're friends now.'

'Thank you so much.' She hugged him a third time and started crying. He helped her into the car, always a Cadillac. Just before she turned the ignition, she said, 'Did he ever forgive you, Ray?'

'I don't think so.'

'I don't think so either.'

'But it's not important now. Let's get him buried.'

'He could be a mean old sumbitch, couldn't he?' she said, smiling through the tears.

Ray had to laugh. His dead father's seventy-year-old former lover had just called the great man a son of a bitch.

'Yes,' he agreed. 'He certainly could be.'

Chapter 12

They rolled Judge Atlee down the center aisle in his fine oak casket and parked him at the altar in front of the pulpit where Reverend Palmer was waiting in a black robe. The casket was left unopened, much to the disappointment of the mourners, most of whom still clung to the ancient Southern ritual of viewing the deceased one last time in a strange effort to maximize the grief. 'Hell no,' Ray had said politely to Mr. Magargel when asked about opening things up. When the pieces were in place, Palmer slowly stretched out his arms, then lowered them, and the crowd sat.

In the front pew to his right was the family, the two sons. Ray wore his new suit and looked tired. Forrest wore jeans and a black suede jacket and looked remarkably sober. Behind them were Harry Rex and the other pallbearers, and behind them was a sad collection of ancient judges, not far from the casket themselves. In the front pew to his left were all sorts of dignitaries – politicians, an ex-governor, a couple of Mississippi Supreme Court justices. Clanton had never seen such power assembled at one time.

The sanctuary was packed, with folks standing along the walls under the stained-glass windows. The balcony above was full. One floor below, the auditorium had been wired for audio and more friends and admirers were down there.

Ray was impressed by the crowd. Forrest was already looking at his watch. He had arrived fifteen minutes earlier and got cursed by Harry Rex, not Ray. His new suit was dirty, he'd said, and besides Ellie had bought him the black suede jacket years ago and she thought it would do just fine for the occasion.

She, at three hundred pounds, would not leave the house, and for that Ray and Harry Rex were grateful. Somehow she'd kept him sober, but a crash was in the air. For a thousand reasons, Ray just wanted to get back to Virginia.

The reverend prayed, a short, eloquent message of thanks for the life of a great man. Then he introduced a youth choir that had won national honors at a music competition in New York. Judge Atlee had given them three thousand dollars for the trip, according to Palmer. They sang two songs Ray had never heard before, but they sang them beautifully.

The first eulogy – and there would be only two short ones per Ray's instructions – was delivered by an old man who barely made it to the pulpit, but once there startled the crowd with a rich and powerful voice. He'd been in law school with the Judge a hundred years ago. He told two humorless stories and the potent voice began to fade.

The reverend read some scripture and delivered words of comfort for the loss of a loved one, even an old one who had lived a full life.

The second eulogy was given by a young black man named Nakita Poole, something of a legend in Clanton. Poole came from a rough family south of town, and had it not been for a chemistry teacher at the high school he would have dropped out in the ninth grade and become another statistic. The Judge met him during an ugly family matter in court, and he took an interest in the kid. Poole had an amazing capacity for science and math. He finished first in his class, applied to the best colleges, and was accepted everywhere. The Judge wrote powerful letters of recommendation and pulled every string he could grab. Nakita picked Yale, and its financial package covered everything but spending money. For four years Judge Atlee wrote him every week, and in each letter there was a check for twenty-five dollars.

'I wasn't the only one getting the letters or the checks,' he said to a silent crowd. 'There were many of us.'

Nakita was now a doctor and headed for Africa for two years of volunteer work. 'I'm gonna miss those letters,' he said, and every lady in the church was in tears.

The coroner, Thurber Foreman, was next. He'd been a fixture at funerals in Ford County for many years, and the Judge specifically wanted him to play his mandolin and sing 'Just a Closer Walk with Thee.' He sang it beautifully, and somehow managed to do so while weeping.

Forrest finally began wiping his eyes. Ray just stared at the casket, wondering where the cash came from. What had the old man done? What, exactly, did he think would happen to the money after he died?

When the reverend finished a very brief message, the pallbearers rolled Judge Atlee out of the sanctuary. Mr. Magargel escorted Ray and Forrest down the aisle and down the front steps to a limo waiting behind the hearse. The crowd spilled out and went to their cars for the ride to the cemetery.

Like most small towns, Clanton loved a funeral procession. All traffic stopped. Those not driving in the procession were on the sidewalks, standing sadly and gazing at the hearse and the endless parade of cars behind it. Every part-time deputy was in uniform and blocking something, a street, an alley, parking spaces.

The hearse led them around the courthouse, where the flag was at half-mast and the county employees lined the front sidewalk and lowered their heads. The merchants around the square came out to bid farewell to Judge Atlee.

He was laid to rest in the Atlee plot, next to his long-forgotten wife and among the ancestors he so revered. He would be the last Atlee returned to the dust of Ford County, though no one knew it. And certainly no one cared. Ray would be cremated and his ashes scattered over the Blue Ridge Mountains. Forrest admitted he was closer to death than his older brother, but he had not nailed down his final details. The only thing for certain was that he would not be buried in Clanton. Ray was lobbying for cremation. Ellie liked the idea of a mausoleum. Forrest preferred not to dwell on the subject.

The mourners crowded under and around a crimson Magargel Funeral Home tent, which was much too small. It covered the grave and four rows of folding chairs. A thousand were needed.

Ray and Forrest sat with their knees almost touching the casket and listened as Reverend Palmer wrapped it all up. Sitting in a folding chair at the edge of his father's open grave, Ray found it odd the things he thought about. He wanted to go home. He missed his classroom and his students. He missed flying and the views of the Shenandoah Valley from five thousand feet. He was tired and irritable and did not want to spend the next two hours lingering in the cemetery making small talk with people who remembered when he was born.

The wife of a Pentecostal preacher had the final words. She sang 'Amazing Grace,' and for five minutes time stood still. In a beautiful soprano, her voice echoed through the gentle hills of the cemetery, comforting the dead, giving hope to the living. Even the birds stopped flying.

An Army boy with a trumpet played 'Taps,' and everybody had a good cry. They folded the flag and handed it to Forrest, who was sobbing and sweating under the damned suede jacket. As the final notes faded into the woods, Harry Rex started bawling behind them. Ray leaned forward and touched the casket. He said a silent farewell, then rested with his elbows on his knees, his face in his hands.

The burial broke up quickly. It was time for lunch. Ray figured that if he just sat there and stared at the casket, then folks would leave him alone. Forrest flung a heavy arm across his shoulders, and together they looked as though they might stay until dark. Harry Rex regained his composure and assumed the role of family spokesman. Standing outside the tent, he thanked the dignitaries for coming, complimented Palmer on a fine service, praised the preacher's wife for such a beautiful rendition, told Claudia that she could not sit with the boys, that she needed to move along, and on and on. The gravediggers waited under a nearby tree, shovels in hand.

When everybody was gone, including Mr.

Magargel and his crew, Harry Rex fell into the chair on the other side of Forrest and for a long time the three of them sat there, staring, not wanting to leave. The only sound was that of a backhoe somewhere in the distance, waiting. But Forrest and Ray didn't care. How often do you bury your father?

And how important is time to a gravedigger?

'What a great funeral,' Harry Rex finally said. He was an expert on such matters.

'He would've been proud,' said Forrest.

'He loved a good funeral,' Ray added. 'Hated weddings though.'

'I love weddings,' said Harry Rex.

'Four or five?' asked Forrest.

'Four, and counting.

A man in a city work uniform approached and quietly asked, 'Would you like for us to lower it now?'

Neither Ray nor Forrest knew how to respond. Harry Rex had no doubt. 'Yes, please,' he said. The man turned a crank under the grave apron. Very slowly, the casket began sinking. They watched it until it came to rest deep in the red soil.

The man removed the belts, the apron, and the crank, and disappeared.

'I guess it's over,' Forrest said.

Lunch was tamales and sodas at a drive-in on the edge of town, away from the crowded places where someone would undoubtedly interrupt them with a few kind words about the Judge. They sat at a wooden picnic table under a large umbrella and watched the cars go by.

'When are you heading back?' Harry Rex asked.

'First thing in the morning,' Ray answered.

'We have some work to do.'

'I know. Let's do it this afternoon.'

'What kinda work?' Forrest asked.

'Probate stuff,' Harry Rex said. 'We'll open the estate in a couple of weeks, whenever Ray can get back. We need to go through the Judge's papers now and see how much work there is.'

'Sounds like a job for the executor.'

'You can help.'

Ray was eating and thinking about his car, which was parked on a busy street near the Presbyterian church. Surely it was safe there. 'I went to a casino last night,' he announced with his mouth full.

'Which one?' asked Harry Rex.

'Santa Fe something or other, the first one I came to. You been there?'

'I've been to all of them,' he said, as if he'd never go back. With the exception of illegal narcotics, Harry Rex had explored every vice.

'Me too,' said Forrest, a man with no exceptions.

'How'd you do?' Forrest asked.

'I won a couple of thousand at blackjack. They comped me a room.'

'I paid for that damned room,' Harry Rex said. 'Probably the whole floor.'

'I love their free drinks,' said Forrest. 'Twenty bucks a pop.'

Ray swallowed hard and decided to set the bait. 'I found some matches from the Santa Fe on the old man's desk. Was he sneaking over there?'

'Sure,' said Harry Rex. 'He and I used to go once a month. He loved the dice.'

'The old man?' Forrest asked. 'Gambling?'

'Yep.'

'So there's the rest of my inheritance. What he didn't give away, he gambled away.'

'No, he was actually a pretty good player.'

Ray pretended to be as shocked as Forrest, but he was relieved to pick up his first clue, slight as it was. It seemed almost impossible that the Judge could've amassed such a fortune shooting craps once a week.

He and Harry Rex would pursue it later.

Chapter 13

As he approached the end, the Judge had been diligent in organizing his affairs. The important records were in his study and easily found.

They went through his mahogany desk first. One drawer had ten years' worth of bank statements, all arranged nearly in chronological order. His tax returns were in another. There were thick ledger books filled with entries of the donations he'd made to everybody who'd asked. The largest drawer was filled with letter-size manila files, dozens of them. Files on property taxes, medical records, old deeds and titles, bills to pay, judicial conferences, letters from his doctors, his retirement fund. Ray flipped through the row of files without opening them, except for the bills to pay. There was one – $13.80 to Wayne's Lawnmower Repair – dated a week earlier.

'It's always weird going through the papers of someone who just died,' Harry Rex said. 'I feel dirty, like a peeping Tom.'

'More like a detective looking for clues,' Ray said. He was on one side of the desk, Harry Rex the other, their ties off and sleeves rolled up, with piles of evidence between them. Forrest was his usual helpful self. He'd drained half a six-pack for dessert after lunch, and was now snoring it off in the swing on the front porch.

But he was there, instead of lost in one of his patented binges. He had disappeared so many times over the years. If he'd blown off his father's funeral, no one in Clanton would've been surprised. Just another black mark against that crazy Atlee boy, another story to tell.

In the last drawer they found personal odds and ends – pens, pipes, pictures of the Judge with his cronies at bar conventions, a few photos of Ray and Forrest from years ago, his marriage license, and their mother's death certificate. In an old, unopened envelope there was her obituary clipped from the *Clanton Chronicle*, dated October 12, 1969, complete with a photograph. Ray read it and handed it to Harry Rex.

'Do you remember her?' Ray asked.

'Yes, I went to her funeral,' he said, looking at it. 'She was a pretty lady who didn't have many friends.'

'Why not?'

'She was from the Delta, and most of those folks have a good dose of blue blood. That's what the Judge wanted in a wife, but it didn't work too well around here. She thought she was marrying money. Judges didn't make squat back

126

then, so she had to work hard at being better than everybody else.'

'You didn't like her.'

'Not particularly. She thought I was unpolished.'

'Imagine that.'

'I loved your father, Ray, but there weren't too many tears at her funeral.'

'Let's get through one funeral at a time.'

'Sorry.'

'What was in the will you prepared for him? The last one.'

Harry Rex laid the obituary on the desk and sat back in his chair. He glanced at the window behind Ray, then spoke softly. 'The Judge wanted to set up a trust so that when this place was sold the money would go there. I'd be the trustee and as such I'd have the pleasure of doling out the money to you and him.' He nodded toward the porch. 'But his first hundred thousand would be paid back to the estate. That's how much the Judge figured Forrest owed him.'

'What a disaster.'

'I tried to talk him out of it.'

'Thank God he burned it.'

'Yes indeed. He knew it was a bad idea, but he was trying to protect Forrest from himself.'

'We've been trying for twenty years.'

'He thought of everything. He was going to leave it all to you, cut him out completely, but he knew that would only cause friction. Then he got mad because neither of you would ever live here, so he asked me to do a will that gave the house to the church. He never signed it, then Palmer pissed him off over the death penalty and he ditched that idea, said he would have it sold after his death and give the money to charity.' He stretched his arms upward until his spine popped. Harry Rex had had two back surgeries and was seldom comfortable. He continued. 'I'm guessing the reason he called you and Forrest home was so the three of you could decide what to do with the estate.'

'Then why did he do a last-minute will?'

'We'll never know, will we? Maybe he got tired of the pain. I suspect he'd grown fond of the morphine, like most folks at the end. Maybe he knew he was about to die.'

Ray looked into the eyes of General Nathan Bedford Forrest, who'd been gazing sternly on the Judge's study from the same perch for almost a century. Ray had no doubt that his father had chosen to die on the sofa so that the general could help him through it. The general knew. He knew how and when the Judge died. He knew where the cash came from. He knew who had broken in last night and trashed the office.

'Did he ever include Claudia in anything?' Ray asked.

'Never. He could hold a grudge, you know that.'

'She stopped by this morning.'

'What'd she want?'

'I think she was looking for money. She said the Judge had always promised to take care of her, and she wanted to know what was in the will.'

'Did you tell her?'

'With pleasure.'

'She'll be all right, never worry about that woman. You remember old Walter Sturgis, out from Karraway, a dirt contractor for years, tight as a tick?' Harry Rex knew everybody in the county, all thirty thousand souls – blacks, whites, and now the Mexicans.

'I don't think so.'

'He's rumored to have a half a million bucks in cash, and she's after it. Got the ole boy wearing golf shirts and eating at the country club. He told his buddies he takes Viagra every day.'

'Atta boy.'

'She'll break him.'

Forrest shifted somehow in the porch swing and the chains creaked. They waited a moment, until all was quiet out there. Harry Rex opened a file and said, 'Here's the appraisal. We had it done late last year by a guy from Tupelo, probably the best appraiser in north Mississippi.'

'How much?'

'Four hundred thousand.'

'Sold.'

'I thought he was high. Of course, the Judge thought the place was worth a million.'

'Of course.'

'I figure three hundred is more likely.'

'We won't get half that much. What's the appraisal based on?'

'It's right here. Square footage, acreage, charm, comps, the usual.'

'Give me a comp.'

Harry Rex flipped through the appraisal. 'Here's one. A house about the same age, same size, thirty acres, on the edge of Holly Springs, sold two years ago for eight hundred grand.'

'This is not Holly Springs.'

'No, it's not.'

'That's an antebellum town, with lots of old houses.'

'You want me to sue the appraiser?'

'Yeah, let's go after him. What would you give for this place?'

'Nothing. You want a beer?'

'No.'

Harry Rex lumbered into the kitchen, and returned with a tall can of Pabst Blue Ribbon. 'I don't know why he buys this stuff,' he mumbled, then gulped a fourth of it.

'Always been his brand.'

Harry Rex peeked through the blinds and saw nothing but Forrest's feet hanging off the swing. 'I don't think he's too worried about his father's estate.'

'He's like Claudia, just wants a check.'

'Money would kill him.'

It was reassuring to hear Harry Rex share this belief. Ray waited until he returned to the desk because he wanted to watch his eyes carefully. 'The Judge earned less than nine thousand dollars last year,' Ray said, looking at a tax return.

'He was sick,' Harry Rex said, stretching and twisting his substantial back, then sitting down. 'But he was hearing cases until this year.'

'What kind of cases?'

'All sorts of stuff. We had this Nazi right-wing governor a few years back –'

'I remember him.'

'Liked to pray all the time when he campaigned, family values, anti-everything but guns. Turned out he liked the ladies, his wife caught him, big stink, really juicy stuff. The local judges down in Jackson wanted no part of the case for obvious reasons, so they asked the Judge to ride in and referee things.'

'Did it go to trial?'

'Oh hell yeah, big ugly trial. The wife had the goods on the governor, who thought he could intimidate the Judge. She got the governor's house and most of the money. Last I heard he was living above his brother's garage, with bodyguards, of course.'

'Did you ever see the old man intimidated?'

'Never. Not once in thirty years.'

Harry Rex worked on his beer and Ray looked at another tax return. Things were quiet, and

131

when he heard Forrest snore again, Ray said, 'I found some money, Harry Rex.'

His eyes conveyed nothing. No conspiracy, no surprise, no relief. They didn't blink and they didn't stare. He waited, then finally shrugged and said, 'How much?'

'A boxful.' The questions would follow, and Ray had tried to predict them.

Again Harry Rex waited, then another innocent shrug. 'Where?'

'Over there, in that cabinet behind the sofa. It was cash in a box, over ninety thousand bucks.'

So far he had not told a lie. He certainly hadn't given the entire truth, but he wasn't lying. Not yet.

'Ninety thousand bucks?' Harry Rex said, a little too loudly and Ray nodded toward the porch.

'Yes, in one-hundred-dollar bills,' he said in a lower voice. 'Any idea where it came from?'

Harry Rex gulped from the can, then squinted his eyes at the wall and finally said, 'Not really.'

'Gambling? You said he could throw the dice.'

Another sip. 'Yeah, maybe. The casinos opened six or seven years ago, and he and I would go once a week, at least in the beginning."

'You stopped?'

'I wish. Between me and you, I was going all the time. I was gambling so much I didn't want the Judge to know it, so whenever he and I went

132

I always played it light. Next night, I'd sneak over and lose my ass again.'

'How much did you lose?'

'Let's talk about the Judge.'

'Okay, did he win?'

'Usually. On a good night he'd win a coupla thousand.'

'On a bad night?'

'Five hundred, that was his limit. If he was losin', he knew when to quit. That's the secret to gamblin', you gotta know when to quit, and you gotta have the guts to walk away. He did. I did not.'

'Did he go without you?'

'Yeah, I saw him once. I sneaked over one night and picked a new casino, hell they got fifteen now, and while I was playin' blackjack things got hot at a craps table not too far away. In the thick of things, I saw Judge Atlee. Had on a baseball cap so folks wouldn't recognize him. His disguises didn't always work because I'd hear things around town. A lot of folks go to the casinos and there were sightings.'

'How often did he go?'

'Who knows? He answered to no one. I had a client, one of those Higginbotham boys who sell used cars, and he told me he saw old Judge Atlee at the craps table at three o'clock one mornin' at Treasure Island. So I figured the Judge sneaked over at odd hours so folks wouldn't see him.'

Ray did some quick math. If the Judge gambled three times a week for five years and won two thousand dollars every time, his winnings would have been somewhere around one and a half million.

'Could he have rat-holed ninety thousand?' Ray asked. It sounded like such a small amount.

'Anything's possible, but why hide it?'

'You tell me.'

They pondered this for a while. Harry Rex finished the beer and lit a cigar. A sluggish ceiling fan above the desk pushed the smoke around. He shot a cloud of exhaust toward the fan and said, 'You gotta pay taxes on your winnings, and since he didn't want anybody to know about his gambling, maybe he just kept it all quiet.'

'But don't the casinos require paperwork if you win a certain amount?'

'I never saw any damned paperwork.'

'But if you'd won?'

'Yeah, they do. I had a client who won eleven thousand at the five-dollar slots. They gave him a form ten-ninety-nine, a notice to the IRS.'

'What about shooting craps?'

'If you cash in more than ten thousand in chips at one time, then there's paperwork. Keep it under ten, and there's nothin'. Same as cash transactions at a bank.'

'I doubt if the Judge wanted records.'

'I'm sure he did not.'

'He never mentioned any cash when y'all were doing his wills?'

'Never. The money is a secret, Ray. I can't

explain it. I have no idea what he was thinkin'. Surely he knew it would be found.'

'Right. The question now is what do we do with it.'

Harry Rex nodded and stuck the cigar in his mouth. Ray leaned back and watched the fan. For a long time they contemplated what to do with the money. Neither wanted to suggest that they simply continue to hide it. Harry Rex decided to fetch another beer. Ray said he'd take one too. As the minutes passed it became obvious that the money would not be discussed again, not that day. In a few weeks, when the estate was opened and an inventory of assets was filled, they could visit the issue again. Or perhaps they would not.

For two days, Ray had debated whether or not to tell Harry Rex about the cash, not the entire fortune, but just a sample of it. After doing so, there were more questions than answers.

Little light had been shed on the money. The Judge enjoyed the dice and was good at gambling, but it seemed unlikely he could have cleared $3.1 million in seven years. And to do so without creating paperwork and leaving a trail seemed impossible.

Ray returned to the tax records while Harry Rex plowed through the ledgers of donations. 'Which CPA are you gonna use?' Ray asked after a long period of silence.

'There are several.'

135

'Not local.'

'No, I stay away from the guys around here. It's a small town.'

'Looks to me like the records are in good shape,' Ray said, closing a drawer.

'It'll be easy, except for the house.'

'Let's put it on the market, the sooner the better. It won't be a quick sell.'

'What's the asking price?'

'Let's start at three hundred.'

'Are we spending money to fix it up?'

'There is no money, Harry Rex.'

Just before dark, Forrest announced he was tired of Clanton, tired of death, tired of hanging around a depressing old house he had never particularly cared for, tired of Harry Rex and Ray, and that he was going home to Memphis where wild women and parties were waiting.

'When are you coming back?' he asked Ray.

'Two or three weeks.'

'For probate?'

'Yes,' Harry Rex answered. 'We'll make a brief appearance before the judge. You're welcome to be there, but it's not required.'

'I don't do court. Been there enough.'

The brothers walked down the drive to Forrest's car. 'You okay?' Ray asked, but only because he felt compelled to show concern.

'I'm fine. See you, Bro,' Forrest said, in a hurry to leave before his brother blurted something stupid. 'Call me when you come back,' he

136

said. He started the car and drove away. Ray knew he would pull over somewhere between Clanton and Memphis, either at a joint with a bar and a pool table, or maybe just a beer store where he would buy a case and slug it as he drove. Forrest had survived his father's funeral in an impressive way, but the pressure had been building. The meltdown would not be pretty.

Harry Rex was hungry, as usual, and asked if Ray wanted fried catfish. 'Not really,' he answered.

'Good, there's a new place on the lake.'

'What's it called?'

'Jeter's Catfish Shack.'

'You're kidding.'

'No, it's delicious.'

They dined on an empty deck jutting over a swamp, on the backwaters of the lake. Harry Rex ate catfish twice a week; Ray, once every five years. The cook was heavy on the batter and peanut oil, and Ray knew it would be a long night, for several reasons.

He slept with a loaded gun in the bed of his old room, upstairs, with the windows and doors locked, and the three garbage bags packed with money at his feet. With such an arrangement, it was difficult to look around in the dark and conjure up any pleasant childhood memories that would normally be just under the surface. The house had been dark and cold back then, especially after his mother died.

Instead of reminiscing, he tried to sleep by

counting little round black chips, a hundred bucks each, hauled by the Judge from the tables to the cashiers. He counted with imagination and ambition, and he got nowhere near the fortune he was in bed with.

Chapter 14

The Clanton square had three cafés, two for the whites and one for the blacks. The Tea Shoppe crowd leaned toward banking and law and retail, more of a white-collar bunch, where the chatter was a bit heavier – the stock market, politics, golf. Claude's, the black diner, had been around for forty years and had the best food.

The Coffee Shop was favored by the farmers, cops, and factory workers who talked football and bird hunting. Harry Rex preferred it, as did a few other lawyers who liked to eat with the people they represented. It opened at five every morning but Sunday, and was usually crowded by six. Ray parked near it on the square and locked his car. The sun was inching above the hills to the east. He would drive fifteen hours or so and hopefully be home by midnight.

Harry Rex had a table in the window and a Jackson newspaper that had already been rearranged and folded to the point of being useless to anyone else. 'Anything in the news?' Ray asked. There was no television at Maple Run.

'Not a damned thang,' Harry Rex grumbled with his eyes glued to the editorials. 'I'll send you all the obituaries.' He slid across a crumpled section the size of a paperback. 'You wanna read this?'

'No, I need to go.'

'You're eating first?'

'Yes.'

'Hey, Dell!' Harry Rex yelled across the café. The counter and booths and other tables were crowded with men, only men, all eating and talking.

'Dell is still here?' Ray asked.

'She doesn't age,' Harry Rex said, waving. 'Her mother is eighty and her grandmother is a hundred. She'll be here long after we're buried.'

Dell did not appreciate being yelled at. She arrived with a coffeepot and an attitude, which vanished when she realized who Ray was. She hugged him and said, 'I haven't seen you in twenty years.' Then she sat down, clutched his arm, and began saying how sorry she was about the Judge.

'Wasn't it a great funeral?' Harry Rex said.

'I can't remember a finer one,' she said, as if Ray was supposed to be both comforted and impressed.

'Thank you,' he said, his eyes watering not from sadness but from the medley of cheap perfumes swirling about her.

140

Then she jumped up and said, 'What're y'all eatin'? It's on the house.'

Harry Rex decided on pancakes and sausage, for both of them, a tall stack for him, short for Ray. Dell disappeared, a thick cloud of fragrances lingering behind.

'You got a long drive. Pancakes'll stick to your ribs.'

After three days in Clanton, everything was sticking to his ribs. Ray looked forward to some long runs in the countryside around Charlottesville, and to much lighter cuisine.

To his great relief, nobody else recognized him. There were no other lawyers in the Coffee Shop at that hour, and no one else who'd known the Judge well enough to attend his funeral. The cops and mechanics were too busy with their jokes and gossip to look around. Remarkably, Dell kept her mouth shut. After the first cup of coffee, Ray relaxed and began to enjoy the waves of conversation and laughter around him.

Dell was back with enough food for eight; pancakes, a whole hog's worth of sausage, a tray of hefty biscuits with a bowl of butter, and a bowl of somebody's homemade jam. Why would anyone need biscuits to eat with pancakes? She patted his shoulder again and said, 'And he was such a sweet man.' Then she was gone.

'Your father was a lot of things,' Harry Rex said, drowning his hotcakes with at least a quart of somebody's homemade molasses. 'But he wasn't sweet.'

'No he was not,' Ray agreed. 'Did he ever come in here?'

'Not that I recall. He didn't eat breakfast, didn't like crowds, hated small talk, preferred to sleep as late as possible. I don't think this was his kind of place. For the past nine years, he hasn't been seen much around the square.'

'Where'd Dell meet him?'

'In court. One of her daughters had a baby. The daddy already had a family. A real mess.' He somehow managed to shovel into his mouth a serving of pancakes that would choke a horse. Then a bite of sausage.

'And of course you were in the middle of it.'

'Of course. Judge treated her right.' Chomp, chomp.

Ray felt compelled to take a large bite of his food. With molasses dripping everywhere, he leaned forward and lifted a heavy fork to his mouth.

'The Judge was a legend, Ray, you know that. Folks around here loved him. He never got less than eighty percent of the vote in Ford County.'

Ray nodded as he worked on the pancakes. They were hot and buttery, but not particularly tasty.

'If we spend five thousand bucks on the house,' Harry Rex said without showing food, 'then we'll get it back several times over. It's a good investment.'

'Five thousand for what?'

He wiped his mouth with one long swipe. 'Clean the damned thing first. Spray it, wash it, fumigate it, clean the floors and walls and furniture, make it smell better. Then paint the outside and the downstairs. Fix the roof so the ceilings won't spot. Cut the grass, pull the weeds, just spruce it up. I can find folks around here to do it.' He thrust another serving into his jaws and waited for Ray to respond.

'There's only six thousand in the bank,' Ray said.

Dell dashed by and somehow managed to refill both coffee cups and pat Ray on the shoulder without missing a stride.

'You got more in that box you found,' Harry Rex said, carving another wedge of pancakes.

'So we spend it?'

'I been thinking about it,' he said, gulping coffee. 'Fact, I's up all night thinking about it.'

'And?'

'Got two issues, one's important, the other's not.' A quick bite of modest proportions, then using the knife and fork to help him talk, he continued: 'First, where'd it come from? That's what we want to know, but it ain't really that important. If he robbed a bank, he's dead. If he hit the casinos and didn't pay taxes, he's dead. If he simply liked the smell of cash and saved it over the years, he's still dead. You follow?'

Ray shrugged as if he was waiting for something complicated. Harry Rex used the break in his monologue to eat sausage, then began stabbing the air again: 'Second, what are you going to do with it? That's what's important. We're assuming nobody knows about the money, right?'

Ray nodded and said, 'Right. It was hidden.' Ray could hear the windows being rattled. He could see the Blake & Son boxes scattered and crushed.

He couldn't help but glance through the window and look at his TT roadster, packed and ready to flee.

'If you include the money in the estate, half will go to the IRS.'

'I know that, Harry Rex. What would you do?'

'I'm not the right person to ask. I've been at war with the IRS for eighteen years, and guess who's winnin'? Not me. Screw 'em.'

'That's your advice as an attorney?'

'No, as a friend. If you want legal advice, then I will tell you that all assets must be collected and properly inventoried pursuant to the Mississippi Code, as annotated and amended.'

'Thank you.'

'I'd take twenty thousand or so, put it in the estate to pay the up-front bills, then wait a long time and give Forrest his half of the rest.'

'Now, that's what I call legal advice.'

'Nope, it's just common sense.'

The mystery of the biscuits was solved when Harry Rex attacked them. 'How 'bout a biscuit?' he said, though they were closer to Ray.

'No thanks.'

Harry Rex sliced two in half, buttered them, added a thick layer of jam, then, at the last moment, inserted a patty of sausage. 'You sure?'

'Yes, I'm sure. Could the money be marked in any way?'

'Only if it's ransom or drug money. Don't reckon Reuben Atlee was into those sorts of things, you?'

'Okay, spend five thousand.'

'You'll be pleased.'

A small man with matching khaki pants and shirt stopped at the table, and with a warm smile said, 'Excuse me, Ray, but I'm Loyd Darling.' He stuck out a hand as he spoke. 'I have a farm just east of town.'

Ray shook his hand and half-stood. Mr. Loyd Darling owned more land than anybody in Ford County. He had once taught Ray in Sunday School. 'So good to see you,' Ray said.

'Keep your seat,' he said, gently shoving Ray down by the shoulder. 'Just wanted to say how sorry I am about the Judge.'

'Thank you, Mr. Darling.'

'There was no finer man than Reuben Atlee. You have my sympathies.'

Ray just nodded. Harry Rex had stopped eating and appeared to be ready to cry. Then Loyd was gone and breakfast resumed. Harry Rex launched into a war story about IRS abuse. After another bite or two Ray was stuffed, and as he pretended to listen he thought of all the fine

145

folks who so greatly admired his father, all the Loyd Darlings out there who revered the old man.

What if the cash didn't come from the casinos? What if a crime had been committed, some secret horrible sting perpetrated by the Judge? Sitting there among the crowd in the Coffee Shop, watching Harry Rex but not listening to him, Ray Atlee made a decision. He vowed to himself that if he ever discovered that the cash now crammed into the trunk of his car had been collected by his father in some manner that was less than ethical, then no one would ever know it. He would not desecrate the stellar reputation of Judge Reuben Atlee.

He signed a contract with himself, shook hands, made a blood oath, swore to God. Never would anyone know.

They said good-bye on the sidewalk in front of yet another law office. Harry Rex bear-hugged him, and Ray tried to return the embrace but his arms were pinned to his sides.

'I can't believe he's gone,' Harry Rex said, his eyes moist again.

'I know, I know.'

He walked away, shaking his head and fighting back tears. Ray jumped in his Audi and left the square without looking back. Minutes later he was on the edge of town, past the old drive-in where porno had been introduced, past the shoe factory where a strike had been mediated by the Judge. Past everything until he was in the country, away from the traffic, away from the legend. He glanced at his speedometer and realized he was driving almost ninety miles an hour.

Cops should be avoided, as well as rear-end collisions. The drive was long, but the timing of the arrival in Charlottesville was crucial. Too early and there would be foot traffic on the downtown mall. Too late and the night patrol might see him and ask questions.

Across the Tennessee line, he stopped for gas and a rest room break. He'd had too much coffee. And too much food. He tried to call Forrest on his cell phone, but there was no answer. He took it as neither good news or bad – with Forrest nothing was predictable.

Moving again, he kept his speed at fifty-five and the hours began to pass. Ford County faded into another lifetime. Everyone has to be from somewhere, and Clanton was not a bad place to call home. But if he never saw it again, he would not be unhappy.

Exams were over in a week, graduation the week after, then the summer break. Because he was supposed to be researching and writing, he'd have no classes to teach for the next three months. Which meant he had very little to do at all.

He would return to Clanton and take the oath as executor of his father's estate. He would make all the decisions that Harry Rex asked him to

make. And he would try to solve the mystery of
the money.

Chapter 15

With ample time to plan his movements, he was not surprised when nothing went right. His arrival time was suitable, 11:20 P.M., Wednesday, May 10. He had hoped to park illegally at the curb, just a few feet from the ground-level door to his apartment, but other drivers had the same idea. The curb had never been so completely blocked with a line of cars, and, to his anxious satisfaction, every one of them had a citation under a windshield wiper.

He could park in the street while he dashed back and forth, but that would invite trouble. The small lot behind his building had four spaces, one reserved for him, but they locked the gate at eleven.

So he was forced to use a dark and almost completely abandoned parking garage three blocks away, a large cavernous multilevel that was sold out during the day and eerily empty at night. He'd thought about this alternative off and on for many hours, as he drove north and east and plotted the offensive, and it was the least attractive of all options. It was plan D or E, somewhere way down the list of ways he wanted to transfer the money. He parked on level one, got out with his overnight bag, locked the car, and with great anxiety left it there. He hurried away, eyes darting around as if armed gangs were watching and waiting. His legs and back were stiff from the drive, but he had work to do.

The apartment looked precisely the same as when he'd left it, which was an odd relief. Thirty-four messages awaited him, no doubt colleagues and friends calling with their sympathies. He would listen later.

At the bottom of a tiny closet in the hall, under a blanket and a poncho and other things that had been tossed in, as opposed to being placed or stored, he found a red Wimbledon tennis bag that he hadn't touched in at least two years. Aside from luggage, which he thought would appear too suspicious, it was the largest bag he could think of.

If he'd had a gun he would've stuck it in his pocket. But crime was rare in Charlottesville, and he preferred to live without weapons. After the episode Sunday in Clanton, he was even more terrified of pistols and such. He'd left the Judge's guns hidden in a closet at Maple Run.

With the bag slung over a shoulder, he locked his door on the street and tried his best to walk casually along the downtown mall. It was well lit, there was a cop or two always watching, and the pedestrians at this hour were the wayward kids with green hair, an occasional wino, and a few stragglers working their way home. Charlottesville was a quiet town after midnight.

A thundershower had passed through not long before his arrival. The streets were wet and the wind was blowing. He passed a young couple walking hand in hand but saw no one else on the way to the garage.

He'd given some thought to simply hauling the garbage bags themselves, just throwing them over a shoulder like Santa, one at a time, and walking hurriedly from wherever he was parked to his apartment. He could move the money in three trips and cut his exposure on the street. Two things stopped him. First, what if one ripped, and a million bucks hit the pavement? Every thug and wino in town would come out of the alleys, drawn like sharks to blood. Second, the sight of anyone hauling bags of what appeared to be trash into an apartment, as opposed to away from it, might be suspicious enough to attract the attention of the police.

'What's in the bag, sir?' a cop might ask.

'Nothing. Garbage. A million dollars.' No answer seemed correct.

So the plan was to be patient, take all the time that was necessary, move the loot in small loads, and not worry about how many trips might be required because the least important factor was Ray's fatigue. He could rest later.

The terrifying part was the transferring of the

money from one bag to another while crouching over his trunk and trying not to look guilty. Fortunately, the garage was deserted. He crammed money into the tennis bag until it would barely zip, then slammed the trunk down, looked around as if he'd just smothered someone, and left.

Perhaps a third of a garbage bag – three hundred thousand dollars. Much more than enough to get him arrested or knifed. Nonchalance was what he desperately wanted, but there was nothing fluid about his steps and movements. Eyes straight ahead, though the eyes wanted to dart up and down, right and left, nothing could be missed. A frightening teenager with studs in his nose stumbled by, stoned out of his wasted mind. Ray walked even faster, not sure if he had the nerves for eight or nine more trips to the parking garage.

A drunk on a dark bench yelled something unintelligible at him. He lurched forward, then caught himself, and was thankful he had no gun. At that moment, he might've shot anything that moved. The cash got heavier with each block, but he made it without incident. He spilled the money onto his bed, locked every door possible, and took another route back to his car.

During the fifth trip, he was confronted by a deranged old man who jumped from the shadows and demanded, 'What the hell are you doing?' He was holding something dark in his hand. Ray assumed it was a weapon with which to slaughter him.

'Get out of the way,' he said as rudely as possible, but his mouth was dry.

'You keep going back and forth,' the old man yelled. He stank and his eyes were glowing like a demon's.

'Mind your own business.' Ray had never stopped walking, and the old man was in front of him, bouncing along. The village idiot.

'What's the problem?' came a clear crisp voice from behind them. Ray stopped and a policeman ambled over, nightstick in hand.

Ray was all smiles. 'Evening, Officer.' He was breathing hard and his face was sweaty.

'He's up to something!' the old man yelled. 'Keeps going back and forth, back and forth. Goes that way, the bag is empty. Goes that way, the bag is full.'

'Relax, Gilly,' the cop said, and Ray took a deeper breath. He was horrified that someone had been watching, but relieved because that someone was of Gilly's ilk. Of all the characters on the mall, Ray had never seen this one.

'What's in the bag?' the cop asked.

It was a dumb question, far into foul territory, and for a split second Ray, the law professor, considered a lecture on stops, searches, seizures, and permissible police questioning. He let it pass, though, and smoothly delivered the prepared line. 'I played tennis tonight at Boar's Head. Got a bad hamstring, so I'm just walking it off. I live over there.' He pointed to his apartment two blocks down.

The cop turned to Gilly and said, 'You can't be yelling at people, Gilly, I've told you that. Does Ted know you're out?'

'He's got something in that bag,' Gilly said, much softer. The cop was leading him away.

'Yes, it's cash,' said the cop. 'I'm sure the guy's a bank robber, and you caught him. Good work.'

'But it's empty, then it's full.'

'Good night, sir,' the officer said over his shoulder.

'Good night.' And Ray, the wounded tennis player, actually limped for half a block for the benefit of other characters lurking in the darkness. When he dumped the fifth load on his bed, he found a bottle of scotch in his small liquor cabinet and poured a stiff one.

He waited for two hours, ample time for Gilly to return to Ted, who hopefully could keep him medicated and confined for the rest of the night, and time perhaps for a shift change so a different cop would be walking the beat. Two very long hours, in which he imagined every possible scenario involving his car in the parking garage. Theft, vandalism, fire, towed away by some misguided wrecker, everything imaginable.

At 3 A.M., he emerged from his apartment wearing jeans, hiking boots, and a navy sweatshirt with VIRGINIA across the chest. He'd ditched the red tennis bag in favor of a battered

154

leather briefcase, one that would not hold as much money but wouldn't catch the attention of the cop either. He was armed with a steak knife stuck in his belt, under the sweatshirt, ready to be withdrawn in a flash and used on the likes of Gilly or any other assailant. It was foolish and he knew it, but he wasn't himself either and he was quite aware of that. He was dead-tired, sleep-deprived for the third night in a row, just a little tipsy from three scotches, determined to get the money safely hidden, and scared of getting stopped again.

Even the winos had given up at three in the morning. The downtown streets were deserted. But as he entered the parking garage, he saw something that terrified him. At the far end of the mall, passing under a street lamp, was a group of five or six black teenagers. They were moving slowly in his general direction, yelling, talking loudly, looking for trouble.

It would be impossible to make a half-dozen more deliveries without running into them. The final plan was created on the spot.

Ray cranked the Audi and left the garage. He circled around and stopped in the street next to the cars parked illegally on the curb, close to the door to his apartment. He killed the engine and the lights, opened the trunk, and grabbed the money. Five minutes later, the entire fortune was upstairs, where it belonged.

★

At 9 A.M. the phone woke him. It was Harry Rex. 'Wake your ass up, boy,' he growled. 'How was the trip?'

Ray swung to the edge of his bed and tried to open his eyes. 'Wonderful,' he grunted.

'I talked to a Realtor yesterday, Baxter Redd, one of the better ones in town. We walked around the place, kicked the tires, you know, whatta mess. Anyway, he wants to stick to the appraised value, four hundred grand, and he thinks we can get at least two-fifty. He gets the usual six percent. You there?'

'Yeah.'

'Then say something, okay?'

'Keep going.'

'He agrees we need to spend some dough to fix it up, a little paint, a little floor wax, a good bonfire would help. He recommended a cleaning service. You there?'

'Yes.' Harry Rex had been up for hours, no doubt refueled with another feast of pancakes, biscuits, and sausage.

'Anyway, I've already hired a painter and a roofer. We'll need an infusion of capital pretty soon.'

'I'll be back in two weeks, Harry Rex, can't it wait?'

'Sure. You hungover?'

'No, just tired.'

'Well, get your ass in gear, it's after nine there.'

'Thanks.'

'Speaking of hangovers,' he said, his voice suddenly lower, his words softer, 'Forrest called me last night.'

Ray stood and arched his back. 'This can't be good,' he said.

'No, it's not. He's tanked, couldn't tell if it was booze or drugs, probably both. Whatever he's on, there's plenty of it. He was so mellow I thought he was falling asleep, then he'd fire up and cuss me.'

'What did he want?'

'Money. Not now, he says, claims he's not broke, but he's concerned about the house and the estate and wants to make sure you don't screw him.'

'Screw him?'

'He was bombed, Ray, so you can't hold it against him. But he said some pretty bad things.'

'I'm listening.'

'I'm tellin' you so you'll know, but please don't get upset. I doubt he'll remember it this mornin'.'

'Go ahead, Harry Rex.'

'He said the Judge always favored you and that's why he made you the executor of his estate, that you've always gotten more out of the old man, that it's my job to watch you and protect his interests in the estate because you'll try to screw him out of the money, and so on.'

'That didn't take long, did it? We've hardly got him in the ground.'

'No.'

'I'm not surprised.'

'Keep your guard up. He's on a binge and he might call you with the same crap.'

'I've heard it before, Harry Rex. His problems are not his fault. Somebody's always out to get him. Typical addict.'

'He thinks the house is worth a million bucks, and said it's my job to get that much for it. Otherwise, he might have to hire his own lawyer, blah, blah, blah. It didn't bother me. Again, he was blitzed.'

'He's pitiful.'

'He is indeed, but he'll bottom out and sober up in a week or so. Then I'll cuss him. We'll be fine.'

'Sorry, Harry Rex.'

'It's part of my job. Just one of the joys of practicin' law.'

Ray fixed a pot of coffee, a strong Italian blend he was quite attached to and had missed sorely in Clanton. The first cup was almost gone before his brain woke up.

Any trouble with Forrest would run its course. In spite of his many problems, he was basically harmless. Harry Rex would handle the estate and there would be an equal division of everything left over. In a year or so, Forrest would get a check for more money than he had ever seen.

The image of a cleaning service turned loose at Maple Run bothered him for a while. He could see a dozen women buzzing around like ants, happy with so much to clean. What if they stumbled upon another treasure trove fiendishly left behind by the Judge? Mattresses stuffed with cash? Closets filled with loot? But it wasn't possible. Ray had pored over every inch of the house. You find three million bucks tucked away and you get motivated to pry under every board. He'd even clawed his way through spiderwebs in the basement, a dungeon no cleaning lady would enter.

He poured another cup of strong coffee and walked to his bedroom, where he sat in a chair and stared at the piles of cash. Now what?

Through the blur of the last four days, he had concentrated only on getting the money to the spot where it was now located. Now he had to plan the next step, and he had very few ideas. It had to be hidden and protected, he knew that much for sure.

Chapter 16

There was a large floral arrangement in the center of his desk, with a sympathy card signed by all fourteen students in his antitrust class. Each had written a small paragraph of condolences, and he read them all. Beside the flowers was a stack of cards from his colleagues on the faculty.

Word spread fast that he was back, and throughout the morning the same colleagues dropped by with a quick hello, welcome back, sorry about your loss. For the most part the faculty was a close group. They could bicker with the best of them on the trivial issues of campus politics, but they were quick to circle the wagons in times of need. Ray was very happy to see them. Alex Duffman's wife sent a platter of her infamous chocolate brownies, each weighing a pound and proven to add three more to your waist. Naomi Kraig brought a small collection of roses she'd picked from her garden.

Late in the morning Carl Mirk stopped by

and closed the door. Ray's closest friend on the faculty, his journey to the law school had been remarkably similar. They were the same age, and both had fathers who were small-town judges who'd ruled their little counties for decades. Carl's father was still on the bench, and still holding a grudge because his son did not return to practice law in the family firm. It appeared, though, that the grudge was fading with the years, whereas Judge Atlee apparently carried his to his death.

'Tell me about it,' Carl said. Before long he would make the same trip back to his hometown in northern Ohio.

Ray began with the peaceful house, too peaceful, he recalled now. He described the scene when he found the Judge.

'You found him dead?' Carl asked. The narrative continued, then, 'You think he speeded things up a bit?'

'I hope so. He was in a lot of pain.'

'Wow.'

The story unfolded in great detail, as Ray remembered things he had not thought about since last Sunday. The words poured forth, the telling became therapeutic. Carl was an excellent listener.

Forrest and Harry Rex were colorfully described. 'We don't have characters like that in Ohio,' Carl said. When they told their small-town stories, usually to colleagues from the cities, they stretched the facts and the characters

161

became larger. Not so with Forrest and Harry Rex. The truth was sufficiently colorful.

The wake, the funeral, the burial. When Ray closed with 'Taps' and the lowering of the casket, both had moist eyes. Carl bounced to his feet and said, 'What a great way to go. I'm sorry.'

'Just glad it's over.'

'Welcome back. Let's do lunch tomorrow.'

'What's tomorrow?'

'Friday.'

'Lunch it is.'

For his noon antitrust class, Ray ordered pizzas from a carryout and ate them outside in the courtyard with his students. Thirteen of the fourteen were there. Eight would be graduating in two weeks. The students were more concerned about Ray and the death of his father than about their final exams. He knew that would change quickly.

When the pizza was gone, he dismissed them and they scattered. Kaley lingered behind, as she had been doing in the past months. There was a rigid no-fly zone between faculty and students, and Ray Atlee was not about to venture into it. He was much too content with his job to risk it fooling around with a student. In two weeks, though, Kaley would no longer be a student, but a graduate, and thus not covered by the rules. The flirting had picked up a bit – a serious question after class, a drop-in at his office to get a missed assignment, and always

162

that smile with the eyes that lingered for just a second too long.

She was an average student with a lovely face and a rear-end that stopped traffic. She had played field hockey and lacrosse at Brown and kept a lean athletic figure. She was twenty-eight, a widow with no kids and loads of money she'd received from the company that made the glider her deceased husband had been flying when it cracked up a few miles off the coast at Cape Cod. They found him in sixty feet of water, still strapped in, both wings snapped in two. Ray had researched the accident report online. He'd also found the court file in Rhode Island where she had sued. The settlement gave her four million up front and five hundred thousand a year for the next twenty years. He had kept this information to himself.

After chasing the boys for the first two years of law school, she was now chasing the men. Ray knew of at least two other law professors who were getting the same lingering routine as he. One just happened to be married. Evidently, all were as wary as Ray.

They strolled into the front entrance of the law school, chatting aimlessly about the final exam. She was easing closer with each flirtation, warming up to the zone, the only one who knew where she might be headed with this.

'I'd like to go flying sometime,' she announced.

Anything but flying. Ray thought of her young

husband and his horrible death, and for a second could think of nothing to say. Finally, with a smile he said, 'Buy a ticket.'

'No, no, with you, in a small plane. Let's fly somewhere.'

'Anyplace in particular?'

'Just buzz around for a while. I'm thinking of taking lessons.'

'I was thinking of something more traditional, maybe lunch or dinner, after you graduate.' She had stepped closer, so that anyone who walked by at that moment would have no doubt that they, student and professor, were discussing illicit activity.

'I graduate in fourteen days,' she said, as if she might not be able to wait that long before they hopped in the sack.

'Then I'll ask you to dinner in fifteen days.'

'No, let's break the rule now, while I'm still a student. Let's have dinner before I graduate.'

He almost said yes. 'Afraid not. The law is the law. We're here because we respect it.'

'Oh yes. It's so easy to forget. But we have a date?'

'No, we will have a date.'

She flashed another smile and walked away. He tried mightily not to admire her exit, but it was impossible.

The rented van came from a moving company north of town, sixty dollars a day. He tried for a half-day rate because he would need it only for

164

a few hours, but sixty it was. He drove it exactly four tenths of a mile and stopped at Chaney's Self-Storage, a sprawling arrangement of new cinder-block rectangles surrounded by chain link and shiny new razor wire. Video cameras on light poles watched his every move as he parked and walked into the office.

Plenty of space was available. A ten-by-ten bay was forty-eight dollars a month, no heating, no air, a roll-down door, and plenty of lighting.

'Is it fireproof?' Ray asked.

'Absolutely,' said Mrs. Chaney herself, fighting off the smoke from the cigarette stuck between her lips as she filled in forms. 'Nothing but concrete block.' Everything was safe at Chaney's. They featured electronic surveillance, she explained, as she waved at four monitors on a shelf to her left. On a shelf to her right was a small television wherein folks were yelling and fighting, a Springer-style gabfest that was now a brawl. Ray knew which shelf received the most attention.

'Twenty-four-hour guards,' she said, still doing the paperwork. 'Gate's locked at all times. Never had a break-in, and if one happens then we got all kinds of insurance. Sign right here. Fourteen B.'

Insurance on three million bucks, Ray said to himself as he scribbled his name. He paid cash for six months and took the keys to 14B.

He was back two hours later with six new storage boxes, a pile of old clothes, and a stick or two of worthless furniture he'd picked up at a flea market downtown for authenticity. He parked in the alley in front of 14B and worked quickly to unload and store his junk.

The cash was stuffed into forty-two-ounce freezer bags, zipped tight to keep air and water out, fifty-three in all. The freezer bags were arranged in the bottoms of the six storage boxes, then carefully covered with papers and files and research notes that Ray had until very recently deemed useful. Now his meticulous files served a much higher calling. A few old paperbacks were thrown in for good measure.

If, by chance, a thief penetrated 14B, he would probably abandon it after a cursory look into the boxes. The money was well hidden and as well protected as possible. Short of a safety deposit box in a bank, Ray could think of no better place to secure the money.

What would ultimately become of the money was a mystery that grew by the day. The fact that it was now safely tucked away in Virginia provided little comfort, contrary to what he had hoped.

He watched the boxes and the other junk for a while, not really anxious to leave. He vowed to himself that he would not stop by every day to check on things, but as soon as the vow was made he began to doubt it.

He secured the roll-down door with a new padlock. As he drove away, the guard was awake, the video cameras scanning, the gate locked.

Fog Newton was worrying about the weather. He had a student-pilot on a cross-country to Lynchburg and back, and thunderstorms were moving in quickly, according to radar. The clouds had not been expected, and no weather had been forecast during the student's preflight briefing.

'How many hours does he have?' Ray asked.

'Thirty-one,' Fog said gravely. Certainly not enough experience to handle thunderstorms. There were no airports between Charlottesville and Lynchburg, only mountains.

'You're not flying, are you?' Fog asked.

'I want to.'

'Forget it. This storm is coming together quickly. Let's go watch it.'

Nothing frightened an instructor more than a student up in heavy weather. Each cross-country training flight had to be carefully planned – route, time, fuel, weather, secondary airports, and emergency procedures. And each flight had to be approved in writing by the instructor. Fog had once grounded Ray because there was a slight chance of icing at five thousand feet, on a perfectly clear day.

They walked through the hangar to the ramp where a Lear was parking and shutting down its engines. To the west beyond the foothills was the first hint of clouds. The wind had picked up noticeably. 'Ten to fifteen knots, gusting,' Fog said. 'A direct crosswind.' Ray would not want to attempt a landing in such conditions.

Behind the Lear was a Bonanza taxiing to the ramp, and as it got closer Ray noticed that it was the one he'd been coveting for the past two months. 'There's your plane,' Fog said.

'I wish,' Ray said.

The Bonanza parked and shut down near them, and when the ramp was quiet again Fog said, 'I hear he's cut the price.'

'How much?'

'Somewhere around four twenty-five. Four-fifty was a little steep.'

The owner, traveling alone, crawled out and pulled his bags from the rear. Fog was gazing at the sky and glancing at his watch. Ray kept his eyes on the Bonanza, where the owner was locking the door and putting it to rest.

'Let's take it for a spin,' Ray said.

'The Bonanza?'

'Sure. What's the rent?'

'It's negotiable. I know the guy pretty well.'

'Let's get it for a day, fly up to Atlantic City, then back.'

Fog forgot about the approaching clouds and the rookie student. He turned and looked at Ray. 'You're serious?'

'Why not? Sounds like fun.'

Aside from flying and poker, Fog had few other interests. 'When?'

168

'Saturday. Day after tomorrow. Leave early, come back late.'

Fog was suddenly deep in thought. He glanced at his watch, looked once more to the west, then to the south. Dick Docker yelled from a window, 'Yankee Tango is ten miles out.'

'Thank God,' Fog mumbled to himself and visibly relaxed. He and Ray walked to the Bonanza for a closer look. 'Saturday, huh?' Fog said.

'Yep, all day.'

'I'll catch the owner. I'm sure we can work a deal.'

The winds relented for a moment and Yankee Tango landed with little effort. Fog relaxed even more and managed a smile. 'Didn't know you liked the action,' he said as they walked across the ramp.

'Just a little blackjack, nothing serious,' Ray said.

Chapter 17

The solitude of a late Friday morning was broken by the doorbell. Ray had slept late, still trying to shake off the fatigue from the trip home. Three newspapers and four coffees later he was almost fully awake.

It was a FedEx box from Harry Rex, and it was filled with letters from admirers and newspaper clippings. Ray spread them on the dining table and began with the articles. The *Clanton Chronicle* ran a front-page piece on Wednesday that featured a dignified photo of Reuben Atlee, complete with black robe and gavel. The picture was at least twenty years old. The Judge's hair was thicker and darker, and he filled out the robe. The headline read JUDGE REUBEN ATLEE DEAD AT 79. There were three stories on the front page. One was a flowery obituary. One was a collection of comments from his friends. The third was a tribute to the Judge and his amazing gift of charity.

The *Ford County Times* likewise had a picture,

one taken just a few years earlier. In it Judge Atlee was sitting on his front porch holding his pipe, looking much older but offering a rare smile. He wore a cardigan and looked like a grandfather. The reporter had cajoled him into a feature with the ruse of chatting about the Civil War and Nathan Bedford Forrest. There was the hint of a book in the works, one about the general and the men from Ford County who'd fought with him.

The Atlee sons were barely mentioned in the stories about their father. Referring to one would require referring to the other, and most folks in Clanton wanted to avoid the subject of Forrest. It was painfully obvious that the sons were not a part of their father's life.

But we could've been, Ray said to himself. It was the father who'd chosen early on to have limited involvement with the sons, not the other way around. This wonderful old man who'd given so much to so many had had so little time for his own family.

The stories and photos made him sad, which was frustrating because he had not planned to be sad this Friday. He had held up quite well since discovering his father's body five days earlier. In moments of grief and sorrow, he had dug deep and found the strength to bite his lip and push forward without breaking down. The passage of time and the distance to Clanton had helped immensely, and now from nowhere had come the saddest reminders yet.

The letters had been collected by Harry Rex from the Judge's post office box in Clanton, from the courthouse, and from the mailbox at Maple Run. Some were addressed to Ray and Forrest and some to the family of Judge Atlee. There were lengthy letters from lawyers who'd practiced before the great man and had been inspired by his passion for the law. There were cards of sympathy from people who, for one reason or another, had appeared before Judge Atlee in a divorce, or adoption, or juvenile matter, and his fairness had changed their lives. There were notes from people all over the state – sitting judges, old law school pals, politicians Judge Atlee had helped over the years, and friends who wanted to pass along their sympathies and fond memories.

The largest batch came from those who had received the Judge's charity. The letters were long and heartfelt, and all the same. Judge Atlee had quietly sent money that was desperately needed, and in many cases it had made a dramatic change in the life of someone.

How could a man so generous die with more than three million dollars hidden below his bookshelves? He certainly buried more than he gave away. Perhaps Alzheimer's had crept into his life, or some other affliction that had gone undetected. Had he slipped toward insanity? The easy answer was that the old man had simply gone nuts, but how many crazy people could put together that kind of money?

After reading twenty or so letters and cards, Ray took a break. He walked to the small balcony overlooking the downtown mall and watched the pedestrians below. His father had never seen Charlottesville, and though Ray was certain he had asked him to visit, he could not remember a specific invitation. They had never traveled anywhere together. There were so many things they could have done.

The Judge had always talked of seeing Gettysburg, Antietam, Bull Run, Chancellorsville, and Appomatox, and he would have done so had Ray shown an interest. But Ray cared nothing for the refighting of an old war, and he had always changed the subject.

The guilt hit hard, and he couldn't shake it. What a selfish ass he'd been.

There was a lovely card from Claudia. She thanked Ray for talking to her and expressing his forgiveness. She had loved his father for years and would carry her grief to her grave. Please call me, she begged, then signed off with hugs and kisses. And she's got her current boyfriend on Viagra, according to Harry Rex.

The nostalgic journey home came to an abrupt halt with a simple anonymous card that froze his pulse and sent goose bumps down the backs of both legs.

The only pink envelope in the pile contained a card with the words 'With Sympathy' on the outside. Taped to the inside was a small square piece of paper with a typed message that read:

173

'It would be a mistake to spend the money. The IRS is a phone call away.' The envelope had been postmarked in Clanton on Wednesday, the day after the funeral, and was addressed to the family of Judge Atlee at Maple Run.

Ray placed it aside while he scanned the other cards and letters. They were all the same at this point, and he'd read enough. The pink one sat there like a loaded gun, waiting for him to return to it.

He repeated the threat on the balcony as he grasped the railing and tried to analyze things. He mumbled the words in the kitchen as he fixed more coffee. He'd left the note on the table so he could see it from any part of his rambling den.

Back on the balcony he watched the foot traffic pick up as noon approached, and anyone who glanced up was a person who might know about the money. Bury a fortune, then realize you're hiding it from someone, and your imagination can get crazy.

The money didn't belong to him, and it was certainly enough to get him stalked, followed, watched, reported, even hurt.

Then he laughed at his own paranoia. I will not live like this, he said, and went to take a shower.

Whoever it was knew exactly where the Judge had hidden the money. Make a list, Ray told himself as he sat on the edge of his bed, naked, with water dripping onto the floor. The felon who cut the lawn once a week. Perhaps he was a smooth talker who'd befriended the Judge and spent time in the house. Entry was easy. When the Judge sneaked off to the casinos, maybe the grasscutter slinked through the house, pilfering.

Claudia would be at the top of the list. Ray could easily see her easing over to Maple Run whenever the Judge beckoned. You don't sleep with a woman for years then cut her off without a replacement. Their lives had been so connected it was easy to imagine their romance continuing. No one had been closer to Reuben Atlee than Claudia. If anyone knew where the money came from, it was her.

If she wanted a key to the house, she could've had one, though a key was not necessary. Her visit on the morning of the funeral could've been for surveillance and not sympathy, though she'd played it well. Tough, smart, savvy, calloused, and old but not too old. For fifteen minutes he dwelt on Claudia and convinced himself that she was the one tracking the money.

Two other names came to mind, but Ray could not add them to the list. The first was Harry Rex, and as soon as he mumbled the name he felt ashamed. The other was Forrest, and it too was a ridiculous idea. Forrest had not been inside the house for nine years. Assuming, just for the sake of argument, that he somehow had known about the money, he would never have left it. Give Forrest three million in cash and he would've done serious damage to himself and those around him.

The list took great effort but there was little to show for it. He wanted to go for a quick run, but instead stuffed some old clothes into two pillow-cases, then drove to Chaney's, where he unloaded them into 14B. Nothing had been touched, the boxes were just as he'd left them the day before. The money was still well hidden. As he loitered there, not wanting to leave until the last second, he was hit with the thought that perhaps he was creating a trail. Obviously, someone knew he had taken it from the Judge's study. For that kind of money, private investigators could be hired to follow Ray.

They could follow him from Clanton to Charlottesville, from his apartment to Chaney's Self-Storage.

He cursed himself for being so negligent. Think, man! The money doesn't belong to you!

He locked up 14B as tightly as possible. Driving across town to meet Carl for lunch, he glanced at his mirrors and watched other drivers, and after five minutes of this he laughed at himself and vowed that he would not live like wounded prey.

Let them have the damned money! One less thing to worry about. Break into 14B and haul it away. Wouldn't affect his life in the least. No sir.

Chapter 18

The estimated flying time to Atlantic City was eighty-five minutes in the Bonanza, which was exactly thirty-five minutes faster than the Cessna Ray had been renting. Early Saturday morning he and Fog did a thorough preflight under the intrusive and often obnoxious supervision of Dick Docker and Charlie Yates, who walked around the Bonanza with their tall Styrofoam cups of bad coffee as if they were flying instead of just watching. They had no students that morning, but the gossip around the airport was that Ray was buying the Bonanza and they had to see things for themselves. Hangar gossip was as reliable as coffee shop rumors.

'How much does he want now?' Docker asked in the general direction of Fog Newton, who was crouched under a wing draining a fuel sump, checking for water and dirt in the tanks.

'He's down to four-ten,' Fog said, with an air of importance because he was in charge of this flight, not them.

'Still too high,' Yates said.

'You gonna make an offer?' Docker said to Ray.

'Mind your own business,' Ray shot back without looking. He was checking the engine oil.

'This is our business,' Yates said, and they all laughed.

In spite of the unsolicited help, the preflight was completed without a problem. Fog climbed in first and buckled himself into the left seat. Ray followed in the right, and when he pulled the door hard and latched it and put on the headset he knew he had found the perfect flying machine. The two-hundred-horsepower engine started smoothly. Fog slowly went through the gauges, instruments, and radios, and when they finished a pre-takeoff checklist he called the tower. He would get it airborne, then turn it over to Ray.

The wind was light and the clouds were high and scattered, almost a perfect day for flying. They lifted off the runway at seventy miles per hour, retracted the landing gear, and climbed eight hundred feet per minute until they reached their assigned cruising altitude of six thousand feet. By then, Ray had the controls and Fog was explaining the autopilot, the radar weather, the traffic collision avoidance system. 'She's loaded,' Fog said more than once.

Fog had flown Marine fighters for one career, but for the past ten years he'd been relegated to the little Cessnas in which he'd taught Ray and a thousand others to fly. A Bonanza was the Porsche of single engines, and Fog was delighted for the rare chance to fly one. The route assigned by air traffic control took them just south and east of Washington, away from the busy airspace around Dulles and Reagan National. Thirty miles away and more than a mile up, they could see the dome of the Capitol, then they were over the Chesapeake with the skyline of Baltimore in the distance. The bay was beautiful, but the inside of the airplane was far more interesting. Ray was flying it himself without the help of the autopilot. He maintained a course, kept the assigned altitude, talked to Washington control, and listened to Fog chat incessantly about the performance ratings and features of the Bonanza.

Both pilots wanted the flight to last for hours, but Atlantic City was soon ahead. Ray descended to four thousand feet, then to three thousand, and then switched to the approach frequency. With the runway in sight, Fog took the controls and they glided to a soft touchdown. Taxiing to the general aviation ramp, they passed two rows of small Cessnas and Ray couldn't help but think that those days were behind him. Pilots were always searching for the next plane, and Ray had found his.

Fog's favorite casino was the Rio, on the boardwalk with several others. They agreed to meet for lunch in a second-floor cafeteria, then quickly lost each other. Each wanted to keep his gambling private. Ray wandered among the slots and scoped out the tables. It was Saturday and the Rio was busy. He circled around and eased up on the poker tables. Fog was in a crowd around a table, lost in his cards with a stack of chips under his hands.

Ray had five thousand dollars in his pocket – fifty of the hundred-dollar bills picked at random from the stash he'd hauled back from Clanton. His only goal that day was to drop the money in the casinos along the boardwalk and make certain it was not counterfeit, not marked, not traceable in any way. After his visit to Tunica last Monday night, he was fairly certain the money was for real.

Now he almost hoped it was marked. If so, then maybe the FBI would track him down and tell him where the money came from. He'd done nothing wrong. The guilty party was dead. Bring on the feds.

He found an empty chair at a blackjack table and laid five bills down for chips. 'Greens,' he said like a veteran gambler.

'Changing five hundred,' the dealer said, barely looking up.

'Change it,' came the reply from a pit boss. The tables were busy. Slots were ringing in the background. A crap game was hot off in the distance, men were yelling at the dice.

The dealer picked up the bills as Ray froze for a second. The other players watched with detached admiration. All were playing five- and ten-dollar chips. Amateurs.

The dealer stuffed the Judge's bills, all perfectly valid, into the money box and counted twenty twenty-five-dollar green chips for Ray, who lost half of them in the first fifteen minutes and left to find some ice cream. Down two hundred fifty and not the least bit worried about it.

He ventured near the crap tables and watched the confusion. He could not imagine his father mastering such a complicated game. Where did one learn to shoot dice in Ford County, Mississippi?

According to a thin little gambling guide he'd picked up in a bookstore, a basic wager is a come-bet, and when he mustered the courage he wedged his way between two other gamblers and placed the remaining ten chips on the pass line. The dice rolled twelve, the money was scraped away by the dealer, and Ray left the Rio to visit the Princess next door.

Inside, the casinos were all the same. Old folks staring hopelessly at the slots. Just enough coins rattling in the trays to keep them hooked. Blackjack tables crowded with subdued players slugging free beer and whiskey. Serious gamblers packed around the crap tables hollering at the dice. A few Asians playing roulette. Cocktail waitresses in silly costumes showing skin and hauling drinks.

He picked out a blackjack table and repeated

the procedure. His next five bills passed the dealer's inspection. Ray bet a hundred dollars on the first hand, but instead of quickly losing his money, he began winning.

He had too much untested cash in his pocket to waste time accumulating chips, so when he'd doubled his money, he pulled out ten more bills and asked for hundred-dollar chips. The dealer informed the pit boss, who offered a gapped smile, and said, 'Good luck.' An hour later, he left the table with twenty-two chips.

Next on his tour was the Forum, an older-looking establishment with an odor of stale cigarette smoke partially masked by cheap disinfectant. The crowd was older too because, as he soon realized, the Forum's specialty was quarter slots and those over sixty-five got a free breakfast, lunch, or dinner, take your pick. The cocktail waitresses were on the downhill side of forty and had given up the notion of showing flesh. They hustled about in what appeared to be track suits with matching sneakers.

The limit at blackjack was ten dollars a hand. The dealer hesitated when he saw Ray's cash hit the table, and he held the first bill up to the light as if he'd finally caught a counterfeiter. The pit boss inspected it too, and Ray was rehearsing his lines about procuring that particular bill down the street at the Rio. 'Cash it,' said the pit boss, and the moment passed. He lost three hundred dollars in an hour.

Fog claimed to be breaking the casino when they met for a quick sandwich. Ray was down a hundred dollars, but like all gamblers lied and said he was up slightly. They agreed to leave at 5 P.M. and fly back to Charlottesville.

The last of Ray's cash was converted to chips at a fifty-dollar table in Canyon Casino, the newest of those on the boardwalk. He played for a while but soon grew tired of cards and went to the sports bar, where he sipped a soda and watched boxing from Vegas. The five thousand he brought to Atlantic City had been thoroughly flushed through the system. He would leave with forty-seven hundred, and a wide trail. He had been filmed and photographed in seven casinos. At two of them he had filled in paperwork when cashing in chips at the cashiers' windows. At two others he had used his credit cards to make small withdrawals, just to leave more evidence behind.

If the Judge's cash was traceable, then they would know who he was and where to find him.

Fog was quiet as they rode back to the airport. His luck had turned south during the afternoon. 'Lost a couple hundred,' he finally admitted, but his demeanor suggested he'd lost much more.

'You?' he asked.

'I had a good afternoon,' Ray said. 'Won enough to pay for the charter.'

'That's not bad.'

'Don't suppose I could pay for it in cash, could I?'

'Cash is still legal,' Fog said, perking up a bit. 'Then cash it is.'

During the preflight, Fog asked if Ray wanted to fly in the left seat. 'We'll call it a lesson,' he said. The prospect of a cash transaction had raised his spirits.

Behind two commuter flights, Ray taxied the Bonanza into position and waited for traffic to clear. Under the close eye of Fog, he began the takeoff roll, accelerated to seventy miles per hour, then lifted smoothly into the air. The turbocharged engine seemed twice as powerful as the Cessna's. They climbed with little effort to seventy-five hundred feet and were soon on top of the world.

Dick Docker was napping in the Cockpit when Ray and Fog walked in to log the trip and turn in headsets. He jumped to attention and made his way to the counter. 'Didn't expect you back so soon,' he mumbled, half-asleep, as he pulled paperwork from a drawer.

'We broke the casino,' Ray said.

Fog had disappeared down into the study room of the flight school.

'Gee, I never heard that before.'

Ray was flipping through the logbook.

'You paying now?' Dick asked, scribbling numbers.

'Yes, and I want the cash discount.'

'Didn't know we had one.'

'You do now. It's ten percent.'

'We can do that. Yep, it's the old cash discount.' He figured again, then said, 'Total's thirteen hundred and twenty bucks.'

Ray was counting money from his wad of bills. 'I don't carry twenties. Here's thirteen.' As Dick was recounting the money, he said, 'Some guy came poking around today, said he wanted to take lessons and somehow your name came up.'

'Who was he?'

'Never saw him before.'

'Why was my name used?'

'It was kinda weird. I was giving him the spiel about costs and such, and out of the blue he asked if you owned an airplane. Said he knew you from someplace.'

Ray had both hands on the counter. 'Did you get his name?'

'I asked. Dolph something or other, wasn't real clear. Started acting suspicious and finally left. I watched him. He stopped by your car in the parking lot, walked around it like he might break in or something, then left. You know a Dolph?'

'I've never known a Dolph.'

'Me neither. I've never heard of a Dolph. Like I said, it was weird.'

'What'd he look like?'

'Fiftyish, small, thin, head full of grey hair slicked back, dark eyes like a Greek or something, used-car-salesman type, pointed-toe boots.'

Ray was shaking his head. Not a clue.

'Why didn't you just shoot him?' Ray asked.

'Thought he was a customer.'

'Since when are you nice to your customers?'

'You buying the Bonanza?'

'Nope. Just dreaming.'

Fog was back and they congratulated each other on a wonderful trip, promised to do it again, the usual. Driving away, Ray watched every car and every turn.

They were following him.

Chapter 19

A week passed, a week without FBI or Treasury agents knocking on his door with badges and questions about bad money tracked down in Atlantic City, a week with no sign of Dolph or anyone else following him, a week of the normal routine of running five miles in the morning and being a law professor after that.

He flew the Bonanza three times, each a lesson with Fog at his right elbow, and each lesson paid for on the spot with cash. 'Casino money,' he said with a grin, and it wasn't a lie. Fog was anxious to return to Atlantic City to reclaim his lost assets. Ray had no interest, but it wasn't a bad idea. He could boast of another good day at the tables and keep paying cash for his flying lessons.

The money was now in 37F – 14B was still rented to Ray Atlee, and it still held the old clothes and the cheap furniture; 37F was rented to NDY Ventures, named in honor of the three flight instructors at Docker's. Ray's name was nowhere on the paperwork for 37F. He leased it for three months, in cash.

'I want this confidential,' he'd said to Mrs. Chaney.

'Everything's confidential around here. We get all types.' She gave him a conspiratorial look as if to say, 'I don't care what you're hiding. Just pay me.'

He'd moved it one box at a time, hauling it at night, under the cover of darkness, with a security guard watching from a distance. Storage space 37F was identical to 14B, and when the six boxes were safely tucked away he had vowed once again to leave it alone and not stop by every day. It had never occurred to him that hauling around three million bucks could be such a chore.

Harry Rex had not called. He'd sent another overnight package with more of the same letters of sympathy and such. Ray was compelled to read them all, or least scan them just in case there was a second cryptic note. There was not.

Exams came and went and after graduation the law school would be quiet for the summer. Ray said good-bye to his students, all but Kaley, who, after her last exam, informed Ray she had decided to stay in Charlottesville through the summer. She pressed him again for a pregraduation rendezvous of some sort. Just for the hell of it.

'We are waiting until you are no longer a student,' Ray said, holding his ground but

188

wanting to yield. They were in his office with the door open.

'That's a few days away,' she said.

'Yes it is.'

'Then let's pick a date.'

'No, let's graduate first, then we'll pick a date.'

She left him with the same lingering smile and look, and Ray knew that she was trouble. Carl Mirk caught him gazing down the hall as she walked away in very tight jeans. 'Not bad,' Carl said.

Ray was slightly embarrassed, but kept watching anyway. 'She's after me,' he said.

'You're not alone. Be careful.'

They were standing in the hallway next to the door to Ray's office. Carl handed him an odd-looking envelope and said, 'Thought you'd get a kick out of this.'

'What is it?'

'It's an invitation to the Buzzard Ball.'

'The what?' Ray was pulling out the invitation.

'The first ever Buzzard Ball, probably the last too. It's a black-tie gala to benefit the preservation of bird life in the Piedmont. Look at the hosts.'

Ray read it slowly. 'Vicki and Lew Rodowski cordially invite you to . . . '

'The Liquidator is now saving our birds. Touching, huh?'

'Five thousand bucks a couple!'

'I think that's a record for Charlottesville. It was sent to the Dean. He's on the A list, we are not. Even his wife was shocked at the price.'

'Suzie's shockproof, isn't she?'

'Or so we thought. They want two hundred couples. They'll raise a million or so and show everybody how it's done. That's the plan anyway. Suzie says they'll be lucky to get thirty couples.'

'She's not going?'

'No, and the Dean is very relieved. He thinks it's the first black-tie shindig they'll miss in the last ten years.'

'Music by the Drifters?' Ray said as he scanned the rest of the invitation.

'That'll cost him fifty grand.'

'What a fool.'

'That's Charlottesville. Some clown bails out from Wall Street, gets a new wife, buys a big horse farm, starts throwing money around, and wants to be the big man in a small town.'

'Well, I'm not going.'

'You're not invited. Keep it.'

Carl was off, and Ray returned to his desk, invitation in hand. He put his feet on his desk, closed his eyes, and began daydreaming. He could see Kaley in a slinky black dress with no back at all, slits up past her thighs, very low V-neck, drop-dead gorgeous, thirteen years younger than Vicki, a helluva lot fitter, out there on the dance floor with Ray, who was not a bad dancer himself, bobbing and jerking to the Motown rhythms of the Drifters, while everybody watched and whispered, 'Who's that?'

And in response Vicki would be forced to drag old Lew out onto the floor, Lew in his designer tux, which could not hide his dumpy little belly; Lew with shrubs of bright grey hair above his ears; Lew the old goat trying to buy respect by saving the birds; Lew with the arthritic back and slow feet who moves like a dump truck; Lew proud of his trophy wife in her million-dollar dress, which reveals too much of her magnificently starved bones.

Ray and Kaley would look much better, dance much better, and, well, what would all that prove?

A nice scene to visit, but give it up. Now that he had the money he wouldn't waste it on nonsense like that.

The drive to Washington was only two hours, and more than half of it was fairly scenic and enjoyable. But his preferred method of travel had changed. He and Fog flew the Bonanza for thirty-eight minutes to Reagan National, where they were reluctantly allowed to land, even with a preapproved slot. Ray jumped in a taxi and fifteen minutes later was at the Treasury Department on Pennsylvania Avenue.

A colleague at the law school had a brother-in-law with some clout in Treasury. Phone calls had been made, and Mr. Oliver Talbert welcomed Professor Atlee into his rather comfortable office in the BEP, Bureau of Engraving and Printing. The professor was doing research on a vaguely defined project and needed less than an hour of someone's time. Talbert was not the brother-in-law, but he was asked to fill in.

They began with the topic of counterfeiting, and in broad strokes Talbert laid out the current problems, almost all blamed on technology – primarily inkjet printers and computer-generated counterfeit currency. He had samples of some of the best imitations. With a magnifier, he pointed out the flaws – the lack of detail in Ben Franklin's forehead, the missing thin thread lines running through the design background, the bleeding ink in the serial numbers. 'This is very good stuff,' he said. 'And counterfeiters are getting better.'

'Where'd you find this?' Ray asked, though the question was completely irrelevant. Talbert looked at the tag on the back of the display board. 'Mexico,' he said, and that was all.

To outpace the counterfeiters, Treasury was investing heavily in its own technology. Printers that gave the bills an almost holographic effect, watermarks, color-shifting inks, fine line printing patterns, enlarged off-center portraits, and scanners that could spot a fake in less than a second. The most effective method so far was one that had not yet been used. Simply change the color of the money. Go from green to blue to yellow then to pink. Gather up the old, flood the banks with the new, and the counterfeiters could not catch up, at least not in Talbert's opinion. 'But Congress won't allow it,' he said, shaking his head.

Tracing real money was Ray's primary concern, and they eventually got around to it. Money is not actually marked, Talbert explained, for obvious reasons. If the crook could look at the bills and see markings, then the sting would fall apart. Marking simply meant recording serial numbers, once a very tedious task because it was done manually. He told a kidnapping and ransom story. The cash arrived just minutes before the drop was planned. Two dozen FBI agents worked furiously to write down the serial numbers of the hundred-dollar bills. 'The ransom was a million bucks,' he was saying, 'and they simply ran out of time. Got about eighty thousand recorded, but it was enough. They caught the kidnappers a month later with some of the marked bills, and that broke the case.'

But a new scanner had made the job much easier. It photographs ten bills at a time, one hundred in forty seconds.

'Once the serial numbers are recorded, how do you find the money?' Ray asked, taking notes on a yellow legal pad. Would Talbert have expected anything else?

'Two ways. First, if you find the crook with the money, you simply put two and two together and nail him. That's how the DEA and FBI catch drug dealers. Bust a street dealer, cut him a deal, give him twenty thousand in marked bills to buy coke from his supplier, then catch the bigger fish holding the government's money.'

'What if you don't catch the crook?' Ray asked, and in doing so could not help but think of his departed father.

'That's the second way, and it's much more diffficult. Once the money is lifted out of circulation by the Federal Reserve, a sample of it is routinely scanned. If a marked bill is found, it can be traced back to the bank that submitted it. By then it's too late. Occasionally, a person with marked money will use it in one general location over a period of time, and we've caught a few crooks that way.'

'Sounds like a long shot.'

'Very much so,' Talbert admitted.

'I read a story a few years ago about some duck hunters who stumbled across a wrecked airplane, a small one,' Ray said casually. The tale had been rehearsed. 'There was some cash on board, seems like it was almost a million bucks. They figured it was drug money, so they kept it. Turns out it they were right, the money was marked, and it soon surfaced in their small town.'

'I think I remember that,' Talbert said.

I must be good, thought Ray. 'My question is this: could they, or could anyone else who finds money, simply submit it to the FBI or DEA or

Treasury and have it scanned to see if it was marked, and if so, where it came from?'

Talbert scratched his cheek with a bony finger and contemplated the question, then shrugged and said, 'I don't see why they couldn't. The problem, though, is obvious. They would run the risk of losing the money.'

'I'm sure it's not a common occurrence,' Ray said, and they both laughed.

Talbert had a story about a judge in Chicago who was skimming from the lawyers, small sums, five hundred and a thousand bucks a pop, to get cases moved up the docket, and for friendly rulings. He'd done it for years before the FBI got a tip. They busted some of the lawyers and convinced them to play along. Serial numbers were taken from the bills, and during the two-year operation three hundred fifty thousand was sneaked across the bench into the judge's sticky fingers. When the raid happened, the money had vanished. Someone tipped the judge. The FBI eventually found the money in the judge's brother's garage in Arizona, and everybody went to jail.

Ray caught himself squirming. Was it a coincidence, or was Talbert trying to tell him something? But as the narrative unfolded he relaxed and tried to enjoy it, close as it was. Talbert knew nothing about Ray's father.

Riding in a cab back to the airport, Ray did the math on his legal pad. For a judge like the one in Chicago, it would take eighteen years, stealing at the rate of a hundred seventy-five thousand a year, to accumulate three million. And that was Chicago, with a hundred courts and thousands of wealthy lawyers handling cases worth much more than the ones in north Mississippi. The judicial system there was an industry where things could slip through, heads could be turned, wheels greased. In Judge Atlee's world a handful of people did everything, and if money was offered or taken folks would know about it. Three million dollars could not be taken from the 25th Chancery District because there wasn't that much in the system to begin with.

He decided that one more trip to Atlantic City was necessary. He would take even more cash and flush it through the system. A final test. He had to be certain the Judge's money wasn't marked.

Fog would be thrilled.

Chapter 20

When Vicki fled and moved in with the Liquidator, a professor friend recommended Axel Sullivan as a divorce specialist. Axel proved to be a fine lawyer, but there wasn't much he could do on the legal front. Vicki was gone, she wasn't coming back, and she didn't want anything from Ray. Axel supervised the paperwork, recommended a good shrink, and did a commendable job of getting Ray through the ordeal. According to Axel, the best private investigator in town was Corey Crawford, a black ex-cop who'd pulled time for a beating.

Crawford's office was above a bar his brother owned near the campus. It was a nice bar, with a menu and unpainted windows, live music on the weekends, no unseemly traffic other than a bookie who worked the college crowd. But Ray parked three blocks away just the same. He did not want to be seen entering the premises. A sign that read CRAWFORD INVESTIGATIONS pointed to stairs on one side of the building.

There was no secretary, or at least none was present. He was ten minutes early but Crawford was waiting. He was in his late thirties with a shaved head and handsome face, no smile whatsoever. He was tall and lean and his expensive clothes were well fitted. A large pistol was strapped to his waist in a black leather holster.

'I think I'm being followed,' Ray began.

'This is not a divorce?' They were on opposite sides of a small table in a small office that overlooked the street.

'No.'

'Who would want to follow you?'

He had rehearsed a story about family trouble back in Mississippi, a dead father, some inheritances that may or may not happen, jealous siblings, a rather vague tale that Crawford seemed to buy none of. Before he could ask questions, Ray told him about Dolph at the airport and gave him his description.

'Sounds like Rusty Wattle,' Crawford said.

'And who's that?'

'Private eye from Richmond, not very good. Does some work around here. Based on what you've said, I don't think your family would hire someone from Charlottesville. It's a small town.'

The name of Rusty Wattle was duly recorded and locked away forever in Ray's memory.

'Is there a chance that these bad guys back in Mississippi would want you to know that you're being followed?' Crawford asked.

Ray looked completely baffled, so Crawford continued. 'Sometimes we get hired to intimidate, to frighten. Sounds like Wattle or whoever it was wanted your buddies at the airport to give you a good description. Maybe he left a trail.'

'I guess it's possible.'

'What do you want me to do?'

'Determine if someone is following me. If so, who is it, and who's paying for it.'

'The first two might be easy. The third might be impossible.'

'Let's give it a try.'

Crawford opened a thin file. 'I charge a hundred bucks an hour,' he said, his eyes staring right through Ray's, looking for indecision. 'Plus expenses. And a retainer of two thousand.'

'I prefer to deal in cash,' Ray said, staring right back. 'If that's acceptable.'

The first hint of a smile. 'In my business, cash is always preferred.'

Crawford filled in some blanks in a contract.

'Would they tap my phones, stuff like that?' Ray asked.

'We'll search everything. Get another cell phone, digital, and don't register it in your name. Most of our correspondence will be by cell phone.'

'What a surprise,' Ray mumbled, taking the contract, scanning it, then signing.

Crawford put it back in the file and returned to his notepad. 'For the first week, we'll coordinate your movements. Everything will be planned. Go about your normal routine, just give us notice so we can have people in place.'

I'll have a traffic jam behind me, Ray thought. 'It's a pretty dull life,' Ray said. 'I jog, I go to work, sometimes I go fly an airplane, I go home, alone, no family.'

'Other places?'

'Sometimes I do lunch, dinner, not a breakfast guy though.'

'You're putting me to sleep,' Crawford said and almost smiled. 'Women?'

'I wish. Maybe a prospect or two, nothing serious. If you find one, give her my name.'

'These bad guys in Mississippi, they're looking for something. What is it?'

'It's an old family with lots of stuff handed down. Jewelry, rare books, crystal, and silver.' It sounded natural and this time Crawford bought it.

'Now we're getting somewhere. And you have possession of the family heirloom?'

'That's right.'

'It's here?'

'Tucked away in Chaney's Self-Storage, on Berkshire Road.'

'What's it worth?'

'Not nearly as much as my relatives think.'

'Gimme a ballpark.'

'Half a million, on the high side.'

'And you have a legitimate claim to it?'

'Let's say the answer is yes. Otherwise, I'll be forced to give you the family history, which

200

could take the next eight hours and give us both a migraine.'

'Fair enough.'

Crawford finished a lengthy paragraph and was ready to wrap things up. 'When can you get a new cell phone?'

'I'll go now.'

'Great. And when can we check your apartment?'

'Anytime.'

Three hours later, Crawford and a sidekick he called Booty finished what was known as a sweep. Ray's phones were clear, no taps or bugs. The air vents hid no secret cameras. In the cramped attic they found no receivers or monitors hidden behind boxes.

'You're clean,' Crawford said as he left.

He didn't feel very clean as he sat on his balcony. You open up your life to complete strangers, albeit some selected and paid by you, and you feel compromised.

The phone was ringing.

Forrest sounded sober – strong voice, clear words. As soon as he said 'Hello, Bro,' Ray listened to see what kind of shape he was in. It was instinctive now, after years of phone calls at all hours, from all places, many of which he, Forrest, never remembered. He said he was fine, which meant he was sober and clean, no booze or drugs, but he did not say for how long. Ray was not about to ask.

201

Before either could mention the Judge or his estate or the house or Harry Rex, Forrest blurted out, 'I got a new racket.'

'Tell me about it,' Ray said, settling into his recliner. The voice on the other end was full of excitement. Ray had plenty of time to listen.

'Ever heard of Benalatofix?'

'No.'

'Me neither. The nickname is Skinny Ben. Ring a bell?'

'No, sorry.'

'It's a diet pill put out by a company called Luray Products, out of California, a big private outfit that no one's ever heard of. For the last five years doctors have been prescribing Skinny Bens like crazy because the drug works. It's not for the woman who needs to drop twenty pounds, but it does wonders for the really obese, talking linebackers, defensive ends. You there?'

'I'm listening.'

'Trouble is, after a year or two these poor women develop leaky heart valves. Tens of thousands of them have been treated, and Luray is getting sued like crazy in California and Florida. Food and Drug stepped in eight months ago, and last month Luray yanked Skinny Bens off the market.'

'Where, exactly, do you come in, Forrest?'

'I am now a medical screener.'

'And what does a medical screener do?'

'Thanks for asking. Today, for example, I was

202

in a hotel suite in Dyersburg, Tennessee, helping these hefty darlings on to a treadmill. The
doctor, paid by the lawyers who pay me, checks
their heart capacity, and if they're not up to
snuff, guess what?'

'You have a new client.'

'Absolutely. Signed up forty today.'

'What's the average case worth?'

'About ten thousand bucks. The lawyers I'm
now working with have eight hundred cases.
That's eight million bucks, the lawyers get half,
the women get screwed again. Welcome to the
world of mass torts.'

'What's in it for you?'

'A base salary, a bonus for new clients, and a
piece of the back end. There could be a half a
million cases out there, so we're scrambling to
round them up.'

'That's five billion dollars in claims.'

'Luray's got eight in cash. Every plaintiff's
lawyer in the country is talking about Skinny
Bens.'

'Aren't there some ethical problems?'

'There are no ethics anymore, Bro. You're in
la-la land. Ethics are only for people like you to
teach to students who'll never use them. I hate
to be the one to break it to you.'

'I've heard it before.'

'Anyway, I'm mining for gold. Just thought
you'd want to know.'

'That's good to hear.'

'Is anybody up there doing Skinny Bens?'

'Not to my knowledge.'

'Keep your eyes open. These lawyers are teaming up with other lawyers around the country. That's how mass tort stuff works, as I'm learning. The more cases you have in a class, the bigger the settlement.'

'I'll put out the word.'

'See you, Bro.'

'Be careful, Forrest.'

The next call came shortly after 2:30 A.M., and like every call at such an hour the phone seemed to ring forever, both during sleep and afterward. Ray finally managed to grab it and switch on a light.

'Ray, this is Harry Rex, sorry to call.'

'What is it?' he said, knowing too well that it was not good.

'Forrest. I've spent the last hour talking to him and some nurse at Baptist Hospital in Memphis. They've got him there, I think with a broken nose.'

'Back up, Harry Rex.'

'He went to a bar, got drunk, got in a fight, the usual. Looks like he picked on the wrong guy, now he's getting his face stitched up. They want to keep him overnight. I had to talk to the staff there and guarantee payment. I also asked them not to give him painkillers and drugs. They have no idea who they've got there.'

'I'm sorry you're in the middle of this, Harry Rex.'

'I've been here before, and I don't mind. But he's crazy, Ray. He started again about the estate and how he's getting screwed out of his rightful share, all that crap. I know he's drunk and all, but he just won't leave it alone.'

'I talked to him five hours ago. He was fine.'

'Well, he must've been headed for the bar. They finally had to sedate him to reset his nose, otherwise it would've been impossible. I'm just worried about all the drugs and stuff. What a mess.'

'I'm sorry, Harry Rex,' Ray said again because he could think of nothing else to say. There was a pause as Ray tried to collect his thoughts. 'He was fine, just a few hours ago, clean, sober, seemed so anyway.'

'Did he call you?' Harry Rex asked.

'Yeah, he was excited about a new job.'

'That Skinny Ben crap?'

'Yeah, is it a real job?'

'I think so. There are a bunch of lawyers down here chasing those cases. Quantity's crucial. They hire guys like Forrest to go out and round 'em up.'

'They ought to be disbarred.'

'Half of us should. I think you need to come home. The sooner we can open the estate the sooner we can get Forrest calmed down. I hate these accusations.'

'Do you have a court date?'

'We can do it Wednesday of next week. I think you ought to stay for a few days.'

'I was planning on it. Book it, I'll be there.'

'I'll notify Forrest in a day or so, try to catch him sober.'

'Sorry, Harry Rex.'

Not surprisingly, Ray couldn't sleep. He was reading a biography when his new cell phone rang. Had to be a wrong number. 'Hello,' he said suspiciously.

'Why are you awake?' asked the deep voice of Corey Crawford.

'Because my phone keeps ringing. Where are you?'

'We're watching. You okay?'

'I'm fine. It's almost four in the morning. You guys ever sleep?'

'We nap a lot. I'd keep the lights out if I were you.'

'Thank you. Anybody else watching my lights?'

'Not yet.'

'That's good.'

'Just checking in.'

Ray turned off the lights in the front of his apartment and retreated to his bedroom, where he read with aid of a small lamp. Sleep was made even more difficult with the knowledge that he was being billed a hundred dollars an hour through the night.

It's a wise investment, he kept telling himself.

At exactly 5 A.M. he sneaked down his hallway as if someone on the ground down there might see him, and he brewed coffee in the dark.

Waiting for the first cup, he called Crawford, who, not surprisingly, sounded groggy.

'I'm brewing coffee, you want some?' Ray asked.

'Not a good idea, but thanks.'

'Look, I'm flying to Atlantic City this afternoon. You got a pen?'

'Yeah, let's have it.'

'I'm leaving from general aviation in a white Beech Bonanza, tail number eight-one-five-romeo, at three P.M., with a flight instructor named Fog Newton. We'll stay tonight at the Canyon Casino, and return around noon tomorrow. I'll leave my car at the airport, locked as usual. Anything else?'

'You want us in Atlantic City?'

'No, that's not necessary. I'll move around a lot up there and try to watch my rear.'

Chapter 21

The consortium was put together by one of Dick Docker's flying buddies. It was built around two local ophthalmologists who had clinics in West Virginia. Both had just learned to fly and needed to shuttle back and forth at a faster pace. Docker's pal was a pension consultant who needed the Bonanza for about twelve hours a month. A fourth partner would get the deal off the ground. Each would put up $50,000 for a quarter interest, then sign a bank loan for the balance of the purchase price, which was currently at $390,000 and not likely to move lower. The note was spread over six years and would cost each partner $890 per month.

That was about eleven hours in a Cessna for Pilot Atlee.

On the plus side, there was depreciation and potential charter business when the partners were not using the plane. On the negative, there were hangar fees, fuel, maintenance, and a list that seemed to go on too long. Unsaid by the pal of Dick Docker, and also very much on the negative side, was the possibility of getting into business with three strangers, two of whom were doctors.

But Ray had $50,000, and he could swing $890 a month, and he wanted desperately to own the airplane that he secretly considered to be his.

Bonanzas held their value, according to a rather persuasive report that was attached to the proposal. Demand had remained high in the used-aircraft market. The Beech safety record was second only to Cessna and practically as strong. Ray carried the consortium deal around with him for two days, reading it at the office, in his apartment, at the lunch counter. The other three partners were in. Just sign his name in four places, and he would own the Bonanza.

The day before he left for Mississippi, he studied the deal for the last time, said to hell with everything else, and signed the papers.

If the bad guys were watching him, they were doing an excellent job of covering their tracks. After six days of trying to find the surveillance, Corey Crawford was of the opinion that there was nobody back there. Ray paid him thirty-eight hundred in cash and promised to call if he got suspicious again.

Under the guise of storing more junk, he went to Chaney's Self-Storage every day to check on the money. He hauled in boxes filled with anything he could find around his apartment. Both 14B and 37F were slowly taking on the appearance of an old attic.

The day before he left town, he went to the front office and asked Mrs. Chaney if someone had vacated 18R. Yes, two days ago.

'I'd like to rent it,' he said.

'That makes three,' she said.

'I'm going to need the space.'

'Why don't you just rent one of our larger units?'

'Maybe later. For now, I'll use the three small ones.'

It really didn't matter to her. He rented 18R in the name of Newton Aviation and paid cash for a six-month lease. When he was certain no one was watching, he moved the money out of 37F and into 18R, where new boxes were waiting. They were made of aluminum-coated vinyl and guaranteed to resist fire up to three hundred degrees Fahrenheit. They were also waterproof, and they locked. The money fit into five of them. For good measure, Ray threw some old quilts and blankets and clothes over the boxes so things would look a little more normal. He wasn't sure whom he was trying to impress with the randomness of his little room, but he felt better when it looked disheveled.

A lot of what he was doing these days was for the benefit of someone else. A different route from his apartment to the law school. A new jogging trail. A different coffee bar. A new downtown bookstore to browse through. And always with an eye for the unusual, an eye in the rearview mirror, a quick turnaround when he walked or jogged, a peek through shelves after he entered a shop. Someone was back there, he could feel it.

He had decided to have dinner with Kaley before he went South for a while, and before she technically became a former student. Exams were over, what was the harm? She would be around for the summer and he was determined to pursue her, with great caution. Caution because that's what every female got from him. Caution because he thought he saw potential in this one.

But the first phone call to her number was a disaster. A male voice answered, a younger voice, Ray thought, and whoever he was, he wasn't too pleased that Ray had called. When Kaley got on the phone she was abrupt. Ray asked if he could call at a better time. She said no, she'd ring him back.

He waited three days then wrote her off, something he could do as easily as flipping the calendar to the next month.

So he departed Charlottesville with nothing left undone. With Fog in the Bonanza, he flew four hours to Memphis, where he rented a car and went to look for Forrest.

His first and only visit to the home of Ellie Crum had been for the same purpose as this one.

211

Forrest had cracked up, disappeared, and his family was curious as to whether he might be dead or thrown in jail somewhere. The Judge was still presiding back then, and life was normal, including the hunt for Forrest. Of course the Judge had been too busy to search for his youngest son, and why should he when Ray could do it?

The house was an old Victorian in midtown Memphis, a hand-me-down from Ellie's father, who'd once been prosperous. Not much else was inherited. Forrest had been attracted to the notion of trust funds and real family money, but after fifteen years he'd given up hope. In the early days of the arrangement he had lived in the main bedroom. Now his quarters were in the basement. Others lived in the house too, all rumored to be struggling artists in need of refuge.

Ray parked by the curb in the street. The shrubs needed trimming and the roof was old, but the house was aging nicely. Forrest painted it every October, always in a dazzling color scheme he and Ellie would argue over for a year. Now it was a pale blue trimmed with reds and oranges. Forrest said he'd painted it teal one year.

A young woman with snow-white skin and black hair greeted him at the door with a rude, 'Yes?'

Ray was looking at her through a screen.

Behind her the house was dark and eerie, same as last time. 'Is Ellie in?' Ray asked, as rudely as possible.

'She's busy. Who's calling?'

'I'm Ray Atlee, Forrest's brother.'

'Who?'

'Forrest, he lives in the basement.'

'Oh, that Forrest.' She disappeared and Ray heard voices somewhere in the back of the house.

Ellie was wearing a bedsheet, white with streaks and spots of clay and water and slits for her head and arms. She was drying her hands on a dirty dish towel and looked frustrated that her work had been interrupted. 'Hello, Ray,' she said like an old friend and opened the door.

'Hello, Ellie.' He followed her through the foyer and into the living room.

'Trudy, bring us some tea, will you?' she called out. Wherever Trudy was, she didn't answer. The walls of the room were covered with a collection of the wackiest pots and vases Ray had ever seen. Forrest said she sculpted ten hours a day and couldn't give the stuff away.

'I'm sorry about your father,' she said. They sat across a small glass table from each other. The table was unevenly mounted on three phallic cylinders, each a different shade of blue. Ray was afraid to touch it.

'Thank you,' he said stiffly. No calls, no cards, no letters, no flowers, not one word of sympathy uttered until now, in this happenstance meeting. An opera could barely be heard in the background.

'I guess you're looking for Forrest,' she said.
'Yes.'

'I haven't seen him lately. He lives in the basement, you know, comes and goes like an old tomcat. I sent a girl down this morning to have a look – she said she thinks he's been gone for a week or so. The bed hasn't been made in five years.'

'That's more than I wanted to know.'

'And he hasn't called.'

Trudy arrived with the tea tray, another of Ellie's hideous creations. And the cups were mismatched little pots with large handles. 'Cream and sugar?' she asked, pouring and stirring.

'Just sugar.'

She handed him his brew and he took it with both hands. Dropping it would've crushed a foot.

'How is he?' Ray asked when Trudy was gone.

'He's drunk, he's sober, he's Forrest.'

'Drugs?'

'Don't go there. You don't want to know.'

'You're right,' Ray said and tried to sip his tea. It was peach-flavored something and one drop was enough. 'He was in a fight the other night, did you know about it? I think he broke his nose.'

'It's been broken before. Why do men get

214

drunk and beat up each other?' It was an excellent question and Ray had no answer. She gulped her tea and closed her eyes to savor it. Many years ago, Ellie Crum had been a lovely woman. But now, in her late forties, she had stopped trying.

'You don't care for him, do you?' Ray asked.

'Of course I do.'

'No, really?'

'Is it important?'

'He's my brother. No one else cares about him.'

'We had great sex in the early years, then we just lost interest. I got fat, now I'm too involved with my work.'

Ray glanced around the room.

'And besides, there's always sex,' she said, nodding to the door from which Trudy had come and gone.

'Forrest is a friend, Ray. I suppose I love him, at some level. But he's also an addict who seems determined to always be an addict. After a point, you get frustrated.'

'I know. Believe me, I know.'

'And I think he's one of the rare ones. He's strong enough to pick himself up at the last possible moment.'

'But not strong enough to kick it.'

'Exactly. I kicked it, Ray, fifteen years ago. Addicts are tough on each other. That's why he's in the basement.'

He's probably happier down there, Ray

thought. He thanked her for the tea and the time, and she walked him to the door. She was still standing there, behind the screen, when he raced away.

Chapter 22

The estate of Reuben Vincent Atlee was opened for probate in the courtroom where he had presided for thirty-two years. High on the oak-paneled wall behind the bench, a grim-faced Judge Atlee looked down upon the proceedings from between the Stars and Stripes and the state flag of Mississippi. It was the same portrait they had placed near his coffin during the courthouse wake three weeks earlier. Now it was back where it belonged, in a place where it would undoubtedly hang forever.

The man who had ended his career, and sent him into exile and seclusion at Maple Run, was Mike Farr from Holly Springs. He'd been reelected once and according to Harry Rex was doing a credible job. Chancellor Farr reviewed the petition for letters of administration, and he studied the one-page will attached to the filings.

The courtroom was busy with lawyers and clerks milling about, filing papers and chatting with clients. It was a day set aside for uncontested matters and quick motions. Ray sat in the front row while Harry Rex was at the bench, whispering back and forth with Chancellor Farr. Next to Ray was Forrest, who, other than the faded bruises under his eyes, looked as normal as possible. He had insisted that he would not be present when probate was opened, but a tongue-lashing from Harry Rex had persuaded him otherwise.

He'd finally come home to Ellie's, the usual return from the streets without a word to anyone about where he'd been or what he'd been up to. No one wanted to know. There was no mention of a job, so Ray was assuming his brief career as a medical screener for the Skinny Ben lawyers was over.

Every five minutes, a lawyer would crouch in the aisle, stick out a hand, and tell Ray what a fine man his father had been. Of course Ray was supposed to know all of them because they knew him. No one spoke to Forrest.

Harry Rex motioned for Ray to join them at the bench. Chancellor Farr greeted him warmly. 'Your father was a fine man and a great judge,' he said, leaning down.

'Thank you,' Ray replied. Then why, during the campaign, did you say he was too old and out of touch? Ray wanted to ask. It had been nine years earlier and seemed like fifty. With the passing of his father, everything in Ford County was now decades older.

'You teach law?' Chancellor Farr asked.

'Yes, at the University of Virginia.'

He nodded his approval and asked, 'All the heirs are present?'

'Yes sir,' answered Ray. 'It's just my brother, Forrest, and myself.'

'And both of you have read this one-page document that purports to be the last will and testament of Reuben Atlee?'

'Yes sir.'

'And there is no objection to this will being probated?'

'No sir.'

'Very well. Pursuant to this will, I will appoint you as the executor of your late father's estate. Notice to creditors will be filed today and published in a local paper. I'll waive the bond. Inventory and accounting will be due pursuant to the statute.'

Ray had heard his father utter those same instructions a hundred times. He glanced up at Judge Farr.

'Anything further, Mr. Vonner?'

'No, Your Honor.'

'I'm very sorry, Mr. Atlee,' he said.

'Thank you, Your Honor.'

For lunch they went to Claude's and ordered fried catfish. Ray had been back for two days and he could already feel his arteries choking. Forrest had little to say. He was not clean and his system was polluted.

Ray's plans were vague. He wanted to visit

some friends around the state, he said. There was no hurry to return to Virginia. Forrest left them after lunch, said he was going back to Memphis.

'Will you be at Ellie's?' Ray asked.

'Maybe.' was his only reply.

Ray was sitting on the porch, waiting for Claudia when she arrived promptly at 5 P.M. He met her beside her car where she stopped and looked at the Realtor's For Sale sign in the front yard, near the street.

'Do you have to sell it?' she asked.

'Either that or give it away. How are you?'

'I'm fine, Ray.' They managed to hug with just the minimum of contact. She was dressed for the occasion in slacks, loafers, a checkered blouse, and a straw hat, as if she'd just stepped from the garden. The lips were red, the mascara perfect. Ray had never seen her when she wasn't properly turned out.

'I'm so glad you called,' she said as they slowly walked up the drive to the house.

'We went to court today, opened the estate.'

'I'm sorry, must've been tough on you.'

'It wasn't too bad. I met Judge Farr.'

'Did you like him?'

'Nice enough, I guess, in spite of the history.'

He took her arm and led her up the steps, though Claudia was fit and could climb hills, in spite of the two packs a day. 'I remember when he was fresh out of law school,' she said. 'Didn't know a plaintiff from a defendant. Reuben could've won that race, you know, if I'd been around.'

'Let's sit here,' Ray said, pointing to two rockers.

'You've cleaned up the place,' she said, admiring the porch.

'It's all Harry Rex. He's hired painters, roofers, a cleaning service. They had to sandblast the dust off the furniture, but you can breathe now.'

'Mind if I smoke?' she said.

'No.' It didn't matter. She was smoking regardless.

'I'm so happy you called,' she said again, then lit a cigarette.

'I have tea and coffee,' Ray said.

'Ice tea, please, lemon and sugar,' she said, and crossed her legs. She was perched in the rocker like a queen, waiting for her tea. Ray recalled the tight dresses and long legs of many years ago as she sat just below the bench, scribbling elegantly away in her shorthand while every lawyer in the courtroom watched.

They talked about the weather, as folks do in the South when there's a gap in the conversation, or when there's nothing else to talk about. She smoked and smiled a lot, truly happy to be remembered by Ray. She was clinging. He was trying to solve a mystery.

They talked about Forrest and Harry Rex, two loaded topics, and when she'd been there for half an hour Ray finally got to the point.

'We've found some money, Claudia,' he said, and let the words hang in the air. She absorbed them, analyzed them, and proceeded cautiously. 'Where?'

It was an excellent question. Found where, as in the bank with records and such? Found where, as in stuffed in the mattress with no trail?

'In his study, cash. Left behind for some reason.'

'How much?' she asked, but not too quickly.

'A hundred thousand.' He watched her face and eyes closely. Surprise registered, but not shock. He had a script so he pressed on. 'His records are meticulous, checks written, deposits, ledgers with every expense, and this money seems to have no source.'

'He never kept a lot of cash,' she said slowly.

'That's what I remember too. I have no idea where it came from, do you?'

'None,' she said with no doubts whatsoever. 'The Judge didn't deal in cash. Period. Everything went through the First National Bank. He was on the board for a long time, remember?'

'Yes, very well. Did he have anything on the side?'

'Such as?'

'I'm asking you, Claudia, you knew him better than anyone. And you knew his business.'

'He was completely devoted to his work. To him, being a chancellor was a great calling, and he worked very hard at it. He had no time for anything else.'

'Including his family,' Ray said, then immediately wished he had not.

'He loved his boys, Ray, but he was from a different generation.'

'Let's stay away from that.'

'Let's.'

They took a break and each regrouped. Neither wanted to dwell on the family. The money had their attention. A car eased down the street and seemed to pause just long enough for the occupants to see the For Sale sign and take a long look at the house. One look was enough because it sped away.

'Did you know he was gambling?' Ray asked.

'The Judge? No.'

'Hard to believe, isn't it? Harry Rex took him to the casinos once a week for a while. Seems as if the Judge had a knack for it and Harry Rex did not.'

'You hear rumors, especially about the lawyers. Several of them have gotten into trouble over there.'

'But you've heard nothing about the Judge?'

'No. I still don't believe it.'

'The money came from somewhere, Claudia. And something tells me it was dirty, otherwise he would have included it with the rest of his assets.'

'And if he won at gambling he would have considered that dirty, don't you think?' Indeed, she knew the Judge better than anyone.

'Yes, and you?'

'Sounds like Reuben Atlee to me.'

They finished that round of conversation and took a break, both rocking gently in the cool shade of the front porch, as if time had stopped, neither bothered by the silence. Porch-sitting allowed great lapses while thoughts were gathered, or while there was no thinking at all.

Finally Ray, still plodding through an unwritten script, mustered the courage to ask the toughest question of the day. 'I need to know something, Claudia, and please be honest.'

'I'm always honest. It's one of my faults.'

'I have never questioned my father's integrity.'

'Nor should you now.'

'Help me out here, okay.'

'Go on.'

'Was there anything on the side – a little extra from a lawyer, a slice of the pie from a litigant, a nice backhander as the Brits like to say?'

'Absolutely not.'

'I'm throwing darts, Claudia, hoping to hit something. You don't just find a hundred thousand dollars in nice crisp bills tucked away on a shelf. When he died he had six thousand dollars in the bank. Why keep a hundred buried?'

'He was the most ethical man in the world.'

'I believe that.'

'Then stop talking about bribes and such.'

'Gladly.'

She lit another cigarette and he left to fill up the tea glasses. When he returned to the porch

Claudia was deep in thought, her gaze stretching far beyond the street. They rocked for a while.

Finally, he said, 'I think the Judge would want you to have some of it.'

'Oh you do?'

'Yes. We'll need some of it now to finish fixing up the place, probably twenty-five thousand or so. What if you, me, and Forrest split the remainder?'

'Twenty-five each?'

'Yep. What do you think?'

'You're not running it through the estate?' she asked. She knew the law better than Harry Rex.

'Why bother? It's cash, nobody knows about it, and if we report it then half will go for taxes.'

'And how would you explain it?' she asked, as always, one step ahead. They used to say that Claudia would have the case decided before the lawyers began their opening statements.

And the woman loved money. Clothes, perfume, always a late-model car, and all these things from a poorly paid court reporter. If she was drawing a state pension, it couldn't be much.

'It cannot be explained,' Ray said.

'If it's from gambling, then you'll have to go back and amend his tax returns for the past years,' she said, quickly on board. 'What a mess.'

'A real mess.'

The mess was quietly put to rest. No one would ever know about her share of the money.

'We had a case once,' she said, gazing across the front lawn. 'Over in Tippah County, thirty years ago. A man named Childers owned a scrap yard. He died with no will.' A pause, a long drag on the cigarette. 'Had a bunch of kids, and they found money hidden all over the place, in his office, in his attic, in a utility shed behind his house, in his fireplace. It was a regular Easter egg hunt. Once they'd scoured every inch of the place, they counted it up and it was about two hundred thousand dollars. This, from a man who wouldn't pay his phone bill and wore the same pair of overalls for ten years.' Another pause, another long puff. She could tell these stories forever. 'Half the kids wanted to split the money and run, the other half wanted to tell the lawyer and include the money in the probate. Word leaked out, the family got scared, and the money got added to the old man's estate. The kids fought bitterly. Five years later all the money was gone – half to the government, half to the lawyers.'

She stopped, and Ray waited for the resolution. 'What's the point?' he asked.

'The Judge said it was a shame, said the kids should've kept the money quiet and split it. After all, it was the property of their father.'

'Sounds fair to me.'

'He hated inheritance taxes. Why should the government get a large portion of your wealth just because you die? I heard him grumble about it for years.'

226

Ray took an envelope from behind his rocker and handed it to her. 'That's twenty-five thousand in cash.'

She stared at it, then looked at him in disbelief.

'Take it,' he said, inching it closer to her. 'No one will ever know.'

She took it and for a second was unable to speak. Her eyes watered, and for Claudia that meant serious emotions were at work. 'Thank you,' she whispered, and clutched the money even tighter.

Long after she left, Ray sat in the same chair, rocking in the darkness, quite pleased with himself for eliminating Claudia as a suspect. Her ready acceptance of twenty-five thousand dollars was convincing proof that she knew nothing of the much larger fortune.

But there was no suspect to take her place on the list.

Chapter 23

The meeting had been arranged through a Virginia law alumnus who was now a partner in a New York megafirm, which in turn was counsel to a gaming group that operated Canyon Casinos across the country. Contacts had been made, favors exchanged, arms twisted slightly and very diplomatically. It was in the delicate area of security, and no one wanted to step over the line. Professor Atlee needed just the basics.

Canyon had been on the Mississippi River, in Tunica County, since the mid-nineties, arriving in the second wave of construction and surviving the first shakeout. It had ten floors, four hundred rooms, eighty thousand square feet of gaming opportunities, and had been very successful with old Motown acts. Mr. Jason Piccolo, a vice president of some sort from the home office in Vegas, was on hand to greet Ray, and with him was Alvin Barker, head of security. Piccolo was in his early thirties and dressed like an Armani model. Barker was in his fifties and had the look of a weathered old cop in a bad suit.

They began by offering a quick tour, which Ray declined. He'd seen enough casino floors in the past month to last him forever. 'How much of the upstairs is off-limits?' he asked.

'Well, let's see,' Piccolo said politely, and they led him away from the slots and tables to a hallway behind the cashiers' booths. Up the stairs and down another hallway, and they stopped in a narrow room with a long wall of one-way mirrors. Through it, there was a large, low room filled with round tables covered with closed-circuit monitors. Dozens of men and women were glued to the screens, seemingly afraid to miss anything.

'This is the eye-in-the-sky,' Piccolo was saying. 'Those guys on the left are watching the blackjack tables. In the center, craps and roulette, to the right, slots and poker.'

'And what are they watching?'

'Everything. Absolutely everything.'

'Give me the list.'

'Every player. We watch the big hitters, the pros, the card counters, the crooks. Take blackjack. Those guys over there can watch ten hands and tell if a player is counting cards. That man in the gray jacket studies faces, looking for the serious players. They bounce around, here today, Vegas tomorrow, then they'll lay low for a week and surface in Atlantic City or the

Bahamas. If they cheat or count cards, he'll spot them when they sit down.' Piccolo was doing the talking. Barker was watching Ray as if he might be a potential cheater.

'How close is the camera view?' Ray asked.

'Close enough to read the serial number of any bill. We caught a cheater last month because we recognized a diamond ring he'd worn before.'

'Can I go in there?'

'Sorry.'

'What about the craps tables?'

'The same. It's a bigger problem because the game is faster and more complicated.'

'Are there professional cheaters at craps?'

'They're rare. Same with poker and roulette. Cheating is not a huge problem. We worry more about employee theft and mistakes at the table.'

'What kind of mistakes?'

'Last night a blackjack player won a forty-dollar hand, but our dealer made a mistake and pulled the chips. The player objected and called the pit boss over. Our guys up here saw it happen and we corrected the situation.'

'How?'

'We sent a security guy down with instructions to pay the customer his forty bucks, give him an apology, and comp a dinner.'

'What about the dealer?'

'He has a good record, but one more screwup and he's gone.'

'So everything's recorded?'

'Everything. Every hand, every throw of the dice, every slot. We have two hundred cameras rolling right now.'

Ray walked along the wall and tried to absorb the level of surveillance. There seemed to be more people watching above than gambling below.

'How can a dealer cheat with all this?' he asked, waving a hand.

Piccolo said, 'There are ways,' and gave Barker a knowing look. 'Many ways. We catch one a month.'

'Why do you watch the slots?' Ray asked, changing the subject. He would kill some time scatter-shooting since he'd been promised only one visit upstairs.

'Because we watch everything,' Piccolo said. 'And because there have been some instances where minors won jackpots. The casinos refused to pay, and they won the lawsuits because they had videos showing the minors ducking away while adults stepped in. Would you like something to drink?'

'Sure.'

'We have a secret little room with a better view.'

Ray followed them up another flight of stairs to a small enclosed balcony with views of the gaming floor and the surveillance room. A waitress materialized from thin air and took their drink orders. Ray asked for cappuccino. Waters for his hosts.

'What's your biggest security concern?' Ray asked. He was looking at a list of questions he'd pulled from his coat pocket.

'Card counters and sticky-fingered dealers,' Piccolo answered. 'Those little chips are very easy to drop into cuffs and pockets. Fifty bucks a day is a thousand dollars a month, tax free, of course.'

'How many card counters do you see in here?'

'More and more. There are casinos in forty states now, so more people are gambling. We keep extensive files on suspected counters, and when we think we have one here, then we simply ask them to leave. We have that right, you know.'

'What's your biggest one-day winner?' Ray asked.

Piccolo looked at Barker, who said, 'Excluding slots?'

'Yes.'

'We had a guy win a buck eighty in craps one night.'

'A hundred and eighty thousand?'

'Right.'

'And your biggest loser?'

Barker took his water from the waitress and scratched his face for a second. 'Same guy dropped two hundred grand three nights later.'

'Do you have consistent winners?' Ray asked, looking at his notes as if serious academic research was under way.

'I'm not sure what you mean,' Piccolo said.

'Let's say a guy comes in two or three times every week, plays cards or dice, wins more than he loses, and over time racks up some nice gains. How often do you see that?'

'It's very rare,' said Piccolo. 'Otherwise, we wouldn't be in business.'

'Extremely rare,' Barker said. 'A guy might get hot for a week or two. We'll zero in on him, watch him real close, nothing suspicious, but he is taking our money. Sooner or later he's gonna take one chance too many, do something stupid, and we'll get our money back.'

'Eighty percent lose over time,' Piccolo added.

Ray stirred his cappuccino and glanced at his notes. 'A guy walks in, complete stranger, lays down a thousand bucks on a blackjack table and wants hundred-dollar chips. What happens up here?'

Barker smiled and cracked his thick knuckles. 'We perk up. We'll watch him for a few minutes, see if he knows what he's doing. The pit boss'll ask him if he wants to be rated, or tracked, and if so then we'll get his name. If he says no, then we'll offer him a dinner. The cocktail waitress will keep the drinks coming, but if he doesn't drink then that's another sign that he might be serious.'

'The pros never drink when they gamble,' Piccolo added. 'They might order a drink for cover, but they'll just play with it.'

'What is rating?'

'Most gamblers want some extras,' explained Piccolo. 'Dinner, tickets to a show, room discounts, all kinds of goodies we can throw in. They have membership cards that we monitor to see how much they're gambling. The guy in your hypothetical has no card, so we'll ask him if he wants to be rated.'

'And he says no.'

'Then it's no big deal. Strangers come and go all the time.'

'But we sure try to keep up with them,' Barker admitted.

Ray scribbled something meaningless on his folded sheet of paper. 'Do the casinos pool their surveillance?' he asked, and for the first time Piccolo and Barker squirmed in unison.

'What do you mean by pool?' Piccolo asked with a smile, which Ray returned, Barker quickly joining in.

While all three were smiling, Ray said, 'Okay, another hypothetical about our consistent winner. Let's say the guy plays one night at the Monte Carlo, the next night at Treasure Cove, the next night at Aladdin, and so on down the strip here. He works all the casinos, and he wins a lot more than he loses. And this goes on for a year. How much will you know about this guy?'

Piccolo nodded at Barker, who was pinching his lips between a thumb and an index finger. 'We'll know a lot,' he admitted.

'How much?' Ray pressed.

'Go on,' Piccolo said to Barker, who reluctantly began talking.

'We'll know his name, his address, his occupation, phone number, automobile, bank. We'll know where he is each night, when he arrives, when he leaves, how much he wins or loses, how much he drinks, did he have dinner, did he tip the waitress, and if so then how much, how much did he tip the dealer.'

'And you keep records on these people?'

Barker looked at Piccolo, who nodded yes, very slowly, but said nothing. They were clamming up because he was getting too close. On second thought, a tour was just what he needed. They walked down to the floor where, instead of looking at the tables, Ray was looking up at the cameras. Piccolo pointed out the security people. They stood close to a blackjack table where a kid who seemed like a young teenager was playing with stacks of hundred-dollar chips.

'He's from Reno,' Piccolo whispered. 'Hit Tunica last week, took us for thirty grand. Very very good.'

'And he doesn't count cards,' Barker whispered, joining the conspiracy.

'Some people just have the talent for it, like golf or heart surgery,' Piccolo said.

'Is he working all the casinos?' Ray asked.

'Not yet, but they're all waiting for him.' The kid from Reno made both Barker and Piccolo very nervous.

The visit was finished in a lounge where they

drank sodas and wrapped things up. Ray had completed his list of questions, all of which had been leading up to the grand finale.

'I have a favor,' he asked the two of them. Sure, anything.

'My father died a few weeks ago, and we have reason to believe he was sneaking over here, shooting dice, perhaps winning a lot more than he was losing. Can this be confirmed?'

'What was his name?' asked Barker.

'Reuben Atlee, from Clanton.'

Barker shook his head no while pulling a phone from his pocket.

'How much?' asked Piccolo.

'Don't know, maybe a million over a period of years.'

Barker was still shaking his head. 'No way. Anybody who wins or loses that kinda money, we'll know him well.' And then, into the phone, Barker asked the person on the other end if he could check on a Reuben Atlee.

'You think he won a million dollars?' Piccolo asked.

'Won and lost,' Ray replied. 'Again, we're just guessing.'

Barker slammed his phone shut. 'No record of any Reuben Atlee anywhere. There's no way he gambled that much around here.'

'What if he never came to this casino?' Ray asked, certain of the answer.

'We would know,' they said together.

Chapter 24

He was the only morning jogger in Clanton, and for this he got curious stares from the ladies in their flower beds and the maids sweeping the porches and the summer help cutting grass at the cemetery when he ran past the Atlee family plot. The soil was settling around the Judge, but Ray did not stop or even slow down to inspect it. The men who'd dug the grave were digging another. There was a death and a birth every day in Clanton. Things changed little.

It was not yet eight o'clock and the sun was hot and the air heavy. The humidity didn't bother him because he'd grown up with it, but he certainly didn't miss it either.

He found the shaded streets and worked his way back to Maple Run. Forrest's Jeep was there, and his brother was slouched in the swing on the porch. 'Kinda early for you, isn't it?' Ray said.

'How far did you run? You're covered in sweat.'

'That happens when you jog in the heat. Five miles. You look good.'

And he did. Clear, unswollen eyes, a shave, a shower, clean white painter's pants.

'I'm on the wagon, Bro.'

'Wonderful.' Ray sat in a rocker, still sweating, still breathing heavily. He would not ask how long Forrest had been sober. Couldn't have been more than twenty-four hours.

Forrest bounced from the swing and pulled the other rocker near Ray. 'I need some help, Bro,' he said, sitting on the edge of the chair.

Here we go again, Ray said to himself. 'I'm listening.'

'I need some help,' he blurted again, rubbing his hands fiercely as if the words were painful.

Ray had seen it before and had no patience. 'Let's go, Forrest, what is it?' It was money, first of all. After that, there were several possibilities.

'There's a place I want to go, about an hour from here. It's way out in the woods, close to nothing, very pretty, a nice little lake in the center, comfortable rooms.' He pulled a wrinkled business card from his pocket and handed it to Ray.

Alcorn Village. Drug and Alcohol Treatment Facility. A Ministry of the Methodist Church.

'Who's Oscar Meave?' Ray asked, looking at the card.

'A guy I met a few years ago. He helped me, now he's at that place.'

'It's a detox center.'

'Detox, rehab, drug unit, dry-out tank, spa, ranch, village, jail, prison, mental ward, call it whatever you want. I don't care. I need help, Ray. Now.' He covered his face with his hands and began crying.

'Okay, okay.' Ray said. 'Give me the details.'

Forrest wiped his eyes and his nose and sucked in a heavy load of air. 'Call the guy and see if they have a room,' he said, his voice quivering.

'How long will you stay?'

'Four weeks, I think, but Oscar can tell you.'

'And what's the cost?'

'Somewhere around three hundred bucks a day. I was thinking maybe I could borrow against my share of this place, get Harry Rex to ask the judge if there's a way to get some money now.' Tears were dripping from the corners of his eyes.

Ray had seen the tears before. He'd heard the pleas and the promises, and no matter how hard and cynical he tried to be at that moment, he melted. 'We'll do something,' he said. 'I'll call this guy now.'

'Please, Ray, I want to go right now.'

'Today?'

'Yes, I, uh, well, I can't go back to Memphis.' He lowered his head and ran his fingers through his long hair.

'Somebody looking for you?'

'Yeah,' he nodded. 'Bad guys.'

'Not cops?'

'No, they're a helluva lot worse than cops.'

'Do they know you're here?' Ray asked, glancing around. He could almost see heavily armed drug dealers hiding behind the bushes.

'No, they have no idea where I am.'

Ray stood and went into the house.

Like most folks, Oscar Meave remembered Forrest well. They had worked together in a federal detox program in Memphis, and while he was sad to hear that Forrest was in need of help, he was nonetheless delighted to talk to Ray about him. Ray tried his best to explain the urgency of the matter, though he had no details and was not likely to get any. Their father had died three weeks earlier, Ray said, already making excuses.

'Bring him on,' Meave said. 'We'll find a place.'

They left town thirty minutes later, in Ray's rental car. Forrest's Jeep was parked behind the house, for good measure.

'Are you sure these guys won't be snooping around here?' Ray said.

'They have no idea where I'm from,' Forrest replied. His head was back on the headrest, his eyes hidden behind funky sunshades.

'Who are they, exactly?'

'Some really nice guys from south Memphis. You'd like them.'

'And you owe them money?'

'Yes.'

'How much?'

'Four thousand dollars.'

'And where did this four thousand bucks go?'

Forrest gently tapped his nose. Ray shook his head in frustration and anger and bit his tongue to hold back another bitter lecture. Let some miles pass, he told himself. They were in the country now, farmland on both sides.

Forrest began snoring.

This would be another Forrest tale, the third time Ray actually loaded him up and hauled him away for detox. The last time had been almost twelve years earlier – the Judge was still presiding, Claudia still at his side, Forrest doing more drugs than anyone in the state. Things had been normal. The narcs had cast a wide net around him, and through blind luck Forrest had sneaked through it. They suspected he was dealing, which was true, and had they caught him he would still be in prison. Ray had driven him to a state hospital near the coast, one the Judge had pulled strings to get him into. There, he slept for a month then walked away.

The first brotherly journey to rehab had been during Ray's law school years at Tulane. Forrest had overdosed on some vile combination of pills. They pumped his stomach and almost pronounced him dead. The Judge sent them to a compound near Knoxville with locked gates and razor wire. Forrest stayed a week before escaping.

He'd been to jail twice, once as a juvenile, once as an adult, though he was only nineteen.

His first arrest was just before a high school football game, Friday night, the playoffs, in Clanton with the entire town waiting for kickoff. He was sixteen, a junior, an all-conference quarterback and safety, a kamikaze who loved to hit late and spear with his helmet. The narcs plucked him from the dressing room and led him away in handcuffs. The backup was an untested freshman, and when Clanton got slaughtered the town never forgave Forrest Atlee.

Ray had been sitting in the stands with the Judge, anxious as everyone else about the game. 'Where's Forrest?' folks began asking during pregame. When the coin was tossed he was in the city jail getting fingerprinted and photographed. They found fourteen ounces of marijuana in his car.

He spent two years in a juvenile facility and was released on his eighteenth birthday.

How does the sixteen-year-old son of a prominent judge become a dope pusher in a small Southern town with no history of drugs? Ray and his father had asked each other that question a thousand times. Only Forrest knew the answer, and long ago he had made the decision to keep it to himself. Ray was thankful that he buried most of his secrets.

After a nice nap, Forrest jolted himself awake and announced he needed something to drink.

'No,' Ray said.

'A soft drink, I swear.'

242

They stopped at a country store and bought sodas. For breakfast Forrest had a bag of peanuts.

'Some of these places have good food,' he said when they were moving again. Forrest the tour guide for detox centers. Forrest the Michelin critic for rehab units. 'I usually lose a few pounds,' he said, chomping.

'Do they have gyms and such?' Ray asked, aiding the conversation. He really didn't want to discuss the perks of various drug tanks.

'Some do,' Forrest said smugly. 'Ellie sent me to this place in Florida near a beach, lots of sand and water, lots of sad rich folks. Three days of brainwashing, then they worked our asses off. Hikes, bikes, power walks, weights if we wanted. I got a great tan and dropped fifteen pounds. Stayed clean for eight months.'

In his sad little life, everything was measured by stints of sobriety.

'Ellie sent you?' Ray asked.

'Yeah, it was years ago. She had a little dough at one point, not much. I'd hit the bottom, and it was back when she cared. It was a nice place, though, and some of the counselors were those Florida chicks with short skirts and long legs.'

'I'll have to check it out.'

'Kiss my ass.'

'Just kidding.'

'There's this place out West where all the stars go, the Hacienda, and it's the Ritz. Plush rooms, spas, daily massages, chefs who can fix

243

great meals at one thousand calories a day. And the counselors are the best in the world. That's what I need, Bro, six months at the Hacienda.'

'Why six months?'

'Because I need six months. I've tried two months, one month, three weeks, two weeks, it's not enough. For me, it's six months of total lockdown, total brainwashing, total therapy, plus my own masseuse.'

'What's the cost?'

Forrest whistled and rolled his eyes. 'Pick a number. I don't know. You gotta have a zillion bucks and two recommendations to get in. Imagine that, a letter of recommendation. "To the Fine Folks at the Hacienda: I hereby heartily recommend my friend Doofus Smith as a patient in your wonderful facility. Doofus drinks vodka for breakfast, snorts coke for lunch, snacks on heroin, and is usually comatose by dinner. His brain is fried, his veins are lacerated, his liver is shot to hell. Doofus is your kind of person and his old man owns Idaho." '

'Do they keep people for six months?'

'You're clueless, aren't you?'

'I guess.'

'A lot of cokeheads need a year. Even more for heroin addicts.'

And which is your current poison? Ray wanted to ask. But then he didn't want to. 'A year?' he said.

'Yep, total lockdown. And then the addict has to do it himself. I know guys who've been to prison for three years with no coke, no crack, no drugs at all, and when they were released they called a dealer before they called their wives or girlfriends.'

'What happens to them?'

'It's not pretty.' He threw the last of the peanuts into his mouth, slapped his hands together, and sent salt flying.

There were no signs directing traffic to Alcorn Village. They followed Oscar's directions until they were certain they were lost deep in the hills, then saw a gate in the distance. Down a tree-lined drive, a complex spread before them. It was peaceful and secluded, and Forrest gave it good marks for first impressions.

Oscar Meave arrived in the lobby of the administration building and guided them to an intake office, where he handled the initial paper-work himself. He was a counselor, an administrator, a psychologist, an ex-addict who'd cleaned himself up years ago and received two Ph.D.s. He wore jeans, a sweatshirt, sneakers, a goatee, and two earrings, and had the wrinkles and chipped tooth of a rough prior life. But his voice was soft and friendly. He exuded the tough compassion of one who'd been where Forrest was now.

The cost was $325 a day and Oscar was recommending a minimum of four weeks. 'After that, we'll see where he is. I'll need to ask some pretty rough questions about what Forrest has been doing.'

'I don't want to hear that conversation,' Ray said.

'You won't,' Forrest said. He was resigned to the flogging that was coming.

'And we require half the money up front,' Oscar said. 'The other half before his treatment is complete.'

Ray flinched and tried to remember the balance in his checking account back in Virginia. He had plenty of cash, but this was not the time to use it.

'The money is coming out of my father's estate,' Forrest said. 'It might take a few days.'

Oscar was shaking his head. 'No exceptions. Our policy is half now.'

'No problem,' said Ray. 'I'll write a check for it.'

'I want it to come out of the estate,' Forrest said. 'You're not paying for it.'

'The estate can reimburse me. It'll work.' Ray wasn't sure how it would work, but he'd let Harry Rex worry about that. He signed the forms as guarantor of payment. Forrest signed at the bottom of a page listing all the do's and don'ts.

'You can't leave for twenty-eight days,' Oscar said. 'If you do, you forfeit all monies paid and you're never welcome back. Understand?'

'I understand,' Forrest said. How many times had he been through this?

246

'You're here because you want to be here, right?'

'Right.'

'And no one is forcing you?'

'No one.'

Now that the flogging was on, it was time for Ray to leave. He thanked Oscar and hugged Forrest and sped away much faster than he'd arrived.

Chapter 25

Ray was now certain that the cash had been collected since 1991, the year the Judge was voted out of office. Claudia was around until the year before, and she knew nothing of the money. It had not come from graft and it had not come gambling.

Nor had it come from skillful investing on the sly, because Ray found not a single record of the Judge ever buying or selling a stock or a bond. The accountant hired by Harry Rex to reconstruct the records and put together the final tax return had found nothing either. He said that the Judge's trail was easy to follow because everything had been run through the First National Bank of Clanton.

That's what you think, Ray thought to himself.

There were almost forty boxes of old, useless files scattered throughout the house. The cleaning service had gathered and stacked them in the Judge's study and in the dining room. It took a few hours but he finally found what he was looking for. Two of the boxes held the notes and research – the 'trial files' as the Judge had always referred to them – of the cases he'd heard as a special chancellor since his defeat in 1991.

During a trial the Judge wrote nonstop on yellow legal pads. He noted dates, times, relevant facts, anything that would aid him in reaching a final opinion in the case. Often he would interject a question to a witness and he frequently used his notes to correct the attorneys. Ray had heard him quip more than once, in chambers of course, that the notetaking helped him stay awake. During a lengthy trial, he would fill twenty legal pads with his notes.

Because he was a lawyer before he was a judge, he had acquired the lifelong habit of filing and keeping everything. A trial file consisted of his notes, copies of cases the attorneys relied on, copies of code sections, statutes, even pleadings that were not put with the official court file. As the years passed, the trial files became even more useless, and now they filled forty boxes.

According to his tax returns, since 1993, he had picked up income trying cases as a special chancellor, cases no one else wanted to hear. It was not uncommon in the rural areas to have a dispute too hot for an elected judge. One side would file a motion asking the judge to recuse himself, and he would go through the routine of grappling with the issue while proclaiming his ability to be fair and impartial regardless of the facts or litigants, then reluctantly step down and hand it off to an old pal from another part of the state. The special chancellor would ride in without the baggage of any prior knowledge and without one eye on reelection and hear the case.

In some jurisdictions, special chancellors were used to relieve crowded dockets. Occasionally, they would sit in for an ailing judge. Almost all were retired themselves. The state paid them fifty dollars an hour, plus expenses.

In 1992, the year after his defeat, Judge Atlee had earned nothing extra. In 1993, he'd been paid $5,800. The busiest year – 1996 – he'd reported $16,300. Last year, 1999, he was paid $8,760, but he'd been ill most of the time.

The grand total in earnings as a special chancellor was $56,590, over a six-year period, and all earnings had been reported on his tax returns.

Ray wanted to know what kinds of cases Judge Atlee had heard in his last years. Harry Rex had mentioned one – the sensational divorce trial of a sitting governor. That trial file was three inches thick and included clippings from the Jackson newspaper with photos of the governor, his soon to be ex-wife, and a woman thought to be his current flame. The trial lasted two weeks, and Judge Atlee, according to his notes, seemed to enjoy it tremendously.

There was an annexation case near Hatties-burg that lasted for two weeks and had irritated

everyone involved. The city was growing west-
ward and eyeing some prime industrial sites.
Lawsuits got filed and two years later Judge
Atlee gathered everyone together for a trial.
There were also newspaper articles, but after an
hour of review Ray was bored with the whole
mess. He couldn't imagine presiding over it for a
month.

But at least there was money involved in it.

Judge Atlee spent eight days in 1995 holding
court in the small town of Kosciusko, two hours
away, but from his files it looked as though
nothing of consequence went to trial.

There was a horrendous tanker truck collision
in Tishomingo County in 1994. Five teenagers
were trapped in a car and burned to death.
Since they were minors, Chancery Court had
jurisdiction. One sitting chancellor was related
to one of the victims. The other chancellor was
dying of brain cancer. Judge Atlee got the call
and presided over a trial that lasted two days
before it was settled for $7,400,000. One third
went to the attorneys for the teenagers, the rest
to their families.

Ray set the file on the Judge's sofa, next to the
annexation case. He was sitting on the floor of
the study, the newly polished floor, under the
vigilant gaze of General Forrest. He had a vague
idea of what he was doing, but no real plan on
how to proceed. Go through the files, pick out
the ones that involved money, see where the trail
might lead.

The cash he'd found hidden less than ten feet away had come from somewhere.

His cell phone rang. It was a Charlottesville alarm company with a recorded message that a break-in was in progress at his apartment. He jumped to his feet and talked to himself while the message finished. The same call would simultaneously go to the police and to Corey Crawford. Seconds later, Crawford called him. 'I'm on the way there,' he said, and sounded like he was running. It was almost nine-thirty, CST. Ten-thirty in Charlottesville.

Ray paced through the house, thoroughly helpless. Fifteen minutes passed before Crawford called him again. 'I'm here,' he said. 'With the police. Somebody jammed the door downstairs, then jammed the one to the den. That set off the alarm. They didn't have much time. Where do we check?'

'There's nothing particularly valuable there,' Ray said, trying to guess what a thief might want. No cash, jewelry, art, hunting rifles, gold, or silver.

'TV, stereo, microwave, everything's here,' Crawford said. 'They scattered books and magazines, knocked over the table by the kitchen phone, but they were in a hurry. Anything in particular?'

'No, nothing I can think of.' Ray could hear a police radio squawking in the background.

'How many bedrooms?' Crawford asked as he moved through the apartment.

'Two, mine is on the right.'

'All the closet doors are open. They were looking for something. Any idea what?'

'No,' Ray answered.

'No sign of entry in the other bedroom,' Crawford reported, then began talking with two cops. 'Hang on,' he told Ray, who was standing in the front door, looking through the screen, motionless and trying to think of the fastest way home.

The cops and Crawford decided it was a quick strike by a pretty good thief who got surprised by the alarm. He jammed the two doors with minimal damage, realized there was an alarm, raced through the place looking for something in particular, and when he didn't find it he kicked a few things for the hell of it and fled. He or they – could've been more than one.

'You need to be here to tell the police if anything is missing and to do a report,' Crawford said.

'I'll be there tomorrow,' Ray said. 'Can you secure the place tonight?'

'Yeah, we'll think of something.'

'Call me after the cops leave.'

He sat on the front steps and listened to the crickets while yearning to be at Chaney's Self-Storage, sitting in the dark with one of the Judge's guns, ready to blast away at anyone who came near him. Fifteen hours away by car. Three and a half by private plane. He called Fog Newton and there was no answer.

His phone startled him again. 'I'm still in the apartment,' Crawford said.

'I don't think this is random,' Ray said.

'You mentioned some valuables, some family stuff, at Chaney's Self-Storage.'

'Yeah. Any chance you could watch the place tonight?'

'They got security out there, guards and cameras, not a bad outfit.' Crawford sounded tired and not enthusiastic about napping in a car all night.

'Can you do it?'

'I can't get in the place. You have to be a customer.'

'Watch the entrance.'

Crawford grunted and breathed deeply. 'Yeah, I'll check on it, maybe call a guy in to watch it.'

'Thanks. I'll call you when I get to town tomorrow.'

He called Chaney's and there was no answer. He waited five minutes, called again, counted fourteen rings then heard a voice.

'Chancey's, security, Murray speaking.'

He very politely explained who he was and what he wanted. He was leasing three units and there was a bit of concern because someone had vandalized his downtown apartment, and could Mr. Murray please pay special attention to 14B, 37F, and 18R. No problem, said Mr. Murray, who sounded as if he was yawning into the phone.

Just a little jumpy, Ray explained.

'No problem,' mumbled Mr. Murray.

It took one hour and two drinks for the edginess to relent. He was no closer to Charlottesville. There was the urge to hop in the rental car and race through the night, but it passed. He preferred to sleep and try to find an airplane in the morning. Sleep, though, was impossible, so he returned to the trial files.

The Judge had once said he knew little about zoning law because there was so little zoning in Mississippi, and virtually none in the six counties of the 25th Chancery District. But somehow someone had cajoled him into hearing a bitterly fought zoning case in the city of Columbus. The trial lasted for six days, and when it was over an anonymous phone caller threatened to shoot the Judge, according to his notes.

Threats were not uncommon, and he'd been known to carry a pistol in his briefcase over the years. It was rumored that Claudia carried one too. You'd rather have the Judge shooting at you than his court reporter, ran the conventional wisdom.

The zoning case almost put Ray to sleep. But then he found a gap, the black hole he'd been digging for, and he forgot about sleep.

According to his tax records, the Judge was paid $8,110 in January 1999 to hear a case in the 27th Chancery District. The 27th comprised two counties on the Gulf Coast, a part of the state the Judge cared little for. The fact that he would voluntarily go there for a period of days struck Ray as quite odd.

Odder still was the absence of a trial file. He searched the two boxes and found nothing related to a case on the coast, and with his curiosity barely under control he plowed through the other thirty-eight or so. He forgot about his apartment and the self-storage and whether or not Mr. Murray was awake or even alive, and he almost forgot about the money.

A trial file was missing.

Chapter 26

The US Air flight left Memphis at six-forty in the morning, which meant Ray had to leave Clanton no later than five, which meant he slept about three hours, the usual at Maple Run. On the first flight, he dozed off en route, again in the Pittsburgh airport, and again on the commuter flight to Charlottesville. He inspected his apartment, then fell asleep on the sofa.

The money hadn't been touched. No unauthorized entries into any of his little storage units at Chaney's. Nothing was out of the ordinary. He locked himself inside 18R, opened the five fireproof and waterproof boxes, and counted fifty-three freezer bags.

Sitting on the concrete floor with three million dollars strewn around him, Ray Atlee finally admitted how important the money had become. The real horror of last night had been the chance of losing it. Now he was afraid to leave it.

In the past few weeks, he had become more

curious about how much things cost, about what the money could buy, about how it could grow if invested conservatively, or aggressively. At times he thought of himself as wealthy, and then he would dismiss those thoughts. But they were always there, just under the surface and popping up with greater frequency. The questions were slowly being answered – no it was not counterfeit, no it was not traceable, no it had not been won at the casinos, no it had not been filched from the lawyers and litigants of the 25th Chancery District.

And, no, the money should not be shared with Forrest because he would kill himself with it. No, it should not be included in the estate for several excellent reasons.

One by one the options were being eliminated. He might be forced to keep it himself.

There was a loud knock on the metal door, and he almost screamed. He scrambled to his feet and yelled, 'Who is it?'

'Security,' came the reply, and the voice was vaguely familiar. Ray stepped over the cash and reached for the door, which he cracked no more than four inches. Mr. Murray was grinning at him.

'Everything okay in there?' he asked, more of a janitor than an armed guard.

'Fine, thanks,' Ray said, his heart still frozen.

'Need anything, let me know.'

'Thanks for last night.'

'Just doing my job.'

Ray repacked the money, relocked the doors,

and drove across town with one eye on the rearview mirror.

The owner of his apartment sent a crew of Mexican carpenters around to repair the two damaged doors. They hammered and sawed throughout the late afternoon, then said yes to a cold beer when they were finished. Ray chatted with them as he tried to ease them out of his den. There was a pile of mail on the kitchen table, and, after ignoring it for most of the day, he sat down to deal with it. Bills had to be paid. Catalogs and junk mail. Three notes of sympathy.

A letter from the Internal Revenue Service, addressed to Mr. Ray Atlee, Executor of the Estate of Reuben V. Atlee, and postmarked in Atlanta two days earlier. He studied it carefully before opening it slowly. A single sheet of official stationery, from one Martin Gage, Office of Criminal Investigations, in the Atlanta office. It read:

Dear Mr. Atlee:

As executor of your father's estate, you are required by law to include all assets for valuation and taxation purposes. Concealment of assets may constitute tax fraud. The unauthorized disbursement of assets is a violation of the laws of Mississippi and possible federal laws as well.

Martin Gage
Criminal Investigator

His first instinct was to call Harry Rex to see what notice had been given to the IRS. As executor, he had a year from the date of death to file the final return, and, according to the accountant, extensions were liberally granted.

The letter was postmarked the day after he and Harry Rex went to court to open the estate. Why would the IRS be so quick to respond? How would they even know about the death of Reuben Atlee?

Instead, he called the office number on the letterhead. The recorded message welcomed him to the world of the IRS, Atlanta office, but he would have to call back later because it was a Saturday. He went online and in the Atlanta directory found three Martin Gages. The first one he called was out of town, but his wife said he did not work for the IRS, thank heavens. The second call went unanswered. The third found a Mr. Gage eating dinner.

'Do you work for the IRS?' Ray asked, after cordially introducing himself as a professor of law and apologizing for the intrusion.

'Yes, I do.'

'Criminal Investigations?'

'Yep, that's me. Fourteen years now.'

Ray described the letter, then read it verbatim.

'I didn't write that,' Gage said.

'Then who did?' Ray snapped, and immediately wished he had not.

'How am I supposed to know? Can you fax it to me?'

Ray stared at his fax machine, and, thinking quickly, said, 'Sure, but my machine is at the office. I can do it Monday.'

'Scan it and e-mail it,' Gage said.

'Uh, my scanner's broke right now. I'll just fax it to you Monday.'

'Okay, but somebody's pulling your leg, pal. That's not my letter.'

Ray was suddenly anxious to rid himself of the IRS, but Gage was now fully involved. 'I'll tell you something else,' he continued. 'Impersonating an IRS agent is a federal offense, and we prosecute vigorously. Any idea who it is?'

'I have no idea.'

'Probably got my name from our online directory, worst thing we ever did. Freedom of Information and all that crap.'

'Probably so.'

'When was the estate opened?'

'Three days ago.'

'Three days ago! The return's not due for a year.'

'I know.'

'What's in the estate?'

'Nothing. An old house.'

'Just some crackpot. Fax it Monday and I'll give you a call.'

'Thanks.'

Ray put the phone on the coffee table and

asked himself why, exactly, had he called the IRS?

To verify the letter.

Gage would never get a copy of it. And in a month or so he would forget about it. And in a year he wouldn't recall it if anyone mentioned it.

Perhaps not the smartest move so far.

Forrest had settled into the routine of Alcorn Village. He was allowed two calls a day and they were subject to being recorded, he explained. 'They don't want us calling our dealers.'

'Not funny,' Ray said. It was the sober Forrest, with the soft drawl and clear mind.

'Why are you in Virginia?' he asked.

'It's my home.'

'Thought you were visiting some friends around here, old buddies from law school.'

'I'll be back shortly. How's the food?'

'Like a nursing home, Jell-O three times a day but always a different color. Really lousy stuff. For three hundred bucks plus a day it's a rip-off.'

'Any cute girls?'

'One, but she's fourteen, daughter of a judge, if you can believe that. Really some sad people. We have these group bitch meetings once a day where everyone lashes out at whoever got them started on drugs. We talk through our problems. We help one another. Hell, I know more than the counselors. This is my eighth detox, Bro, can you believe it?'

'Seems like more than that,' Ray said.

'Thanks for helping me. You know what's sick?'

'What?'

'I'm happiest when I'm clean. I feel great, I feel smart, I can do anything. Then I hate myself when I'm on the streets doing all that stupid stuff like the other scumbags. I don't know why I do it.'

'You sound great, Forrest.'

'I like this place, aside from the food.'

'Good, I'm proud of you.'

'Can you come see me?'

'Of course I will. Give me a couple of days.'

He checked in with Harry Rex, who was at the office, where he usually spent the weekends. With four wives under his belt, there were good reasons he wasn't home much.

'Do you recall the Judge hearing a case on the coast, early last year?' Ray asked.

Harry Rex was eating something and smacking into the phone. 'The coast?' He hated the coast, thought they were all a bunch of redneck mafia types.

'He was paid for a trial down there, January of last year.'

'He was sick last year,' Harry Rex said, then swallowed something liquid.

'His cancer was diagnosed last July.'

'I don't remember any case on the coast,' he said, and bit into something else. 'That surprises me.'

'Me too.'

'Why are you going through his files?'

'I'm just checking his payroll records against his trial files.'

'Why?'

'Because I'm the executor.'

'Forgive me. When are you coming back?'

'Couple of days.'

'Hey, I bumped into Claudia today, hadn't seen her in months, and she gets to town early, parks a brand-new black Cadillac near the Coffee Shop so everybody can see it, then spends half the morning piddling around town. Whatta piece of work.'

Ray couldn't help but smile at the thought of Claudia racing down to the car dealership with a pocket full of cash. The Judge would be proud.

Sleep came in short naps on the sofa. The walls cracked louder, the vents and ducts seemed more active. Things moved, then they didn't. The night after the break-in, the entire apartment was poised for another one.

Chapter 27

Trying hard to be normal, Ray took a long jog on a favorite trail, along the downtown mall, down Main Street to the campus, up Observatory Hill and back, six miles in all. He had lunch with Carl Mirk at Bizou, a popular bistro three blocks from his apartment, and he drank coffee afterward at a sidewalk café. Fog had the Bonanza reserved for a 3 P.M. training session, but the mail came and everything normal went out the window.

The envelope was addressed to him by hand, nothing on the return, with a postmark in Charlottesville the day before. A stick of dynamite would not have looked more suspicious lying there on the table. Inside was a letter-size sheet of paper, trifolded, and when he spread it open all systems shut down. For a moment, he couldn't think, breathe, feel, hear.

It was a color digital photo of the front of 14B at Chaney's, printed off a computer on regular copier paper. No words, no warnings, no threats. None were needed.

When he could breathe again he also started sweating, and the numbness wore off enough for a sharp pain to knife through his stomach. He was dizzy so he closed his eyes, and when he opened them and looked at the picture again, it was shaking.

His first thought, the first he could remember, was that there was nothing in the apartment he could not do without. He could leave everything. But he filled a small bag anyway.

Three hours later he stopped for gas in Roanoke, and three hours after that he pulled into a busy truck stop just east of Knoxville. He sat in the parking lot for a long time, low in his TT roadster, watching the truckers come and go, watching the movements in and out of the crowded café. There was a table he wanted in the window, and when it was available he locked the Audi and went inside. From the table, he guarded his car, fifty feet away and stuffed with three million in cash.

Because of the aroma, he guessed that grease was the café's specialty. He ordered a burger and on a napkin began scribbling his options.

The safest place for the money was in a bank, in a large lock box behind thick walls, cameras, etc. He could divide the money, scatter it among several banks in several towns between Charlottesville and Clanton, and leave a complicated trail. The money could be discreetly hauled in by briefcase. Once locked away, it would be safe forever.

The trail, though, would be extensive. Lease forms, proper ID, home address, phones, here meet our new vice president, in business with strangers, video cameras, lock box registers, and who knew what else because Ray had never hidden stuff in a bank before.

He had passed several self-storage places along the interstate. They were everywhere these days and for some reason wedged as close to the main roads as possible. Why not pick one at random, pull over, pay cash, and keep the paperwork to a minimum? He could hang around in Podunktown for a day or two, find some more fireproof boxes at a local supply house, secure his money, then sneak away. It was a brilliant idea because his tormentor would not expect it.

And it was a stupid idea because he would leave the money.

He could take it home to Maple Run and bury it in the basement. Harry Rex could alert the sheriff and the police to watch for suspicious outsiders lurking around the town. If an agent showed up to follow him, he'd get nailed in Clanton, and Dell at the Coffee Shop would have the details by sunrise. You couldn't cough there without three people catching your cold.

The truckers came in waves, most of them talking loudly as they entered, anxious to mix it up after miles of solitary confinement. They all looked the same, jeans and pointed-toe boots. A pair of sneakers walked by and caught Ray's attention. Khakis, not jeans. The man was alone and took a seat at the counter. In the mirror Ray saw his face, and it was one he'd seen before. Wide through the eyes, narrow at the chin, long flat nose, flaxen hair, thirty-five years old give or take. Somewhere around Charlottesville but impossible to place.

Or was everyone now a suspect?

Run with your loot, like a murderer with his victim in the trunk, and plenty of faces look familiar and ominous.

The burger arrived, hot and steaming, covered with fries, but he'd lost his appetite. He started on his third napkin. The first two had taken him nowhere.

His options at the moment were limited. Since he was unwilling to let the money out of his sight, he would drive all night, stopping for coffee, perhaps pulling over for a nap, and arrive at Clanton early in the morning. Once he was on his turf again, things would become clearer.

Hiding the money in the basement was a bad idea. An electrical short, a bolt of lightning, a stray match, and the house was gone. It was hardly more than kindling anyway.

The man at the counter had yet to look at Ray, and the more Ray looked at him the more convinced he was that he was wrong. It was a generic face, the kind you see every day and seldom remember. He was eating chocolate pie and drinking coffee. Odd, at eleven o'clock at night.

He rolled into Clanton just after 7 A.M. He was red-eyed, ragged with exhaustion, in need of a shower and two days' rest. Through the night, while he wasn't watching every set of headlights behind him and slapping himself to stay awake, he'd dreamed of the solitude of Maple Run. A large, empty house, all to himself. He could sleep upstairs, downstairs, on the porch. No ringing phones, no one to bother him.

But the roofers had other plans. They were hard at work when he arrived, their trucks and ladders and tools covering the front lawn and blocking the driveway. He found Harry Rex at the Coffee Shop, eating poached eggs and reading two newspapers at once.

'What are you doing here?' he said, barely looking up. He wasn't finished with his eggs or his papers, and didn't appear too excited to see Ray.

'Maybe I'm hungry.'

'You look like hell.'

'Thanks. I couldn't sleep there, so I drove here.'

'You're cracking up.'

'Yes, I am.'

He finally lowered the newspaper and stabbed an egg that appeared to be covered with hot sauce. 'You drove all night from Charlottesville?'

'It's only fifteen hours.'

A waitress brought him coffee. 'How long are those roofers planning on working?'

'They're there?'

'Oh yes. At least a dozen of them. I wanted to sleep for the next two days.'

'It's those Atkins boys. They're fast unless they start drinking and fighting. Had one fall off a ladder last year, broke his neck. Got him thirty thousand in workers' comp.'

'Anyway, why, then, did you hire them?'

'They're cheap, same as you, Mr. Executor. Go sleep in my office. I got a hideaway on the third floor.'

'With a bed?'

Harry Rex glanced around as if the gossip-mongers of Clanton were closing in. 'Remember Rosetta Rhines?'

'No.'

'She was my fifth secretary and third wife. That was where it all started.'

'Are the sheets clean?'

'What sheets? Take it or leave it. It's very quiet, but the floor shakes. That's how we got caught.'

'Sorry I asked.' Ray took a long swig of coffee. He was hungry, but not ready for a feast. He wanted a bowl of flakes with skim milk and fruit, something sensible, but he'd be ridiculed for ordering such light fare in the Coffee Shop.

'You gonna eat?' Harry Rex growled at him.

270

'No. We need to store some stuff. All those boxes and furniture. You know a place?'

'We?'

'Okay, I need a place.'

'It's nothing but crap.' A bite of a biscuit, one loaded with sausage, Cheddar, and what appeared to be mustard. 'Burn it.'

'I can't burn it, at least not now.'

'Then do what all good executors do. Store for two years, then give it to the Salvation Army and burn what they don't want.'

'Yes or no. Is there a storage place in town?'

'Didn't you go to school with that crazy Cantrell boy?'

'There were two of them.'

'No, there were three of them. One got hit by that Greyhound out near Tobytown.' A long pull of coffee, then more eggs.

'A storage place, Harry Rex.'

'Testy, aren't we?'

'No, sleep-deprived.'

'I've offered my love nest.'

'No thanks. I'll try my luck with the roofers.'

'Their uncle is Virgil Cantrell, I handled his first wife's second divorce, and he's converted the old depot into a storage warehouse.'

'Is that the only place in town?"

'No, Lundy Staggs put in some of those ministorage units west of town, but they got flooded. I wouldn't go there.'

'What's the name of this depot?' Ray asked, tired of the Coffee Shop.

'The Depot.' Another bite of biscuit.

'By the railroad tracks?'

'That's it.' He began shaking a bottle of Tabasco sauce over the remaining pile of eggs. 'He's usually got some space, even put in a block room for fire protection. Don't go in the basement, though.'

Ray hesitated, knowing he should ignore the bait. He glanced at his car parked in front of the courthouse and finally said, 'Why not?'

'He keeps his boy down there.'

'His boy?'

'Yeah, he's crazy too. Virgil couldn't get him in Whitfield and couldn't afford a private joint, so he figured he'd just lock him up in the basement.'

'You're serious?'

'Hell yes, I'm serious. I told him it wasn't against the law. Boy's got everythang – bedroom, bathroom, television. Helluva lot cheaper than paying rent in a nuthouse.'

'What's his name?' Ray asked, digging the hole deeper.

'Little Virgil.'

'Little Virgil?'

'Little Virgil.'

'How old is Little Virgil?'

'I don't know, forty-five, fifty.'

To Ray's great relief, no Virgil was present when he walked into the Depot. A stocky woman in overalls said Mr. Cantrell was out running errands and wouldn't be back for two hours. Ray inquired about storage space, and she offered to show him around.

Years before, a remote uncle from Texas had come to visit. Ray's mother scrubbed and polished him to the point of misery. With great anticipation they drove to the depot to fetch the uncle. Forrest was an infant and they left him at home with the nanny. Ray clearly remembered waiting on the platform, hearing the train's whistle, seeing it approach, feeling the excitement as the crowd waited. The depot back then was a busy place. When he was in high school they boarded it up, and the hoodlums used it as a hangout. It was almost razed before the town stepped in with an ill-advised renovation.

Now it was a collection of chopped-up rooms flung over two floors, with worthless junk piled to the ceiling. Lumber and wallboard were stacked throughout, evidence of endless repairs. Sawdust covered the floors. A quick walk-through convinced Ray that the place was more flammable than Maple Run.

'We got more space in the basement,' the woman said.

'No thanks.'

He stepped outside to leave, and flying by on Taylor Street was a brand-new black Cadillac, glistening in the early sun, not a speck of dirt anywhere, Claudia behind the wheel with Jackie O sunglasses.

Standing there in the early morning heat, watching the car race down the street, Ray felt the town of Clanton collapse on top of him. Claudia, the Virgils, Harry Rex and his wives and secretaries, the Atkins boys roofing and drinking and fighting.

Is everybody crazy, or is it just me?

He got in his car and left the Depot, slinging gravel behind. At the edge of town the road stopped. To the north was Forrest, to the south was the coast. Life would get no simpler by visiting his brother, but he had promised.

Chapter 28

Two days later, Ray arrived on the Gulf Coast of Mississippi. There were friends from his law school days at Tulane he wanted to see, and he gave serious thought to spending time in his old haunts. He craved an oyster po'boy from Franky & Johnny's by the levee, a muffaletta from Maspero's on Decatur in the Quarter, a Dixie Beer at the Chart Room on Bourbon Street, and chicory coffee and beignets at Café du Monde, all of his old haunts from twenty years ago.

But crime was rampant in New Orleans, and his handsome little sports car could be a target. Lucky the thief who stole it and yanked open the trunk. Thieves would not catch him, nor would state troopers because he kept precisely at the posted limits. He was a perfect driver – obeying all the laws, closely eyeing every other car.

The traffic slowed him on Highway 90, and for an hour he crept eastward through Long Beach, Gulfport, and Biloxi, hugging the beach, past the shiny new casinos sitting at the water, past new hotels and restaurants. Gambling had hit the coast as fast as it had arrived in the farmlands around Tunica.

He crossed the Bay of Biloxi and entered Jackson County. Near Pascagoula, he saw a flashing rented sign beckoning travelers to stop in for All-You-Can-Eat-Cajun, just $13.99. It was a dive but the parking lot was well lit. He cased it first and realized he could sit at a table in the window and keep an eye on his car. This had become his habit.

There were three counties along the Gulf. Jackson on the east and bordering Alabama, Harrison in the middle, and Hancock on the west next to Louisiana. A local politician had succeeded nicely in Washington and kept the pork flowing back to the shipyards in Jackson County. Gambling was paying the bills and building the schools in Harrison County. And it was Hancock, the least developed and populated, that Judge Atlee had visited in January 1999 for a case that no one back home knew about.

After a slow dinner of crawfish étoufée and shrimp rémoulade, with some raw oysters thrown in, he drifted back across the bay, back through Biloxi and Gulfport. In the town of Pass Christian he found what he was searching for – a new, flat motel with doors that opened to the outside. The surroundings looked safe, the parking lot was half-full. He paid sixty dollars cash for one night and backed the car as close to his door as possible. He'd changed his mind about being without a weapon. One strange sound during the night, and he'd be outside in a flash with the Judge's .38, loaded now. He was perfectly prepared to sleep in the car, if necessary.

Hancock county was named for John, he of the bold signature on the Declaration of Independence. Its courthouse was built in 1911 in the center of Bay St. Louis, and was practically blown away by Hurricane Camille in August 1969. The eye ran right through Pass Christian and Bay St. Louis, and no building escaped severe damage. More than a hundred people died and many were never found.

Ray stopped to read a historical marker on the courthouse lawn, then turned once more to look at his little Audi. Though court records were usually open, he was nervous anyway. The clerks in Clanton guarded their records and monitored who came and went. He wasn't sure what he was looking for or where to begin. The biggest fear, however, was what he might find.

In the Chancery Clerk's office, he loitered just long enough to catch the eye of a pretty young lady with a pencil in her hair. 'May I help you?' she drawled. He was holding a legal pad, as if that would somehow qualify him and open all the right doors.

'Do y'all keep records of trials?' he asked,

trying hard to string out the 'y'all' and overemphasizing it in the process.

She frowned and looked at him as if he had committed a misdemeanor.

'We have minutes from each term of court,' she said slowly, because he obviously was not very bright. 'And we have the actual court files.' Ray was scribbling this down.

'And,' she said after a pause, 'there are the trial transcripts taken down by the court reporter, but we don't keep those here.'

'Can I see the minutes?' he asked, grasping at the first item she'd mentioned.

'Sure. Which term?'

'January of last year.'

She took two steps to her right and began pecking on a keyboard. Ray looked around the large office where several ladies were at their desks, some typing, some filing, some on the phone. The last time he'd seen the Chancery Clerk's office in Clanton there had been only one computer. Hancock County was ten years ahead.

In a corner two lawyers sipped coffee from paper cups and whispered low about important matters. Before them were the property deed books that dated back two hundred years. Both had reading glasses perched on their noses and scuffed wing tips and ties with thick knots. They were checking land titles for a hundred bucks a pop, one of a dozen dreary chores handled by legions of small-town lawyers. One of them noticed Ray and eyed him suspiciously.

That could be me, Ray thought to himself.

The young lady ducked and pulled out a large ledger filled with computer printouts. She flipped pages, then stopped and spun it around on the counter. 'Here,' she said, pointing. 'January '99, two weeks of court. Here's the docket, which goes on for several pages. This column lists the final disposition. As you'll see, most cases were continued to the March term.'

Ray was looking and listening.

'Any case in particular?' she asked.

'Do you remember a case that was heard by Judge Atlee, from Ford County? I think he was here as a special chancellor?' he asked casually. She glared at him as if he'd asked to see her own divorce file.

'Are you a reporter?' she asked, and Ray almost took a step backward.

'Do I need to be?' he asked. Two of the other deputy clerks had stopped whatever they were doing and were frowning at him.

She forced a smile. 'No, but that case was pretty big. It's right here,' she said, pointing again. On the docket it was listed simply as *Gibson v. Miyer-Brack*. Ray nodded approvingly as if he'd found exactly what he wanted. 'And where would the file be located?' he asked.

'It's thick,' she said.

He followed her into a room filled with black metal cabinets that held thousands of files. She knew exactly where to go. 'Sign here,' she said, handing over a clipboard with a ledger on it. 'Just your name, the date. I'll do the rest.'

'What kind of case was it?' he asked as he filled in the blanks.

'Wrongful death.' She opened a long drawer and pointed from one end to the other. 'All this,' she said. 'The pleadings start here, then discovery, then the trial transcript. You can take it to that table over there, but it cannot leave the room. Judge's orders.'

'Which judge?'

'Judge Atlee.'

'He died, you know.'

Walking away, she said, 'That's not such a bad thing.'

The air in the room went with her, and it took a few seconds for Ray to think again. The file was four feet thick, but he didn't care. He had the rest of the summer.

Clete Gibson died in 1997 at the age of sixty-one. Cause of death, kidney failure. Cause of kidney failure, a drug called Ryax, manufactured by Miyer-Brack, according to the allegations of the lawsuit, and found to be true by the Honorable Reuben V. Atlee, sitting as special chancellor.

Mr. Gibson had taken Ryax for eight years to battle high cholesterol. The drug was prescribed by his doctor and sold by his pharmacist, both of whom were also sued by his widow and children. After taking the drug for about five years, he began having kidney problems, which were treated by a different set of doctors. At the time, Ryax, a relatively new drug, had no known side effects. When Gibson's kidneys quit completely, he somehow came to know a Mr. Patton French, attorney-at-law. This happened shortly before his death.

Patton French was with French & French, over in Biloxi. A firm letterhead listed six other lawyers. In addition to the manufacturer, physician, and pharmacist, the defendants also included a local drug salesman and his brokerage company out of New Orleans. Every defendant had a big firm engaged, including some heavyweights from New York. The litigation was contentious, complicated, even fierce at times, and Mr. Patton French and his little firm from Biloxi waged an impressive war against the giants on the other side.

Miyer-Brack was a Swiss pharmaceutical giant, privately owned, with interests in sixty countries, according to the deposition of its American representative. In 1998, its profits were $635 million on revenues of $9.1 billion. That one deposition took an hour to read.

For some reason, Patton French decided to file a wrongful death suit in Chancery Court, the court of equity, instead of Circuit Court, where most trials were by jury. By statute, the only jury trials in Chancery were for will contests. Ray had sat through several of those miserable affairs while clerking for the Judge.

Chancery Court had jurisdiction for two reasons. First, Gibson was dead and his estate was a Chancery matter. Second, he had a child under the age of eighteen. The legal business of minors belonged in Chancery Court.

Gibson also had three children who were not minors. The lawsuit could've been filed in either Circuit or Chancery, one of a hundred great quirks in Mississippi law. Ray had once asked the Judge to explain this enigma, and as usual the answer was simply, 'We have the greatest court system in the country.' Every old chancellor believed this.

Giving lawyers the choice of where to sue was not peculiar to any state. Forum shopping was a game played on the national map. But when a lawsuit by a widow living in rural Mississippi against a mammoth Swiss company that created a drug produced in Uruguay was filed in the Chancery Court of Hancock County, a red flag was raised. The federal courts were in place to deal with such far-flung disputes, and Miyer-Brack and its phalanx of lawyers tried gallantly to remove the case. Judge Atlee held firm, as did the federal judge. Local defendants were included, thus removal to federal court could be denied.

Reuben Atlee was in charge of the case, and as he pushed the matter to trial, his patience with the defense lawyers wore thin. Ray had to smile at some of his father's rulings. They were terse, brutally to the point, and designed to light a fire under the hordes of lawyers scrambling around the defendants. The modern-day rules about speedy trials had never been necessary in Judge Atlee's courtroom.

It became evident that Ryax was a bad product. Patton French found two experts who blasted the drug, and the experts defending it were nothing but mouthpieces for the company. Ryax lowered cholesterol to amazing levels. It had been rushed through the approvals, then dumped into the marketplace, where it became extremely popular. Tens of thousands of kidneys had now been ruined, and Mr. Patton French had Miyer-Brack pinned to the mat.

The trial lasted for eight days. Against the objections of the defense, the proceedings began each morning precisely at eight-fifteen. And they often ran until eight at night, prompting more objections, which Judge Atlee ignored. Ray had seen this many times. The Judge believed in hard work, and, with no jury to pamper, he was brutal.

His final decision was dated two days after the last witness testified, a shocking blow for judicial promptness. Evidently, he had remained in Bay St. Louis and dictated a four-page ruling to the court reporter. This, too, did not surprise Ray. The Judge loathed procrastination in deciding cases.

Plus, he had his notes to rely on. For eight

days of nonstop testimony, the Judge must have filled thirty legal pads. His ruling had enough detail to impress the experts.

The family of Clete Gibson was award $1.1 million in actual damages, the value of his life, according to an economist. And to punish Miyer-Brack for pushing such a bad product, the Judge awarded $10 million in punitive damages. The opinion was a scathing indictment of corporate recklessness and greed, and it was quite obvious that Judge Atlee had become deeply troubled by the practices of Miyer-Brack.

Even so, Ray had never known his father to resort to punitive damages.

There was the usual flurry of post-trial motions, all of which the Judge dismissed with brusque paragraphs. Miyer-Brack wanted the punitive damages taken out. Patton French wanted them increased. Both sides received a written tongue-lashing.

Oddly, there was no appeal. Ray kept waiting for one. He flipped through the post-trial section twice, then dug through the entire drawer again. It was possible the case had been settled afterward, and he made a note to ask the clerk.

A nasty little fight erupted over the fees. Patton French had a contract signed by the Gibson family that gave him fifty percent of any recovery. The Judge, as always, felt that was excessive. In Chancery, the fees were within the sole discretion of the Judge. Thirty-three percent had always been his limit. The math was easy to do, and Mr. French fought hard to collect his well-earned money. His Honor didn't budge.

The Gibson trial was Judge Atlee at his finest, and Ray felt both proud and sentimental. It was difficult to believe it had taken place almost a year and a half earlier, when the Judge was suffering from diabetes, heart disease, and probably cancer, though the latter was six months from being discovered.

He admired the old warrior.

With the exception of one lady who was eating a melon at her desk and doing something else online, the clerks were off at lunch. Ray left the place and went to find a library.

Chapter 29

From a burger joint in Biloxi, he checked his voice mail in Charlottesville and found three messages. Kaley called to say she'd like to have dinner. A quick discard took care of her, forever. Fog Newton called to say the Bonanza was clear for the next week and they needed to go fly. And Martin Gage with the IRS in Atlanta checked in, still looking for the fax of the bogus letter. Keep looking, Ray thought to himself.

He was eating a prepackaged salad at a bright orange plastic table, across the highway from the beach. He could not remember the last time he'd sat alone in a fast-food joint, and he was doing so now only because he could eat with his car close by and in plain sight. Plus the place was crawling with young mothers and their children, usually a low-crime group. He finally gave up on the salad and called Fog.

The Biloxi Public Library was on Lameuse Street. Using a new map he'd purchased at a convenience store, he found it and parked in a row of cars near the main entrance. As was his habit now, he stopped and observed his car and all the elements around it before entering the building.

The computers were on the first floor, in a room encased in glass but with no windows to the outside, to his disappointment. The leading newspaper on the coast was the *Sun Herald*, and through a news-library service its archives could be searched back to 1994. He went to January 24, 1999, the day after Judge Atlee had issued his ruling in the trial. Not surprisingly, there was a story on the front page of the metro section about the $11.1 million verdict over in Bay St. Louis. And it was certainly no surprise to see that Mr. Patton French had a lot to say. Judge Atlee refused comment. The defense lawyers claimed to be shocked and promised to appeal.

There was a photo of Patton French, a man in his mid-fifties with a round face and waves of graying hair. As the story ran on it became obvious that he had called up the paper with the breaking news and had been delighted to chat. It was a 'grueling trial.' The actions of the defendants were 'reckless and greedy.' The decision by the court was 'courageous and fair.' Any appeal would be 'just another attempt to delay justice.'

He'd won many trials, he boasted, but this was his biggest verdict. Quizzed about the recent spate of high awards, he downplayed any suggestion that the ruling was a bit outrageous. 'A jury in Hinds County handed out five hundred million dollars two years ago,' he said. And in other parts of the state, enlightened juries were hitting greedy corporate defendants for ten million here and twenty million there. 'This award is legally defensible on every front,' he declared.

His specialty, he said as the story wound down, was pharmaceutical liability. He had four hundred Ryax cases alone and was adding more each day.

Ray did a word search for Ryax within the *Sun Herald*. Five days after the story, on January 29, there was a bold, full-page ad that began with the ominous question: Have You Taken Ryax? Under it were two paragraphs of dire warnings about the dangers of the drug, then a paragraph detailing the recent victory of Patton French, expert trial attorney, specializing in Ryax and other problematic drugs. A victims' screening session would take place at a Gulfport hotel for the following ten days with qualified medical experts conducting the tests. The screening was at no cost to those who responded. No strings attached, or at least none were mentioned. In clear letters across the bottom of the page was the information that the ad was paid for by the law firm of French & French, with addresses and phone numbers of their offices in Gulfport, Biloxi, and Pascagoula.

The word search produced an almost identical ad dated March 1, 1999. The only difference was the time and place of the screening. Another ad ran in the Sunday edition of the *Sun Herald* on May 2, 1999.

For almost an hour, Ray ventured out from the coast, and found the same ads in the *Clarion-Ledger* in Jackson, the *Times-Picayune* in New Orleans, the *Hattiesburg American*, the *Mobile Register*, the *Commercial Appeal* in Memphis, and *The Advocate* in Baton Rouge. Patton French had launched a massive frontal assault on Ryax and Miyer-Brack.

Convinced that the newspaper ads could spread to all fifty states, Ray grew weary of it. On a guess, he did a Web search for Mr. French, and was welcomed to the firm's own site, a very impressive piece of propaganda.

There were now fourteen lawyers in the firm, with offices in six cities and expanding by the hour. Patton French had a flattering one-page biography that would have embarrassed those with thinner skins. His father, the elder French, looked to be eighty if a day, and had taken senior status, whatever that meant.

The firm's thrust was its rabid representation of folks injured by bad drugs and bad doctors. It had brilliantly negotiated the largest Ryax settlement to date – $900 million for 7,200 clients. Now it was hammering Shyne Medical, makers of Minitrin, the widely used and obscenely profitable hypertension drug that the FDA had pulled because of its side effects. The firm had almost two thousand Minitrin clients and was screening more each week.

Patton French had hit Clark Pharmaceuticals for an eight-million-dollar jury verdict in New Orleans. The drug at war there was Kobril, an antidepressant that had been loosely linked to hearing loss. The firm had settled its first batch of Kobril cases, fourteen hundred of them, for fifty-two million.

Little was said about the other members of the firm, giving the clear impression that it was a one-man show with a squad of minions in the backrooms grappling with thousands of clients who'd been gathered up on the street. There was a page with Mr. French's speaking engagements, one with his extensive trial calendar, and two pages of screening schedules, covering no less than eight drugs, including Skinny Bens, the fat pill Forrest had mentioned earlier.

To better serve its clients, the French firm had purchased a Gulfstream IV, and there was a large color photo of it on the ramp somewhere, with, of course, Patton French posed near the nose in a dark designer suit, with a fierce smile, ready to hop on board and go fight for justice somewhere. Ray knew that such a plane probably cost about thirty million, with two full-time pilots and a list of maintenance expenses that would terrify an accountant.

Patton French was a shameless ego pit.

The airplane was the final straw, and Ray left the library. Leaning on his car, he dialed the number for French & French and worked his way through the recorded menu – client, lawyer, judge, other, screening information, paralegals, the first four letters of your lawyer's last name. Three secretaries working diligently for Mr. French passed him along until he came to the one in charge of scheduling.

Exhausted, Ray said, 'I really would like to see Mr. French.'

'He's out of town,' she said, surprisingly polite.

Of course he was out of town. 'Okay, listen,' Ray said rudely. 'I'm only doing this one time. My name is Ray Atlee. My father was Judge Reuben Atlee. I'm here in Biloxi, and I'd like to see Patton French.'

He gave her his cell phone number and drove away. He went to the Acropolis, a tacky Vegas-style casino with a Greek theme, badly done but absolutely no one cared. The parking lot was busy and there were security guards on duty. Whether they were watching anything was uncertain. He found a bar with a view of the floor, and was sipping a soda when his cell phone beeped. 'Mr. Ray Atlee,' said the voice.

'That's me,' Ray said, pressing the phone closer.

'Patton French here. Delighted you called. Sorry I wasn't in.'

'I'm sure you're a busy man.'

'Indeed I am. You're on the coast?'

'Right now I'm sitting in the Acropolis, a wonderful place.'

'Well, I'm headed back, been down to Naples

291

for a plaintiff's counsel meeting with some big Florida lawyers.'

Here we go, thought Ray.

'Very sorry about your father,' French said, and the signal cracked just a little. Probably at forty thousand feet, streaking home.

'Thank you,' Ray said.

'I was at the funeral, saw you there, but didn't get a chance to speak. A lovely man, the Judge.'

'Thank you,' Ray said again.

'How's Forrest?'

'How do you know Forrest?'

'I know almost everything, Ray. My pretrial preparation is meticulous. We gather information by the truckload. That's how we win. Anyway, is he clean these days?'

'As far as I know,' Ray said, irritated that a private matter would be brought up as casually as the weather. But he knew from the Web site that the man had no finesse.

'Good, look, I'll be in sometime tomorrow. I'm on my yacht, so the pace is a bit slower. Can we do lunch or dinner?'

Didn't see a yacht on the Web page, Mr. French. Must've been an oversight. Ray preferred one hour over coffee, as opposed to a two-hour lunch or an even longer dinner, but he was the guest. 'Either one.'

'Keep them both open, if you don't mind. We're hitting some wind here in the Gulf and I'm not sure when I'll be in. Can I have my girl call you tomorrow?'

'Sure.'

'Are we discussing the Gibson trial?'

'Yes, unless there's something else.'

'No, it all started with Gibson.'

Back at the Easy Sleep Inn, Ray half-watched a muted baseball game and tried to read while waiting for the sun to disappear. He needed sleep but was unwilling to tuck in before dark. He got Forrest on the second try, and they were discussing the joys of rehab when the cell phone erupted. 'I'll call you back,' Ray said and hung up.

An intruder was in his apartment again. A burglary in progress, said the robotic voice from the alarm company. When the recording went dead, Ray opened the door and stared at his car, less than twenty feet away. He held the cell phone and waited.

The alarm company also called Corey Crawford, who called fifteen minutes later with the same report. Crowbar through the door on the street, crowbar through the door to the apartment, a table knocked over, lights on, all appliances accounted for. The same policeman filing the same report.

'There's nothing valuable there,' Ray said.

'Then why do they keep breaking in?' Corey asked.

'I don't know.'

Crawford called the landlord, who promised to find a carpenter and patch up the doors. After the cop left, Corey waited in the apartment and called Ray again. 'This is not a coincidence,' he said.

'Why not?' Ray asked.

'They're not trying to steal anything. It's intimidation, that's all. What's going on?'

'I don't know.'

'I think you do.'

'I swear.'

'I think you're not telling me everything.'

You're certainly right about that, Ray thought, but he held his ground. 'It's random, Corey, relax. Just some of those downtown kids with pink hair and spikes through their jaws. They're druggies looking for a quick buck.'

'I know the area. These aren't kids.'

'A pro wouldn't return if he knew about the alarm. It's two different people.'

'I disagree.'

They agreed to disagree, though both knew the truth.

He rolled in the darkness for two hours, unable even to close his eyes. Around eleven, he went for a drive and found himself back at the Acropolis, where he played roulette and drank bad wine until two in the morning.

He asked for a room overlooking the parking lot, not the beach, and from a third-floor window he guarded his car until he fell asleep.

Chapter 30

He slept until housekeeping got tired of waiting. Checkout was noon, no exceptions, and when the maid banged on the door at eleven forty-five he yelled something through the door and jumped in the shower.

His car looked fine, no pry marks or dents or scrapes around the rear. He unlocked the trunk and quickly peered inside: three black plastic garbage bags stuffed with money. All was normal until he got behind the wheel and saw an envelope tucked under the windshield wiper in front of him. He froze and stared at it, and it seemed to stare back at him from thirty inches away. Plain white, legal size, no visible markings, at least on the side touching the glass.

Whatever it was, it couldn't be good. It wasn't a flyer for a pizza delivery or some clown running for office. It wasn't a ticket for expired parking because parking was free at the Acropolis casino.

It was an envelope with something in it.

He slowly crawled out of the car and looked around on the chance he'd spot someone out there. He lifted the wiper, took the envelope, and examined it as if it might be crucial evidence in a murder trial. Then he got back in the car because he figured someone was watching.

Inside was another trifold, another color digital picture printed off the computer, this one of unit 37F at Chaney's Self-Storage in Charlottesville, Virginia, 930 miles and at least eighteen hours away by car. Same camera, same printer, no doubt the same photographer who no doubt knew that 37F was not the last unit Ray had used to hide the money.

Though he was too numb to move, Ray drove away in a hurry. He sped along Highway 90 watching everything behind him, then suddenly veered to the left and turned onto a street that he followed north for a mile until he abruptly pulled into the parking lot of a Laundromat. No one was following. For an hour he watched every car and saw nothing suspicious. For comfort, his pistol was next to his seat, ready for action. And even more comforting was the money sitting just inches away. He had everything he needed.

The call from Mr. French's scheduling secretary came at eleven-fifteen. Crucial matters had conspired to make lunch impossible, but an early dinner would be his pleasure. She asked if Ray would come to the great man's office around 4 P.M., and the evening would proceed from there.

The office, a flattering photo of which appeared on the Web site, was a stately Georgian home overlooking the Gulf, on a long lot shaded with oaks and Spanish moss. Its neighbors were of similar architecture and age.

The rear had recently been converted into a parking lot with tall brick walls around it and security cameras scanning back and forth. A metal gate was opened for Ray and closed behind him by a guard dressed like a Secret Service agent. He parked in a reserved place, and another guard escorted him up to the rear of the building, where a crew was busy laying tile while another planted shrubs. A major renovation of the office and premises was rapidly winding down.

'The governor's coming in three days,' the guard whispered.

'Wow,' Ray said.

French's personal office was on the second floor, but he was not in it. He was still on his yacht, out in the Gulf, explained a comely young brunette in a tight, expensive dress. She led him into Mr. French's office anyway and asked him to wait in a sitting area by the windows. The room was paneled in blond oak and held enough heavy leather sofas, chairs, and ottomans to furnish a hunting lodge. The desk was the size of a swimming pool and covered with scale models of great yachts.

'He likes boats, huh?' Ray said, looking around. He was expected to be impressed.

'Yes, he does.' With a remote she opened a cabinet and a large flat screen slid out. 'He's in a meeting,' she said, 'but he'll be on in just a moment. Would you like a drink?'

'Thanks, black coffee.'

There was a tiny camera in the top right corner of the screen, and Ray assumed he and Mr. French were about to chat via satellite. His irritation at waiting was slowly building. Normally, it would've been boiling by now, but he was captivated by the show that was unfolding around him. He was a character in it. Relax and enjoy it, he told himself. You have plenty of time.

She returned with the coffee, which, of course, was served in fine china, F&F engraved on the side of the cup.

'Can I step outside?' Ray asked.

'Certainly.' She smiled and returned to her desk.

There was a long balcony through a set of doors. Ray sipped his coffee at the railing and admired the view. The wide front lawn ended at the highway, and beyond it was the beach and the water. No casinos were visible, not much in the way of development. Below him, on the front porch, some painters were chattering back and forth as they moved their ladders. Everything about the place looked and felt new. Patton French had just won the lottery.

'Mr. Atlee,' she called, and Ray stepped inside the office. On the screen was the face of Patton French, hair slightly disheveled, reading glasses perched on his nose, eyes frowning above them. 'There you are,' he barked. 'Sorry for the delay. Have a seat there, if you will, Ray, so I can see you.'

She pointed and Ray sat.

'How are you?' French asked.

'Fine. You?'

'Great, look, sorry for the mix-up, all my fault, but I've been on one of these damned conference calls all afternoon, just couldn't get away. I was thinking it would be a lot quieter here on the boat for dinner, whatta you think? My chef's a damned sight better than anything you'll find on land. I'm only thirty minutes out. We'll have a drink, just the two of us, then a long dinner and we'll talk about your father. It'll be enjoyable, I promise.'

When he finally shut up, Ray said, 'Will my car be secure here?'

'Of course. Hell, it's in a compound. I'll tell the guards to sit on the damned thing if you want.'

'Okay. Do I swim out?'

'No, I've got boats. Dickie'll bring you.'

Dickie was the same thick young man who'd escorted Ray into the building. Now he escorted him out, where a very long silver Mercedes was waiting. Dickie drove it like a tank through the traffic to the Point Cadet Marina, where a hundred small vessels were docked. One of the larger ones just happened to be owned by Patton French. Its name was the *Lady of Justice*.

'The water's smooth, take about twenty-five minutes,' Dickie said as they climbed on board. The engines were running. A steward with a thick accent asked Ray if he'd like a drink. 'Diet soda,' he said. They cast off and puttered through the rows of slips and past the marina until they were away from the pier. Ray climbed to the upper deck and watched the shoreline fade into the distance.

Anchored ten miles from Biloxi was the *King of Torts*, a hundred-forty-foot luxury yacht with a crew of five and plush quarters for a dozen friends. The only passenger was Mr. French, and he was waiting to greet his dinner guest. 'A real pleasure, Ray,' he said as he pumped his hand and then squeezed his shoulder.

'A pleasure for me as well,' Ray said, holding his ground because French liked close contact. He was an inch or two taller, with a nicely tanned face, fierce blue eyes that squinted and did not blink.

'I'm so glad you came,' French said, squeezing Ray's hand. Fraternity brothers couldn't have pawed each other with more affection.

'Stay here, Dickie,' he barked to the deck below. 'Follow me, Ray,' he said, and they were off, up one short flight to the main deck, where a steward in a white jacket was waiting with a

300

starched F&F towel folded perfectly over his arm. 'What'll you have?' he demanded of Ray.

Suspecting that French was not a man who toyed with light booze, Ray said, 'What's the specialty of the house?'

'Iced vodka, with a twist of lime.'

'I'll try it,' Ray said.

'It's a great new vodka from Norway. You'll love it.' The man knew his vodkas.

He was wearing a black linen shirt, buttoned at the neck, and tan linen shorts, perfectly pressed and hanging nicely on his frame. There was a slight belly, but he was thick through the chest and his forearms were twice the normal size. He liked his hair because he couldn't keep his hands out of it.

'How about the boat?' he asked, waving his hands from stern to bow. 'It was built by a Saudi prince, one of the lesser ones, a coupla years ago. Dumb-ass put a fireplace in it, can you believe that? Cost him twenty million or so, and after a year he traded it in for a two-hundred-footer.'

'It's amazing,' Ray said, trying to sound sufficiently awed. The world of yachting was one he had never been near, and he suspected that after this episode he would forever keep his distance.

'Built by the Italians,' French said, tapping a railing made of some terribly expensive wood.

'Why do you stay out here, in the Gulf?' Ray asked.

301

'I'm an offshore kind of guy, ha, ha. If you know what I mean. Sit.' French pointed, and they lowered themselves into two long deck chairs. When they were nestled in, French nodded to the shore. 'You can barely see Biloxi, and this is close enough. I can do more work out here in one day than in a week at the office. Plus I'm transitioning from one house to the next. A divorce is in the works. This is where I hide.'

'Sorry.'

'This is the biggest yacht in Biloxi now, and most folks can spot it. The current wife thinks I've sold it, and if I get too close to the shore then her slimy little lawyer might swim out and take a picture of it. Ten miles is close enough.'

The iced vodkas arrived, in tall narrow glasses, F&F engraved on the sides. Ray took a sip and the concoction burned all the way to his toes. French took a long pull and smacked his lips. 'Whatta you think?' he asked proudly.

'Nice vodka,' Ray said. He couldn't remember the last time he'd had one.

'Dickie brought fresh swordfish out for dinner. Sound okay?'

'Great.'

'And the oysters are good now.'

'I went to law school at Tulane. I had three years of fresh oysters.'

'I know,' French said and pulled a small radio from his shirt pocket and passed along their dinner selections to someone below. He glanced

302

at his watch and decided they would eat in two hours.

'You went to school with Hassel Mangrum,' French said.

'Yes, he was a year ahead of me.'

'We share the same trainer. Hassel has done well here on the coast. Got in early with the asbestos boys.'

'I haven't heard from Hassel in twenty years.'

'You haven't missed much. He's a jerk now, I suspect he was a jerk in law school.'

'He was. How'd you know I went to school with Mangrum?'

'Research, Ray, extensive research.' He swigged the vodka again. Ray's third sip went straight to his brain.

'We spent a bunch of dough investigating Judge Atlee, and his family, and his background, his rulings, his finances, everything we could find. Nothing illegal or intrusive, mind you, but old-fashioned detective work. We knew about your divorce, what's his name, Lew the Liquidator?'

Ray just nodded. He wanted to say something derogatory about Lew Rodowski and he wanted to rebuke French for digging through his past, but for a second the vodka was blocking signals. So he nodded.

'We knew your salary as a law professor, it's public record in Virginia, you know.'

'Yes it is.'

303

'Not a bad salary, Ray, but then it's a great law school.'

'It is indeed.'

'Digging through your brother's past was quite an adventure.'

'I'm sure it was. It's been an adventure for the family.'

'We read every ruling your father issued in damage suits and wrongful death cases. There weren't many, but we picked up clues. He was conservative with his awards, but he also favored the little guy, the working man. We knew he would follow the law, but we also knew that old chancellors often mold the law to fit their notion of fairness. I had clerks doing the grunt work, but I read every one of his important decisions. He was a brilliant man, Ray, and always fair. I never disagreed with one of his opinions.'

'You picked my father for the Gibson case?'

'Yes. When we made the decision to file the case in Chancery Court and try it without a jury, we also decided we did not want a local chancellor to hear it. We have three. One is related to the Gibson family. One refuses to hear any matter other than divorces. One is eighty-four, senile, and hasn't left the house in three years. So we looked around the state and found three potential fill-ins. Fortunately, my father and your father go back sixty years, to Sewanee and then law school at Ole Miss. They weren't close friends over the years, but they kept in touch.'

'Your father is still active?'

'No, he's in Florida now, retired, playing golf every day. I'm the sole owner of the firm. But my old man drove to Clanton, sat on the front porch with Judge Atlee, talked about the Civil War and Nathan Bedford Forrest. They even drove to Shiloh, walked around for two days – the hornet's nest, the bloody pond. Judge Atlee got all choked up when he stood where General Johnston fell.'

'I've been there a dozen times,' Ray said with a smile.

'You don't lobby a man like Judge Atlee. Earwigging is the ancient term.'

'He put a lawyer in jail once for that,' Ray said. 'The guy came in before court began and tried to plead his case. The Judge threw him in jail for half a day.'

'That was that Chadwick fella over in Oxford, wasn't it?' French said smugly, and Ray was speechless.

'Anyway, we had to impress upon Judge Atlee the importance of the Ryax litigation. We knew he wouldn't want to come to the coast and try the case, but he'd do it if he believed in the cause.'

'He hated the coast.'

'We knew that, believe me, it was a huge concern. But he was a man of great principle. After refighting the war up there for two days, Judge Atlee reluctantly agreed to hear the case.'

'Doesn't the Supreme Court assign the special chancellors?' Ray asked. The fourth sip sort of slid down, without burning, and the vodka was tasting better.

French shrugged it off. 'Sure, but there are ways. We have friends.'

In Patton French's world, anyone could be bought.

The steward was back with fresh drinks. Not that they were needed, but they were taken anyway. French was too hyper to sit still for long. 'Lemme show you the boat,' he said, and bounced out of his chair with no effort. Ray climbed out carefully, balancing his glass.

Chapter 31

Dinner was in the captain's galley, a mahogany-paneled dining room with walls adorned with models of ancient clippers and gunboats and maps of the New World and the Far East and even a collection of antique muskets thrown in to give the impression that the *King of Torts* had been around for centuries. It was on the main deck behind the bridge, just down a narrow hallway from the kitchen, where a Vietnamese chef was hard at work. The formal dining area was around an oval marble table that seated a dozen and weighed at least a ton and made Ray ask himself how, exactly, the *King of Torts* stayed afloat.

The captain's table sat only two this evening, and above it was a small chandelier that rocked with the sea. Ray was at one end, French at the other. The first wine of the night was a white burgundy that, following the scalding by two iced vodkas, was tasteless to Ray. Not to his host. French had knocked back three of the

307

vodkas, had in fact drained all three glasses, and his tongue was beginning to thicken slightly. But he tasted every hint of fruit in the wine, even got a whiff of the oak barrels, and, as all wine snobs do, had to pass this useful information along to Ray.

'Here's to Ryax,' French said, reaching forward with his glass in a delayed toast. Ray touched his glass but said nothing. It was not a night for him to say much, and he knew it. He would just listen. His host would get drunk and say enough.

'Ryax saved me, Ray,' French said as he swirled his wine and admired it.

'In what way?'

'In every way. It saved my soul. I worship money, and Ryax has made me rich.' A small sip, followed by the requisite smacking of the lips, a rolling of the eyes. 'I missed the asbestos wave twenty years ago. Those shipyards over in Pascagoula used asbestos for years, and tens of thousands of men became ill. And I missed it. I was too busy suing doctors and insurance companies, and I was making good money but I just didn't see the potential in mass torts. You ready for some oysters?'

'Yes.'

French pushed a button; the steward popped in with two trays of raw oysters on the half shell. Ray mixed horseradish into the cocktail sauce and prepared for the feast. Patton was swirling wine and too busy talking.

'Then came tobacco,' he said sadly. 'Many of the same lawyers, from right here. I thought they were crazy, hell, everybody did, but they sued the big tobacco companies in almost every state. I had the chance to jump into the pit with them, but I was too scared. It's hard to admit that, Ray. I was just too damned scared to roll the dice.'

'What did they want?' Ray asked, then shoved the first oyster and saltine into his mouth.

'A million bucks to help finance the litigation. And I had a million bucks at the time.'

'How much was the settlement?' Ray asked, chewing.

'More than three hundred billion. The biggest financial and legal scam in history. The tobacco companies basically bought off the lawyers, who sold out. One huge bribe, and I missed it.' He appeared to be ready to cry because he'd missed a bribe, but he rallied quickly with a long pull on the wine.

'Good oysters,' Ray said, with a mouthful.

'Twenty-four hours ago, they were fifteen feet down.' French poured more wine and settled over his platter.

'What would've been the return on your one million dollars?' Ray asked.

'Two hundred to one.'

'Two hundred million bucks?'

'Yep. I was sick for a year, lots of lawyers around here were sick. We knew the players and we had chickened out.'

'Then along came Ryax.'

'Yes indeed.'

'How'd you find it?' Ray asked, knowing the question would require another windy answer, and he'd be free to eat.

'I was at a trial lawyers' seminar in St. Louis. Missouri is a nice place and all, but miles behind us when it comes to tort litigation. I mean, hell, we've had the asbestos and tobacco boys running around here for years, burning money, showing everybody else how it's done. I had a drink with this old lawyer from a small town in the Ozarks. His son teaches medicine at the university in Columbia, and the son was on to Ryax. His research was showing some horrible results. The damned drug just eats up the kidneys, and because it was so new there was not a history of litigation. I found an expert in Chicago, and he found Clete Gibson through a doctor in New Orleans. Then we started screening, and the thing snowballed. All we needed was a big verdict.'

'Why didn't you want a jury trial?'

'I love juries. I love to pick them, talk to them, sway them, manipulate them, even buy them, but they're unpredictable. I wanted a lock, a guarantee. And I wanted a speedy trial. Ryax rumors were spreading like crazy, you can imagine a bunch of hungry tort lawyers with the gossip that a new drug had gone bad. We were signing up cases by the dozens. The guy with the first big verdict would be in the driver's seat, especially if it came from the Biloxi area. Miyer-Brack is a Swiss company –'

'I've read the file.'

'All of it?'

'Yes, yesterday in the Hancock County Court-house.'

'Well, these Europeans are terrified of our tort system.'

'Shouldn't they be?'

'Yes, but in a good way. Keeps 'em honest. What should terrify them is the possibility that one of their damned drugs is defective and might harm people, but that's not a concern when billions are at stake. It takes people like me to keep 'em honest.'

'And they knew Ryax was bad?'

French choked down another oyster, swallowed hard, gulped a half pint of wine, and finally said, 'Early on. The drug was so effective at lowering cholesterol that Miyer-Brack, along with the FDA, rushed it to the market. It was another miracle drug, and it worked great for a few years with no side effects. Then, bam! The tissue of the nephrons – do you understand how the kidneys work?'

'For the sake of this discussion, let's say I don't.'

'Each kidney has about a million little filtering units called nephrons, and Ryax contained a synthetic chemical that basically melted them. Not everybody dies, like poor Mr. Gibson, and there are varying degrees of damage. It's all

311

permanent, though. The kidney is an amazing organ that can often heal itself, but not after a five-year bout with Ryax.'

'When did Miyer-Brack know it had a problem?'

'Hard to say exactly, but we showed Judge Atlee some internal documents from their lab people to their suits urging caution and more research. After Ryax had been on the market for about four years, with spectacular results, the company's scientists were worried. Then folks started getting real sick, even dying, and by then it was too late. From my standpoint, we had to find the perfect client, which we did, the perfect forum, which we did, and we had to do it quick before some other lawyer got a big verdict. That's where your father came in.'

The steward cleared the oyster shells and presented a crabmeat salad. Another white burgundy had been selected from the onboard cellar by Mr. French himself.

'What happened after the Gibson trial?' Ray asked.

'I could not have scripted it better. Miyer-Brack absolutely crumbled. Arrogant shitheads were reduced to tears. They had a zillion bucks in cash and couldn't wait to buy off the plaintiffs' lawyers. Before the trial I had four hundred cases and no clout. Afterward, I had five thousand cases and an eleven-million-dollar verdict. Hundreds of lawyers called me. I spent a month flying around the country, in a Learjet,

312

signing co-rep agreements with other lawyers. A guy in Kentucky had a hundred cases. One in St. Paul had eighty. On and on. Then, about four months after the trial, we flew to New York for the big settlement conference. In less than three hours we settled six thousand cases for seven hundred million bucks. A month later we settled another twelve hundred for two hundred million.'

'What was your cut?' Ray asked. It would've been a rude question if posed to a normal person, but French couldn't wait to talk about his fees.

'Fifty percent off the top for the lawyers, then expenses, the rest went to the clients. That's the bad part of a contingency contract – you have to give half to the client. Anyway, I had other lawyers to deal with, but I walked away with three hundred million and some change. That's the beauty of mass torts, Ray. Sign 'em up by the truckload, settle 'em by the trainload, take half off the top.'

They weren't eating. There was too much money in the air.

'Three hundred million in fees?' Ray said in disbelief.

French was gargling with wine. 'Ain't it sweet? It's coming so fast I can't spend it all.'

'Looks like you're giving it a good shot.'

'This is the tip of the iceberg. Ever hear of a drug called Minitrin?'

'I checked your Web site.'

313

'Really? What'd you think?'

'Pretty slick. Two thousand Minitrin cases.'

'Three thousand now. It's a hypertension drug that has dangerous side effects. Made by Shyne Medical. They've offered fifty thousand a case and I said no. Fourteen hundred Kobril cases, antidepressant that causes hearing loss, we think. Ever hear of Skinny Bens?'

'Yes.'

'We have three thousand Skinny Ben cases. And fifteen hundred –'

'I saw the list. I assume the Web site is updated.'

'Of course. I'm the new King of Torts in this country, Ray. Everybody's calling me. I have thirteen other lawyers in my firm and I need forty.'

The steward was back to collect their latest leftovers. He placed the swordfish in front of them and brought the next wine, though the last bottle was half full. French went through the tasting ritual and finally, almost reluctantly, nodded his approval. To Ray it tasted very similar to the first two.

'I owe it all to Judge Atlee,' French said.

'How?'

'He had the guts to make the right call, to keep Miyer-Brack in Hancock County instead of allowing them to escape to federal court. He understood the issues, and he was unafraid to punish them. Timing is everything, Ray. Less than six months after he handed down his

314

ruling, I had three hundred million bucks in my hands.'

'Did you keep all of it?'

French had a bite on a fork close to his mouth. He hesitated for a second, then took the fish, chewed for a while, then said, 'I don't understand the question.'

'I think you do. Did you give any of the money to Judge Atlee?'

'Yes.'

'How much?'

'One percent.'

'Three million bucks?'

'And change. This fish is delicious, don't you think?'

'It is. Why?'

French put down his knife and fork and stroked his locks again with both hands. Then he wiped them on his napkin and swirled his wine. 'I suppose there are a lot of questions. Why, when, how, who.'

'You're good at stories, let's hear it.'

Another swirl, then a satisfied sip. 'It's not what you think, though I would've bribed your father or any judge for that ruling. I've done it before, and I'll happily do it again. It's just part of the overhead. Frankly, though, I was so intimidated by him and his reputation that I just couldn't approach him with a deal. He would've thrown me in jail.'

'He would've buried you in jail.'

'Yes, I know, and my father convinced me of

315

this. So we played it straight. The trial was an all-out war, but truth was on my side. I won, then I won big, now I'm winning even bigger. Late last summer, after we settled and the money was wired in, I wanted to give him a gift. I take care of those who help me, Ray. A new car here, a condo there, a sack full of cash for a favor. I play the game hard and I protect my friends.'

'He wasn't your friend.'

'We weren't amigos, or fraternity brothers, but in my world I've never had a greater friend. It all started with him. Do you realize how much money I'll make in the next five years?'

'Shock me again.'

'Half a billion. And I owe it all to your old man.'

'When will you have enough?'

'There's a tobacco lawyer here who made a billion. I need to catch him first.'

Ray needed a drink. He examined the wine as if he knew what to look for, then sucked it down. French was into the fish.

'I don't think you're lying,' Ray said.

'I don't lie. I cheat and bribe, but I don't lie. About six months ago, while I was shopping for airplanes and boats and beach homes and mountain cabins and new offices, I heard that your father had been diagnosed with cancer, and that it was serious. I wanted to do something nice for him. I knew he didn't have much

316

money, and what he did have he seemed hell-bent on giving away.'

'So you sent him three million in cash?'

'Yes.'

'Just like that?'

'Just like that. I called him and told him a package was on the way. Four packages as it turned out, four large cardboard boxes. One of my boys drove them up in a van, left them on the front porch. Judge Atlee wasn't home.'

'Unmarked bills?'

'Why would I mark them?'

'What did he say?' Ray asked.

'I never heard a word, and I didn't want to.'

'What did he do?'

'You tell me. You're his son, you know him better than me. You tell me what he did with the money.'

Ray pushed back from the table, and holding his wineglass, he crossed his legs and tried to relax. 'He found the money on the porch, and when he realized what it was, I'm sure he gave you a thorough cursing.'

'God, I hope so.'

'He moved it into the foyer, where the boxes joined dozens of others. He planned to load it up and haul it back to Biloxi, but a day or two passed. He was sick and weak, and not driving too well. He knew he was dying, and I'm sure that burden changed his outlook on a lot of things. After a few days he decided to hide the money, which he did, and all the while he planned to get it back down here and flog your corrupt ass in the process. Time passed, and he got sicker.'

'Who found the money?'

'I did.'

'Where is it?'

'In the trunk of my car, at your office.'

French laughed long and hard. 'Back where it started from,' he said between breaths.

'It's had quite a tour. I found it in his study just after I found him dead. Someone tried to break in and get it. I took it to Virginia, now it's back, and that someone is following me.'

The laughter stopped immediately. He wiped his mouth with a napkin. 'How much did you find?'

'Three million, one hundred and eighteen thousand.'

'Damn! He didn't spend a dime.'

'And he didn't mention it in his will. He just left it, hidden in stationer's boxes in a cabinet beneath his bookshelves.'

'Who tried to break in?'

'I was hoping you might know.'

'I have a pretty good idea.'

'Please tell me.'

'It's another long story.'

318

Chapter 32

The steward brought a selection of single malts to the top deck where French had settled them in for a nightcap and another story, with a view of Biloxi flickering in the distance. Ray did not drink whiskey and certainly knew nothing about single malts, but he went along with the ritual because he knew French would get even drunker. The truth was flowing in torrents now, and Ray wanted all of it.

They settled on Lagavulin because of its smokiness, whatever that meant. There were four others, lined like proud old sentries in distinctive regalia, and Ray vowed he'd had enough to drink. He'd sip and spit and if he got the chance he'd toss it overboard. To his relief, the steward poured tiny servings in short thick glasses heavy enough to crack floors.

It was almost ten but felt much later. The Gulf was dark, no other boats were visible. A gentle wind blew from the south and rocked the *King of Torts* just slightly.

'Who knows about the money?' French asked, smacking his lips.

'Me, you, whoever hauled it up there.'

'That's your man.'

'Who is he?'

A long sip, more smacking. Ray brought the whiskey to his lips and wished he hadn't. Numb as they were, they burned all over again.

'Gordie Priest. He worked for me for eight or so years, first as a gofer, then a runner, then a bagman. His family has been on the coast forever, always on the edges. His father and uncles ran numbers, whores, moonshine, honky-tonks, nothing legal. They were part of what was once known as the coast mafia, a bunch of thugs who disdained honest work. Twenty years ago they controlled some things around here, now they're history. Most of them went to jail. Gordie's father, a man I knew very well, got shot outside a bar near Mobile. A pretty miserable lot, really. My family has known them for years.'

He was implying that his family had been part of the same bunch of crooks, but he couldn't say it. They'd been the front guys, the lawyers who smiled for the cameras and cut the backroom deals.

'Gordie went to jail when he was about twenty, a stolen car ring that covered a dozen states. I hired him when he got out, and over time he became one of the best runners on the coast. He was particularly good at the offshore cases. He knew the guys on the rigs, and when there was a death or injury he'd get the case. I'd give him a nice percentage. Gotta take care of your runners. One year I paid him almost eighty thousand, all of it in cash. He blew it, of course, casinos and women. Loved to go to Vegas and stay drunk for a week, throw money around like a big shot. He acted like an idiot but he wasn't stupid. He was always up and down. When he was broke he'd scramble and make some money. When he had money, he'd manage to lose it.'

'I'm sure this is all headed my way,' Ray said.

'Hang on,' French said. 'After the Gibson case early last year, the money hit like a tidal wave. I had favors to repay. Lots of cash got hauled around. Cash to lawyers who were sending me their cases. Cash to doctors who were screening thousands of new clients. Not all of it was illegal, mind you, but a lot of folks didn't want records. I made the mistake of using Gordie as the delivery boy. I thought I could trust him. I thought he would be loyal. I was wrong.'

French had finished one sample and was ready for another. Ray declined and pretended to work on the Lagavulin.

'And he drove the money up to Clanton and left it on the front porch?' Ray said.

'He did, and three months after that he stole a million dollars from me, in cash, and disappeared. He has two brothers, and at any given time during the past ten years one of the three has been in prison. Except for now. Now they're all on parole, and they're trying to extort big money out of me. Extortion is a serious crime, you know, but I can't exactly go to the FBI.'

'What makes you think he's after the three million bucks?'

'Wiretaps. We picked it up a few months ago. I've hired some pretty serious characters to find Gordie.'

'What will you do if you find him?'

'Oh, there's a price on his head.'

'You mean, like a contract?'

'Yes.'

And with that, Ray reached for another single malt.

He slept on the boat, in a large room somewhere under the water, and when he found his way to the main deck the sun was high in the east and the air was already hot and sticky. The captain said good morning and pointed forward, where he found French yelling into a phone.

The faithful steward materialized out of thin air and presented a coffee. Breakfast was up on the top deck at the scene of the single malts, now under a canopy for shade.

'I love to eat outdoors,' French announced as he joined Ray. 'You slept for ten hours.'

'Did I really?' Ray asked, looking again at his watch, which was still on Eastern time. He was on a yacht in the Gulf of Mexico, unsure of the

322

day or time, a million miles from home, and now burdened with the knowledge that some very nasty people were chasing him.

The table was spread with breads and cereals. 'Tin Lu down there can fix anything you want,' French was saying. 'Bacon, eggs, waffles, grits.'

'This is fine, thanks.'

French was fresh and hyper, already tackling another grueling day with the energy that could only come from the prospect of a half a billion or so in fees. He was wearing a white linen shirt, buttoned at the top like the black one last night, shorts, loafers. His eyes were clear and dancing around. 'Just picked up another three hundred Minitrin cases,' he said as he dumped a generous portion of flakes into a large bowl. Every dish had the obligatory F&F monogram splashed on it.

Ray had had enough of mass torts. 'Good, but I'm more interested in Gordie Priest.'

'We'll find him. I'm already making calls.'

'He's probably in town.' Ray pulled a folded sheet of paper from his rear pocket. It was the photo of 37F he'd found yesterday morning on his windshield. French looked at it and stopped eating.

'And this is up in Virginia?' he asked.

'Yep, the second of three units I rented. They've found the first two, I'm sure they know about the third. And they knew exactly where I was yesterday morning.'

'But they obviously don't know where the

323

money is. Otherwise, they would have simply taken it from the trunk of your car while you were asleep. Or they would've pulled you over somewhere between here and Clanton and put a bullet in your ear.'

'You don't know what they're thinking.'

'Sure I do. Think like a crook, Ray. Think like a thug.'

'It may come easy for you, but it's harder for some folks.'

'If Gordie and his brothers knew you had three million bucks in the trunk of your car, they would take it. Simple as that.' He put the photo down and attacked his flakes.

'Nothing is simple,' Ray said.

'What do you wanna do? Leave the money with me?'

'Yes.'

'Don't be stupid, Ray. Three million tax-free dollars.'

'Useless if I get the ole bullet in the ear. I have a very nice salary.'

'The money is safe. Keep it where it is. Give me some time to find these boys, and they'll be neutralized.'

The neutralization sapped any appetite Ray had.

'Eat, man!' French barked when Ray grew still.

'I don't have the stomach for this. Dirty money, bad guys breaking into my apartment, chasing me all over the Southeast, wiretaps, contract killers. What the hell am I doing here?'

French never stopped chewing. His intestines were lined with brass. 'Keep cool,' he said. 'And the money'll be yours.'

'I don't want the money.'

'Of course you do.'

'No I don't.'

'Then give it to Forrest.'

'What a disaster.'

'Give it to charity. Give it your law school. Give it to something that makes you feel good.'

'Why don't I just give it to Gordie so he won't shoot me?'

French gave his spoon a rest and looked around as if others were lurking. 'All right, we spotted Gordie last night over in Pascagoula,' he said, an octave lower. 'We're hot on his trail, okay? I think we'll have him within twenty-four hours.'

'And he'll be neutralized?'

'He'll be iced.'

'Iced?'

'Gordie'll be history. Your money'll be safe. Just hang on, okay.'

'I'd like to leave now.'

French wiped skim milk off his bottom lip, then picked up his mini radio and told Dickie to get the boat ready. Minutes later, they were ready to board.

'Take a look at these,' French said, handing over an eight-by-twelve manila envelope.

'What is it?'

'Photos of the Priest boys. Just in case you bump into them.'

Ray ignored the envelope until he stopped in Hattiesburg, ninety minutes north of the coast. He bought gas and a dreadful shrink-wrapped sandwich, then was off again, in a hurry to get to Clanton, where Harry Rex knew the sheriff and all his deputies.

Gordie had a particularly menacing sneer, one that had been captured by a police photographer in 1991. His brothers, Slatt and Alvin, were certainly no prettier. Ray couldn't tell the oldest from the youngest, not that it mattered. None of the three resembled the others. Bad breeding. Same mother, no doubt different fathers.

They could have a million each, he didn't care. Just leave me alone.

Chapter 33

The hills began between Jackson and Memphis, and the coast seemed time zones away. He had often wondered at how a state so small could be so diverse: the Delta region along the river with the wealth of its cotton and rice farms and the poverty that still astonished outsiders; the coast with its blend of immigrants and laidback, New Orleans casualness; and the hills where most counties were still dry and most folks still went to church on Sundays. A person from the hills would never understand the coast and never be accepted in the Delta. Ray was just happy he lived in Virginia.

Patton French was a dream, he kept telling himself. A cartoonish character from another world. A pompous jerk being eaten alive by his own ego. A liar, a briber, a shameless crook.

Then he would glance over at the passenger's seat and see the sinister face of Gordie Priest. One glance and there was no doubt this brute and his brothers would do anything for the money Ray was still hauling around the country.

An hour from Clanton, and again within range of a tower, his cell phone rang. It was Fog Newton and he was quite agitated. 'Where the hell have you been?' he demanded.

'You wouldn't believe me.'

'I've been calling all morning.'

'What is it, Fog?'

'We've had a little excitement around here. Last night, after general aviation closed, somebody sneaked onto the ramp and put an incendiary device on the left wing of the Bonanza. Boom. A janitor in the main terminal just happened to see the blaze, and they got the fire truck out pretty fast.'

Ray had pulled onto the shoulder of Interstate 55 and stopped. He grunted something into the phone and Fog kept going. 'Severe damage though. No doubt it was an act of arson. You there?'

'Just listening,' Ray said. 'How much damage?'

'Left wing, the engine, and most of the fuselage, probably a total loss for insurance purposes. The arson investigator is already here. Insurance guy's here too. If the tanks had been full it would've been a bomb.'

'The other owners know about it?'

'Yes, everyone's been out. Of course they're first on the suspect list. Lucky you were out of town. When are you coming back?'

'Soon.'

He made it to an exit and pulled into the gravel lot of a truck stop, where he sat in the heat for a long time and occasionally glanced down at Gordie. The Priest gang moved fast – Biloxi yesterday morning, Charlottesville last night. Where are they now?

Inside, he drank coffee and listened to the chatter of the truckers. To change the subject, he called Alcorn Village to check on Forrest. He was in his room, sleeping the sleep of the righteous, as he described it. It was always amazing, he said, how much he slept in rehab. He'd complained about the food, and things had improved slightly. Either that or he had developed a taste for pink Jell-O. He asked how long he could stay, like a kid at Disney World. Ray said he wasn't sure. The money that had once seemed endless was now very much in jeopardy.

'Don't let me out, Bro,' he pleaded. 'I want to stay in rehab for the remainder of my life.'

The Atkins boys had finished the roof at Maple Run without incident. The place was deserted when Ray arrived. He called Harry Rex and checked in. 'Let's drink some beer on the porch tonight,' Ray suggested.

Harry Rex had never said no to such an invitation.

There was a level spot of thick grass just beyond the front sidewalk, directly in front of the house, and after careful deliberation Ray decided it was the place for a washing. He parked the little Audi there, facing the street, its rear and its trunk just a step from the porch. He found an old tin bucket in the basement and a leaky water hose in the back shed. Shirtless and shoeless, he sloshed around for two hours in the hot afternoon sun, scrubbing the roadster. Then he waxed and polished it for an hour. At 5 P.M., he opened a cold bottle of beer and sat on the steps, admiring his work.

He called the private cell phone number given to him by Patton French, but of course the great man was too busy. Ray wanted to thank him for his hospitality, but what he really wanted was to see if they had made any progress down there icing the Priest gang. He would never ask that question directly, but a blowhard like French would happily deliver the news if he had it.

French had probably forgotten about him. He didn't really care if the Priest boys nailed Ray or the next guy. He needed to make a half a billion or so in mass tort schemes, and that took all his energies. Indict a guy like French, for payoffs or contract killings, and he'd hire fifty lawyers and buy every clerk, judge, prosecutor, and juror.

He called Corey Crawford and got the news that the landlord had once again repaired the doors. The police had promised to keep an eye on the place for the next few days, until he returned.

The van pulled into the driveway shortly after

6 P.M. A smiling face jumped out with a thin overnight envelope, which Ray stared at long after it had been delivered. The airbill was a preprinted form from the University of Virginia School of Law, hand-addressed to Mr. Ray Atlee, Maple Run, 816 Fourth Street, Clanton, MS, dated June 2, the day before. Everything about it was suspicious.

No one at the law school had been given the address in Clanton. Nothing from there would be so urgent as to require an overnight delivery. And he could think of no reason whatsoever that the school would be sending him anything. He opened another beer and returned to the front steps, where he grabbed the damned thing and ripped it open.

Plain white legal-size envelope, with the word 'Ray' hand-scrawled on the outside. And on the inside, another of the now familiar color photos of Chaney's Self-Storage, this time the front of unit 18R. At the bottom, in a wacky font of mismatched letters, was the message: 'You don't need an airplane. Stop spending the money.'

These guys were very, very good. It was tough enough to track down the three units at Chaney's and take pictures of them. It was gutsy and also stupid to burn up the Bonanza. Oddly, though, what was most impressive at the moment was their ability to swipe an airbill from the business office at the law school.

After a prolonged moment of shock, he

realized something that should have been immediately obvious. Since they'd found 18R, then they knew the money wasn't there. It wasn't at Chaney's, nor at his apartment. They'd followed him from Virginia to Clanton, and if he'd stopped somewhere along the way to hide the money, they would know it. They'd probably rummaged through Maple Run again, while he was on the coast.

Their net was tightening by the hour. All clues were being linked, all dots connected. The money had to be with him, and Ray had no place to run.

He had a very comfortable salary as a professor of law, with benefits. His lifestyle was not expensive, and he decided right there on the porch, still shirtless and shoeless, sipping a beer in the early evening humidity of a long hot June day, that he preferred to continue that lifestyle. Leave the violence for the likes of Gordie Priest and hit men hired by Patton French. Ray was out of his element.

The cash was dirty anyway.

'Why'd you park in the front yard?' Harry Rex grumbled as he lumbered up the steps.

'I washed it and left it there,' Ray said. He had showered and was wearing shorts and a tee shirt.

'You just can't get the redneck outta some people. Gimme a beer.'

Harry Rex had been brawling in court all day, a nasty divorce where the weighty issues were which spouse had smoked the most dope ten years ago and which one had slept with the most people. The custody of four children was at stake, and neither parent was fit.

'I'm too old for this,' he said, very tired. By the second beer he was nodding off.

Harry Rex controlled the divorce docket in Ford County and had for twenty-five years. Feuding couples often raced to hire him first. One farmer over at Karraway kept him on retainer so he would be available for the next split. He was very bright, but could also be vile and vicious. This had wide appeal in the heat of divorce wars.

But the work was taking its toll. Like all small-town lawyers, Harry Rex longed for the big kill. The big damage suit with a forty percent contingency fee, something to retire on.

The night before, Ray had been sipping expensive wines on a twenty-million-dollar yacht built by a Saudi prince and owned by a member of the Mississippi bar who was plotting billion-dollar schemes against multinationals. Now he was sipping Bud in a rusted swing with a member of the Mississippi bar who'd spent the day bickering over custody and alimony.

'The Realtor showed the house this morning,' Harry Rex said. 'He called me during lunch, woke me up.'

'Who's the prospect?'

'Remember those Kapshaw boys up near Rail Springs?'

'No.'

'Good boys. They started buildin' chairs in an old barn ten years ago, maybe twelve. One thang led to another, and they sold out to some big furniture outfit up in the Carolinas. Each of 'em walked away with a million bucks. Junkie and his wife are lookin' for houses.'

'Junkie Kapshaw?'

'Yeah, but he's tight as Dick's hatband and he ain't payin' four hundred thousand for this place.'

'I don't blame him.'

'His wife's crazy as hell and thinks she wants an old house. The Realtor is pretty sure they'll make an offer, but it'll be low, probably about a hundred seventy-five thousand.' Harry Rex was yawning.

They talked about Forrest for a spell, then things were silent. 'Guess I'd better go,' he said. After three beers, Harry Rex began his exit.

'When are you going back to Virginia?' he asked, struggling to his feet and stretching his back.

'Maybe tomorrow.'

'Gimme a call,' he said, yawning again, and walked down the steps.

Ray watched the lights of his car disappear down the street, and he was suddenly and completely alone again. The first noise was a rustling in the shrubbery near the property line, probably an old dog or cat on the prowl, but regardless of how harmless it was it spooked Ray and he ran inside.

Chapter 34

The attack began shortly after 2 A.M., at the darkest hour of the night, when sleep is heaviest and reactions slowest. Ray was dead to the world, though the world had weighed heavily on his weary mind. He was on a mattress in the foyer, pistol by his side, the three garbage bags of cash next to his makeshift bed.

It began with a brick through the window, a blast that rattled the old house and rained glass and debris across the dining room table and the newly polished wooden floors. It was a well-placed and well-timed throw from someone who meant business and had probably done it before. Ray clawed his way upright like a wounded alley cat and was lucky not to shoot himself as he groped for his gun. He darted low across the foyer, hit a light switch, and saw the brick resting ominously next to a baseboard near the china cabinet.

Using a quilt, he swept away the debris and carefully picked up the brick, a new red one with sharp edges. Attached was a note held in place by two thick rubber bands. He removed them while looking at the remains of the window. His hands were shaking to the point of not being able to read the note. He swallowed hard, tried to breathe, tried to focus on the handwritten warning.

It read simply: 'Put the money back where you found it, then leave the house immediately.'

His hand was bleeding, a small nick from a piece of glass. It was his shooting hand, if in fact he had such a thing, and in the horror of the moment he wondered how he could protect himself. He crouched in the shadows of the dining room, telling himself to breathe, to think clearly.

Suddenly, the phone rang, and he jumped out of his skin again. A second ring, and he scrambled into the kitchen where a dim light above the stove helped him grapple for the phone. 'Hello!' he barked into the receiver.

'Put the money back, and leave the house,' said a calm but rigid voice, one he'd never heard, one he thought, in the blur of the moment, carried a slight trace of a coast accent. 'Now! Before you get hurt.'

He wanted to scream, 'No,' or 'Stop it,' or 'Who are you?' But his indecision caused him to hesitate, and the line went dead. He sat on the floor, and with his back to the refrigerator he quickly ran through his options, slim as they were.

He could call the police – hustle and hide the money, stuff the bags under a bed, move the mattress, conceal the note but not the brick, and carry on as if some delinquents were vandalizing an old house just for the hell of it. The cop would walk around with a flashlight and linger for an hour or two, but he would leave at some point.

The Priest boys were not leaving. They had stuck to him like glue. They might duck for a moment, but they were not leaving. And they were far more nimble than the Clanton night-watchman. And far more inspired.

He could call Harry Rex – wake him up, tell him it was urgent, get him back over to the house and unload the entire story. Ray yearned for someone to talk to. How many times had he wanted to come clean with Harry Rex? They could split the money, or include it in the estate, or take it to Tunica and roll dice for a year.

But why endanger him too? Three million was enough to provoke more than one killing.

Ray had a gun. Why couldn't he protect himself? He could fend off the attackers. When they came through the door, he'd light the place up. The gunfire would alert the neighbors, the whole town would be there.

It just took one bullet, though, one well-aimed, pointed little missile that he would never see and probably feel only for a moment, or two. And he was outnumbered by some fellas who'd fired a helluva lot more of them than Professor

338

Ray Atlee. He had already decided that he was not willing to die. Life back home was too good.

Just as his heart rate peaked and he felt his pulse start to decline, another brick came crashing through the small window above the kitchen sink. He jerked and yelled and dropped his gun, then kicked it as he scrambled toward the foyer. On hands and knees he dragged the three bags of cash into the Judge's study. He yanked the sofa away from the bookshelves and began throwing the stacks of bills back into the cabinet where he'd found the wretched loot in the first place. He was sweating and cursing and expecting another brick or maybe the first round of ammo. When all of it had been crammed back into its hiding place, he picked up the pistol and unlocked the front door. He darted to his car, cranked it, spun ruts down the front lawn, and finished his escape.

He was unharmed, and at the moment that was his only concern.

North of Clanton, the land dipped in the backwaters of Lake Chatoula, and for a two-mile stretch the road was straight and flat. Known simply as The Bottoms, it had long been the turf of late-night drag racers, boozers, ruffians, and hell-raisers in general. His nearest brush with death, prior to that moment, had been in high school when he found himself in the backseat of a packed Pontiac Firebird driven by a drunken Bobby Lee West and drag racing a Camaro driven by an even drunker Doug Terring, both cars flying at a hundred miles an hour through The Bottoms. He had walked away from it, but Bobby Lee had been killed a year later when his Firebird left the road and met a tree.

When he hit the flat stretch of The Bottoms, he pressed the accelerator of his TT and let it unwind. It was two-thirty in the morning, surely everyone else was asleep.

Elmer Conway had indeed been asleep, but a fat mosquito had taken blood from his forehead and awakened him in the process. He saw lights, a car was approaching rapidly, he turned on his radar. It took almost four miles to get the funny little foreign job pulled over, and by then Elmer was angry.

Ray made the mistake of opening his door and getting out, and that was not what Elmer had in mind.

'Freeze, asshole!' Elmer shouted, over the barrel of his service revolver, which, as Ray quickly realized, was aimed at his head.

'Relax, relax,' he said, throwing up his hands in complete surrender.

'Get away from the car,' Elmer growled, and with the gun pointed to a spot somewhere around the center line.

'No problem, sir, just relax,' Ray said, shuffling sideways.

'What's your name?'

'Ray Atlee, Judge Atlee's son. Could you put that gun down, please?'

Elmer lowered the gun a few inches, enough so that a discharge would hit Ray in the stomach, but not the head. 'You got Virginia plates,' Elmer said.

'That's because I live in Virginia.'

'Is that where you're headed?'

'Yes sir.'

'What's the big hurry?'

'I don't know, I just –'

'I clocked you doing ninety-eight.'

'I'm very sorry.'

'Sorry's ass. That's reckless driving.' Elmer took a step closer. Ray had forgotten about the cut on his hand and he was not aware of the one on his knee. Elmer removed a flashlight and did a body scan from ten feet away. 'Why are you bleedin'?'

It was a very good question, and, at that moment, standing in the middle of the dark highway with a light flashed in his face, Ray could not think of an adequate response. The truth would take an hour and fall on unbelieving ears. A lie would only make matters worse. 'I don't know,' he mumbled.

'What's in the car?' Elmer asked.

'Nothing.'

'Sure.'

He handcuffed Ray and put him in the backseat of his Ford County patrol car, a brown Impala with dust on the fenders, no hubcaps, a collection of antennae mounted on the rear bumper. Ray watched as he walked around the

TT and looked inside. When Elmer was finished he crawled into the front seat, and without turning around said, 'What's the gun for?'

Ray had tried to slide the pistol under the passenger's seat. Evidently it was visible from the outside.

'Protection.'

'You got a permit?'

'No.'

Elmer called the dispatcher and made a lengthy report of his latest stop. He concluded with, 'I'm bringin' him in,' as if he had just collared one of the ten most wanted.

'What about my car?' Ray asked, as they turned around.

'I'll send a wrecker out.'

Elmer turned on the red and blue lights and pushed the speedometer to eighty.

'Can I call my lawyer?' Ray asked.

'No.'

'Come on. It's just a traffic offense. My lawyer can meet me at the jail, post bond, and in an hour I'm back on the road.'

'Who's your lawyer?'

'Harry Rex Vonner.'

Elmer grunted and his neck grew thicker. 'Sumbitch cleaned me out in my divorce.'

And with that Ray sat back and closed his eyes.

Ray had actually seen the inside of the Ford County jail on two occasions, he recalled as

Elmer led him up the front sidewalk. Both times he had taken papers to deadbeat fathers who'd been years behind in child support, and Judge Atlee had locked them up. Haney Moak, the slightly retarded jailer in an oversized uniform, was still there at the front desk, reading detective magazines. He also served as the dispatcher for the graveyard shift, so he knew of Ray's transgressions.

'Judge Atlee's boy, huh?' Haney said with a crooked grin. His head was lopsided and his eyes were uneven, and whenever Haney spoke it was a challenge to maintain a visual.

'Yes sir,' Ray said politely, looking for friends.

'He was a fine man,' he said as he moved behind Ray and unlocked the cuffs.

Ray rubbed his wrists and looked at Deputy Conway, who was busy filling in forms and being very officious. 'Reckless, and no gun permit.'

'You ain't lockin' him up, are you?' Haney said to Elmer, quite rudely as if Haney were in charge of the case now, and not the deputy.

'Damned right,' Elmer shot back, and the situation was immediately tense.

'Can I call Harry Rex Vonner?' Ray pleaded.

Haney nodded toward a wall-mounted phone as if he could not care less. He was glaring at Elmer. The two obviously had a history that was not pretty. 'My jail's full now,' Haney said.

'That's what you always say.'

Ray quickly punched Harry Rex's home number. It was after 3 A.M., and he knew the interruption would not be appreciated. The current Mrs. Vonner answered after the third ring. Ray apologized for the call and asked for Harry Rex.

'He's not here,' she said.

He's not out of town, Ray thought. He was on the front porch six hours ago. 'May I ask where he is?'

Haney and Elmer were practically yelling at each other in the background.

'He's over at the Atlee place,' she said slowly.

'No, he left there hours ago. I was with him.'

'No, they just called. The house is burning.'

With Haney in the backseat, they flew around the square, lights and sirens fully engaged. From two blocks away, they could see the blaze. 'Lord have mercy,' Haney said from the back.

Few events excited Clanton like a good fire. The town's two pumpers were there. Dozens of volunteers were darting about, all seemed to be yelling. The neighbors were gathering on the sidewalks across the street.

Flames were already shooting through the roof. As Ray stepped over a water line and eased onto the front lawn, he breathed the unmistakable odor of gasoline.

Chapter 35

The love nest wasn't a bad place for a nap after all. It was a long narrow room with dust and spiderwebs and one light hanging in the center of the vaulted ceiling. The lone window had been painted sometime in the last century and overlooked the square. The bed was an iron antique with no sheets or blankets, and he tried not to think about Harry Rex and his misadventures on that very mattress. Instead, he thought of the old house at Maple Run and the glorious way it went into history. By the time the roof collapsed, half of Clanton was there. Ray had sat alone, on the low limb of a sycamore across the street, hidden from all, trying in vain to pull cherished memories from a wonderful childhood that simply had not happened. When the flames were shooting from every window, he had not thought of the cash or the Judge's desk or his mother's dining room table, but only of old General Forrest glaring down with those fierce eyes.

Three hours of sleep, and he was awake by eight. The temperature was rising rapidly in the den of iniquity, and heavy steps were coming his way.

Harry Rex swung the door open and turned on the light. 'Wake up, felon,' he growled. 'They want you down at the jail.'

Ray swung his feet to the floor. 'My escape was fair and square.' He had lost Elmer and Haney in the crowd and simply left with Harry Rex.

'Did you tell them they could search your car?'

'I did.'

'That was a dumb-ass thing to do. What kinda lawyer are you?' He pulled a wooden folding chair from the wall and sat down near the bed.

'There was nothing to hide.'

'You're stupid, you know that? They searched the car and found nothing.'

'That's what I expected.'

'No clothes, no overnight bag, no luggage, no toothbrush, no evidence whatsoever that you were simply leaving town and going home, per your official story.'

'I did not burn the house down, Harry Rex.'

'Well, you're an excellent suspect. You flee in the middle of the night, no clothes, no nothing, you drive away like a bat outta hell. Old lady Larrimore down the street sees you in your funny little car go flyin' by, then about ten minutes later here come the fire trucks. You're

caught by the dumbest deputy in the state doin'
ninety-eight, drivin' like hell to get away from
here. Defend yourself.'

'I didn't torch it.'

'Why did you leave at two-thirty?'

'Someone threw a rock through the dining
room window. I got scared.'

'You had a gun.'

'I didn't want to use it. I'd rather run away
than shoot somebody.'

'You've been up North too long.'

'I don't live up North.'

'How'd you get cut up like that?'

'The brick broke the window, you see, and
when I checked it out, I got cut.'

'Why didn't you call the police?'

'I panicked. I wanted to go home, so I left.'

'And ten minutes later somebody soaks the
place with gasoline and throws a match.'

'I don't know what they did.'

'I'd convict you.'

'No, you're my lawyer.'

'No, I'm the lawyer for the estate, which by
the way just lost its only asset.'

'There's fire insurance.'

'Yeah, but you can't get it.'

'Why not?'

'Because if you file a claim, then they'll
investigate you for arson. If you say you didn't
do it, then I believe you. But I'm not sure
anybody else will. If you go after the insurance,

then those boys will come after you with a vengeance.'

'I didn't torch it.'

'Great, then who did?'

'Whoever threw the brick.'

'And who might that be?'

'I have no idea. Maybe some guy who got the bad end of a divorce.'

'Brilliant. And he waits nine years to get revenge on the Judge, who, by the way, is dead. I will not be in the courtroom when you offer that to the jury.'

'I don't know, Harry Rex. I swear I didn't do it. Forget the insurance money.'

'It's not that easy. Only half is yours, the other half belongs to Forrest. He can file a claim for the insurance coverage.'

Ray breathed deeply and scratched his stubble. 'Help me here, okay?'

'The sheriff's downstairs, with one of his investigators. They'll ask some questions. Answer slowly, tell the truth, blah, blah. I'll be there, so let's go slow.'

'He's here?'

'In my conference room. I asked him to come over so we can do this now. I really think you need to get out of town.'

'I was trying.'

'The reckless driving and the gun charge will be put off for a few months. Give me some time to work the docket. You got bigger problems right now.'

'I did not torch the house, Harry Rex.'

'Of course you didn't.'

They left the room and started down the unsteady steps to the second floor. 'Who's the sheriff?' Ray asked, over his shoulder.

'Guy named Sawyer.'

'Good guy?'

'It doesn't matter.'

'You close to him?'

'I did his son's divorce.'

The conference room was a wonderful mess of thick law books thrown about on shelves and credenzas and the long table itself. The impression was given that Harry Rex spent hours in tedious research. He did not.

Sawyer was not the least bit polite, nor was his assistant, a nervous little Italian named Sandroni. Italians were rare in northeast Mississippi, and during the tense introductions Ray detected a Delta accent. The two were all business, with Sandroni taking careful notes while Sawyer sipped steaming coffee from a paper cup and watched every move Ray made.

The fire call was made by Mrs. Larrimore at two thirty-four, approximately ten to fifteen minutes after she'd seen Ray's car leave Fourth Street in a hurry. Elmer Conway radioed at two thirty-six that he was in pursuit of some idiot doing a hundred miles an hour down in The Bottoms. Since it was established that Ray was driving very fast, Sandroni spent a long time nailing down his route, his estimated speeds,

349

traffic lights, anything to slow him down at that hour of the morning.

Once Ray's exit route was determined, Sawyer radioed a deputy, who was sitting in front of the rubble at Maple Run, and told him to drive the exact course at the same estimated speeds and to stop out in The Bottoms where Elmer was once again waiting.

Twelve minutes later, the deputy called back and said he was with Elmer.

'So in less than twelve minutes,' Sandroni said as he began his recap, 'Someone – and we're assuming this someone was not already in the house, aren't we, Mr. Atlee? – entered with what evidently was a large supply of gasoline and soaked the place thoroughly, so thoroughly that the fire captain said he'd never smelled such a strong odor of gas, then threw a match or maybe two, because the fire captain was almost certain the fire had more than one point of origin, and once the matches were thrown this unknown arsonist fled into the night. Right, Mr. Atlee?'

'I don't know what the arsonist did,' Ray said.

'But the times are accurate?'

'If you say so.'

'I say so.'

'Move along,' Harry Rex growled from the end of the table.

Motive was next. The house was insured for $380,000, including contents. According to the Realtor, who'd already been consulted, he'd been writing up an offer to purchase it for $175,000.

'That's a nice gap, isn't it, Mr. Atlee?' Sandroni inquired.

'It is.'

'Have you notified your insurance company?' Sandroni asked.

'No, I thought I'd wait until their offices open,' Ray responded. 'Believe it or not, some folks don't work on Saturday.'

'Hell, the fire truck's still there,' Harry Rex added helpfully. 'We got six months to file a claim.'

Sandroni's cheeks turned crimson but he held his tongue. Moving right along, he studied his notes and said, 'Let's talk about other suspects.'

Ray didn't like the use of the word 'other.' He told the story about the brick through the window, or at least most of the story. And the phone call, warning him to leave immediately. 'Check the phone records,' he challenged them. And for good measure, he threw in the earlier adventures with some demented soul rattling windows the night the Judge died.

'Y'all had enough,' Harry Rex said after thirty minutes. In other words, my client will answer no more questions.

'When are you leaving town?' asked Sawyer.

'I've been trying to leave for the past six hours,' Ray replied.

'Real soon,' said Harry Rex.

'We may have some more questions.'

'I'll come back whenever I'm needed,' Ray
said.

Harry Rex shoved them out the front door,
and when he returned to the conference room
he said, 'I think you're a lyin' sonofabitch.'

Chapter 36

The old fire truck was gone, the same one Ray and his friends had followed when they were teenagers and bored on summer nights. A lone volunteer in a dirty tee shirt was folding fire hoses. The street was a mess with mud strewn everywhere.

Maple Run was deserted by midmorning. The chimney on the east end was still standing, as was a short section of charred wall beside it. Everything else had collapsed into a pile of debris. Ray and Harry Rex walked around the rubble and went to the backyard, where a row of ancient pecan trees protected the rear boundary of the property. They sat in the shade, in metal lawn chairs that Ray had once painted red, and ate tamales.

'I didn't burn this place,' Ray finally said.

'Do you know who did?' Harry Rex asked.

'I have a suspect.'

'Tell me, dammit.'

'His name is Gordie Priest.'

'Oh him!'

'It's a long story.'

Ray began with the Judge, dead on the sofa, and the accidental discovery of the money, or was it an accident after all? He gave as many facts and details as he could remember, and he raised all the questions that had been dogging him for weeks. Both stopped eating. They stared at the smoldering debris but were too mesmerized to see it. Harry Rex was stunned by the narrative. Ray was relieved to be telling it. From Clanton to Charlottesville and back. From the casinos in Tunica to Atlantic City, then back to Tunica. To the coast and Patton French and his quest for a billion dollars, all to be credited to Judge Reuben Atlee, humble servant of the law.

Ray held back nothing, and he tried to remember everything. The ransacking of his apartment in Charlottesville, for intimidation only, he thought. The ill-advised purchase of a share in a Bonanza. On and on he went, while Harry Rex said nothing.

When he finished, his appetite was gone and he was sweating. Harry Rex had a million questions, but he began with, 'Why would he burn the house?'

'Cover his tracks, maybe, I don't know.'

'This guy didn't leave tracks.'

'Maybe it was the final act of intimidation.'

They mulled this over. Harry Rex finished a tamale and said, 'You should've told me.'

'I wanted to keep the money, okay? I had

three million bucks in cash in my sticky little hands, and it felt wonderful. It was better than sex, better than anything I'd ever felt. Three million bucks, Harry Rex, all mine. I was rich. I was greedy. I was corrupt. I didn't want you or Forrest or the government or anyone in the world to know that I had the money.'

'What were you gonna do with it?'

'Ease it into banks, a dozen of them, nine thousand dollars at a time, no paperwork that would alert the government, let it pile up over eighteen months, then invest it with a pro. I'm forty-three; in two years the money would be laundered and hard at work. It would double every five years. At the age of fifty, it would be six million. Fifty-five, twelve million. At the age of sixty, I'd have twenty-four million bucks. I had it all planned, Harry Rex. I could see the future.'

'Don't beat yourself up. What you did was normal.'

'It doesn't feel normal.'

'You're a lousy crook.'

'I felt lousy, and I was already changing. I could see myself in an airplane and a fancier sports car and a nicer place to live. There's a lot of money around Charlottesville, and I was thinking about making a splash. Country clubs, fox hunting –'

'Fox hunting?'

'Yep.'

'With those little britches and the hat?'

'Flying over fences on a wild horse, chasing a pack of hounds that are in hot pursuit of a thirty-pound fox that you'll never see.'

'Why would you wanna do that?'

'Why would anyone?'

'I'll stick to huntin' birds.'

'Anyway, it was a burden, literally. I mean, I've been hauling the cash around for weeks.'

'You could've left some at my office.'

Ray finished a tamale and sipped a cola. 'You think I'm stupid?'

'No, lucky. This guy plays for keeps.'

'Every time I closed my eyes, I could see a bullet coming at my forehead.'

'Look, Ray, you've done nothing wrong. The Judge didn't want the money included in his estate. You took it because you thought you were protectin' it, and also guardin' his reputation. You had a crazy man who wanted it more than you. Lookin' back, you're lucky you didn't get hurt in the whole episode. Forget it.'

'Thanks, Harry Rex.' Ray leaned forward and watched the volunteer fireman walk away. 'What about the arson?'

'We'll work it out. I'll file a claim, and the insurance company will investigate. They'll suspect arson and thangs'll get ugly. Let a few months pass. If they don't pay, then we'll sue, in Ford County. They won't risk a jury trial against the estate of Reuben Atlee right here in his own courthouse. I think they'll settle before trial. We

356

may have to compromise some, but we'll get a nice settlement.'

Ray was on his feet. 'I really want to go home,' he said.

The air was thick with heat and smoke as they walked around the house. 'I've had enough,' Ray said, and headed for the street.

He drove a perfect fifty-five through The Bottoms. Elmer Conway was nowhere to be seen. The Audi seemed lighter with the trunk empty. Indeed, life itself was shedding burdens. Ray longed for the normalcy of home.

He dreaded the meeting with Forrest. Their father's estate had just been wiped out, and the arson issue would be difficult to explain. Perhaps he should wait. Rehab was going so smoothly, and Ray knew from experience that the slightest complication could derail Forrest. Let a month go by. Then another.

Forrest would not be going back to Clanton, and in his murky world he might never hear of the fire. It might be best if Harry Rex broke the news to him.

The receptionist at Alcorn Village gave him a curious look when he signed in. He read magazines for a long time in the dark lounge where the visitors waited. When Oscar Meave eased in with a gloomy look, Ray knew exactly what had happened.

'He walked away late yesterday afternoon,' Meave began as he crouched on the coffee table in front of Ray. 'I've tried to reach you all morning.'

'I lost my cell phone last night,' Ray said. Of all the things he'd left behind when the rocks were falling, he couldn't believe he'd forgotten his cell phone.

'He signed in for the ridge walk, a five-mile nature trail he's been doing every day. It's around the back of the property, no fencing, but then Forrest was not a security risk. We didn't think so, anyway. I can't believe this.'

Ray certainly could. His brother had been walking away from detox units for almost twenty years.

'This is not really a lockdown facility,' Meave continued. 'Our patients want to stay here, or it doesn't work.'

'I understand,' Ray said softly.

'He was doing so well,' Meave went on, obviously more troubled than Ray. 'Completely clean and very proud of it. He had sort of adopted two teenagers, both in rehab for the first time. Forrest worked with them every morning. I just don't understand this one.'

'I thought you are an ex-addict.'

Meave was shaking his head. 'I know, I know. The addict quits when the addict wants to, and not before.'

'Have you ever seen one who just couldn't quit?' Ray asked.

'We can't admit that.'

'I know you can't. But, off the record, you

and I both know that there are addicts who will never kick it.'

Meave shrugged, with reluctance.

'Forrest is one of those, Oscar. We've lived this for twenty years.'

'I take it as a personal failure.'

'Don't.'

They walked outside and talked for a moment under a veranda. Meave could not stop apologizing. For Ray, it was nothing unexpected.

Along the winding road back to the main highway, Ray wondered how his brother could simply walk away from a facility eight miles from the nearest town. But then, he had fled more secluded places.

He would go back to Memphis, back to his room in Ellie's basement, back to the streets where pushers were waiting for him. The next phone call might be the last, but then Ray had been half-expecting it for many years. As sick as he was, Forrest had shown an amazing ability to survive.

Ray was in Tennessee now. Virginia was next, seven hours away. With a clear sky and no wind, he thought of how nice it would be at five thousand feet, buzzing around in his favorite rented Cessna.

Chapter 37

Both doors were new, unpainted, and much heavier than the old ones. Ray silently thanked his landlord for the extra expense, though he knew that there would be no more break-ins. The pursuit had ended. No more quick looks over the shoulder. No more sneaking to Chaney's to play hide-and-seek. No more hushed conversations with Corey Crawford. And no more illicit money to fret over, and dream about, and haul around, literally. The lifting of that burden made him smile and walk a bit faster.

Life would become normal again. Long runs in the heat. Long solo flights over the Piedmont. He even looked forward to his neglected research for the monopolies treatise he'd promised to deliver by either this Christmas or the one after. He had softened on the Kaley issue and was ready for one last attempt at dinner. She was legal now, a graduate, and she simply looked too fine to write off without a decent effort.

His apartment was the same, its usual condition since no one else lived there. Other than the door, there was no evidence of a forced entry. He now knew that his burglar had not really been a thief after all, just a tormentor, an intimidator. Either Gordie or one of his brothers. He wasn't sure how they had divided their labors, nor did he care.

It was almost 11 A.M. He made some strong coffee and began shuffling through the mail. No more anonymous letters. Nothing now but the usual bills and solicitations.

There were two faxes in the tray. The first was a note from a former student. The second was from Patton French. He'd been trying to call, but Ray's cell phone wasn't working. It was handwritten on the stationery from the *King of Torts*, no doubt faxed from the gray waters of the Gulf where French was still hiding his boat from his wife's divorce lawyer.

Good news on the security front! Not long after Ray had left the coast, Gordie Priest had been 'located,' along with both of his brothers. Could Ray please give him a call? His assistant would find him.

Ray worked the phone for two hours, until French called from a hotel in Fort Worth, where he was meeting with some Ryax and Kobril lawyers. 'I'll probably get a thousand cases up here,' he said, unable to control himself.

'Wonderful,' said Ray. He was determined not to listen to any more crowing about mass torts and zillion-dollar settlements.

'Is your phone secure?' French asked.

'Yes.'

'Okay, listen. Priest is no longer a threat. We found him shortly after you left, laid up drunk with an old gal he's been seeing for a long time. Found both brothers too. Your money is safe.'

'Exactly when did you find them?' Ray asked. He was hovering over the kitchen table with a large calendar spread before him. Time was crucial here. He'd made notes in the margins as he'd waited for the call.

French thought for a second. 'Uh, let's see. What's today?'

'Monday, June the fifth.'

'Monday. When did you leave the coast?'

'Ten o'clock Friday morning.'

'Then it was just after lunch on Friday.'

'You're sure?'

'Of course I'm sure. Why do you ask?'

'And once you found him, there was no way they left the coast?'

'Trust me, Ray, they'll never leave the coast again. They've, uh, found a permanent home there.'

'I don't want those details.' Ray sat at the table and stared at the calendar.

'What's the matter?' French asked. 'Something wrong?'

362

'Yeah, you could say that.'

'What is it?'

'Somebody burned the house down.'

'Judge Atlee's?'

'Yes.'

'When?'

'After midnight, Saturday morning.'

A pause as French absorbed this, then, 'Well, it wasn't the Priest boys, I can promise you that.'

When Ray said nothing, French asked, 'Where's the money?'

'I don't know,' he mumbled.

A five-mile run did nothing to ease his tension. Though, as always, he was able to plot things, to rearrange his thoughts. The temperature was above ninety, and he was soaked with sweat when he returned to his apartment.

Now that Harry Rex had been told everything, it was comforting to have someone with whom to share the latest. He called his office in Clanton and was informed that he was in court over in Tupelo and wouldn't be back until late. He called Ellie's house in Memphis and no one bothered to answer. He called Oscar Meave at Alcorn Village, and, expecting to hear no news of his brother's whereabouts, got exactly what he expected.

So much for the normal life.

After a tense morning of back-and-forth negotiations in the hallways of the Lee County Courthouse, bickering over such issues as who'd get the ski boat and who'd get the cabin on the lake, and how much he would pay in a lump-sum cash settlement, the divorce was settled an hour after lunch. Harry Rex had the husband, an overheated cowboy on wife number three who thought he knew more divorce law than his lawyer. Wife number three was an aging bimbo in her late twenties who'd caught him with her best friend. It was the typical, sordid tale, and Harry Rex was sick of the whole mess when he walked to the bench and presented a hard-fought property settlement agreement.

The chancellor was a veteran who'd divorced thousands. 'Very sorry about Judge Atlee,' he said softly as he began to review the papers. Harry Rex just nodded. He was tired and thirsty and already contemplating a cold one as he drove the backroad to Clanton. His favorite beer store in the Tupelo area was at the county line.

'We served together for twenty-two years,' the chancellor was saying.

'A fine man,' Harry Rex said.

'Are you doing the estate?'

'Yes sir.'

'Give my regards to Judge Farr over there.'

'I will.'

The paperwork was signed, the marriage mercifully terminated, the warring spouses sent to their neutral homes. Harry Rex was out of the courthouse and halfway to his car when a lawyer chased him down and stopped him on the sidewalk. He introduced himself as Jacob Spain,

Attorney-at-Law, one of a thousand in Tupelo. He'd been in the courtroom and overheard the chancellor mention Judge Atlee.

'He has a son, right, Forrest?' Spain asked.

'Two sons, Ray and Forrest.' Harry Rex took a breath and settled in for a quick visit.

'I played high school football against Forrest; in fact he broke my collarbone with a late hit.'

'That sounds like Forrest.'

'I played at New Albany. Forrest was a junior when I was a senior. Did you see him play?'

'Yes, many times.'

'You remember the game over there against us when he threw for three hundred yards in the first half? Four or five touchdowns, I think.'

'I do,' Harry Rex said, and started to fidget. How long was this going to take?

'I was playing safety that night, and he was firing passes all over the place. I picked one off right before half-time, ran it out of bounds, and he speared me while I was on the ground.'

'That was one of his favorite plays.' Hit 'em hard and hit 'em late had been Forrest's motto, especially those defensive backs unlucky enough to intercept one of his passes.

'I think he was arrested the next week,' Spain was saying. 'What a waste. Anyway, I saw him just a few weeks ago, here in Tupelo, with Judge Atlee.'

The fidgeting stopped. Harry Rex forgot about a cold one, at least for the moment. 'When was this?' he asked.

'Right before the Judge died. It was a strange scene.'

They took a few steps and found shade under a tree. 'I'm listening,' Harry Rex said, loosening his tie. His wrinkled navy blazer was already off.

'My wife's mother is being treated for breast cancer at the Taft Clinic. One Monday afternoon back in the spring I drove her over there for another round of chemo.'

'Judge Atlee went to Taft,' Harry Rex said. 'I've seen the bills.'

'Yes, that's where I saw him. I checked her in, there was a wait, so I went to my car to make a bunch of calls. While I was sitting there, I watched as Judge Atlee pulled up in a long black Lincoln driven by someone I didn't recognize. They got the thing parked, just two cars down, and they got out. His driver then looked familiar – big guy, big frame, long hair, kind of a cocky swagger that I've seen before. It hit me that it was Forrest. I could tell by the way he walked and moved. He was wearing sunglasses and a cap pulled low. They went inside, and within seconds Forrest came back out.'

'What kinda cap?'

'Faded blue, Cubs, I think.'

'I've seen that one.'

'He was real nervous, like he didn't want anyone to see him. He disappeared into some trees next to the clinic, except I could barely see his outline. He just hid there. I thought at first he might be relieving himself, but no, he was just hiding. After an hour or so, I went in, waited, finally got my mother-in-law, and left. He was still out in the trees.'

Harry Rex had pulled out his pocket planner. 'What day was this?' Spain removed his, and as all busy lawyers do, they compared their recent movements. 'Monday, May the first,' Spain decided.

'That was six days before the Judge died,' Harry Rex said.

'I'm sure that's the date. It was just a strange scene.'

'Well, he's a pretty strange guy.'

'He's not running from the law or anything, is he?'

'Not at the present,' Harry Rex said, and they both managed a nervous laugh.

Spain suddenly needed to go. 'Anyway, when you see him again, tell him I'm still mad about the late hit.'

'I'll do that,' Harry Rex said, then watched him walk away.

Chapter 38

Mr. and Mrs. Vonner left Clanton on a cloudy June morning in a new sports utility four-wheel drive that promised twelve miles to the gallon and was loaded with enough luggage for a month in Europe. The District of Columbia was the destination, however, since Mrs. Vonner had a sister there whom Harry Rex had never met. They spent the first night in Gatlinburg and the second night at White Sulphur Springs in West Virginia. They arrived in Charlottesville around noon, did the obligatory tour of Jefferson's Monticello, walked the grounds at the university, and had an unusual dinner at a college dive called the White Spot, the house specialty being a fried egg on a hamburger. It was Harry Rex's kind of food.

The next morning, while she slept, he went for a stroll on the downtown mall. He found the address and waited.

A few minutes after 8 A.M., Ray double-tied the laces of his rather expensive running shoes, stretched in the den, and walked downstairs for the daily five-miler. Outside, the air was warm. July was not far away and summer had already arrived.

He turned a corner and heard a familiar voice call, 'Hey, boy.'

Harry Rex was sitting on a bench, a cup of coffee in hand, an unread newspaper next to him. Ray froze and took a few seconds to collect himself. Things were out of place here.

When he could move, he walked over and said, 'What, exactly, are you doing here?'

'Cute outfit,' Harry Rex said, taking in the shorts, old tee shirt, red runner's cap, the latest in athletic eye glasses. 'Me and the wife are passing through, headed for D.C. She has a sister up there she thinks I want to meet. Sit down.'

'Why didn't you call?'

'Didn't want to bother you.'

'But you should've called, Harry Rex. We could do dinner, I'll show you around.'

'It's not that kind of trip. Sit down.'

Smelling trouble, Ray sat next to Harry Rex. 'I can't believe this,' he mumbled.

'Shut up and listen.'

Ray removed his running glasses and looked at Harry Rex. 'Is it bad?'

'Let's say it's curious.' He told Jacob Spain's story about Forrest hiding in the trees at the oncology clinic, six days before the Judge passed away. Ray listened in disbelief and slid lower on the bench. He finally leaned forward with his elbows on his knees, his head hung low.

'According to the medical records,' Harry Rex was saying, 'he got a morphine pack that day, May the first. Don't know if it was the first pack or a refill, the records are not that clear. Looks like Forrest took him to get the good stuff.'

A long pause as a pretty young woman walked by, obviously in a hurry, her tight skirt swaying wonderfully as she sped along. A sip of coffee, then, 'I've always been suspicious of that will you found in his study. The Judge and I talked about his will for the last six months of his life. I don't think he simply cranked out one more right before he died. I've studied the signatures at length, and it's my untrained opinion that the last one is a forgery.'

Ray cleared his voice and said, 'If Forrest drove him to Tupelo, then it's safe to assume Forrest was in the house.'

'All over the house.'

Harry Rex had hired an investigator in Memphis to find Forrest, but there was no trail, no trace. From somewhere within the newspaper, he pulled out an envelope. 'Then, this came three days ago.'

Ray pulled out a sheet of paper and unfolded it. It was from Oscar Meave at Alcorn Village, and it read: 'Dear Mr. Vonner: I have been unable to reach Ray Atlee. I know the whereabouts of Forrest, if by chance the family does not. Call if you would like to talk. Everything is confidential. Best wishes, Oscar Meave.'

'So I called him right away,' Harry Rex said, eyeing another young woman. 'He has a former patient who's now a counselor at a rehab ranch out West. Forrest checked in there a week ago, and was adamant about his privacy, said he did not want his family to know where he was. Evidently this happens from time to time, and the clinics are always caught in a bind. They have to respect the wishes of their patient, but on the other hand, the family is crucial to the overall rehabilitation. So these counselors whisper among themselves. Meave made the decision to pass along the information to you.'

'Where out West?'

'Montana. A place called Morningstar Ranch. Meave said it's what the boy needs – very nice, very remote, a lockdown facility for the hard cases, said he'll be there for a year.'

Ray sat up and began rubbing his forehead as if he'd finally been shot there.

'And of course the place is pricey,' Harry Rex added.

'Of course,' Ray mumbled.

There was no more talk, not about Forrest anyway. After a few minutes, Harry Rex said he was leaving. He had delivered his message, he had nothing more to say, not then. His wife was anxious to see her sister. Perhaps next time they could stay longer, have dinner, whatever. He patted Ray on the shoulder, and left him there. 'See you in Clanton' were his last words.

Too weak and too winded for a run, Ray sat on the bench in the middle of the downtown mall, his apartment above him, lost in a world of rapidly moving pieces. The foot traffic picked up as the merchants and bankers and lawyers hustled to work, but Ray did not see them.

Carl Mirk taught two sections of insurance law each semester, and he was a member of the Virginia bar, as was Ray. They discussed the interview over lunch, and both came to the conclusion that it was just part of a routine inquiry, nothing to worry about. Mirk would tag along and pretend to be Ray's lawyer.

The insurance investigator's name was Ratterfield. They welcomed him into the conference room at the law school. He removed his jacket as if they might be there for hours. Ray was wearing jeans and a golf shirt. Mirk was just as casual.

'I usually record these,' Ratterfield said, all business as he pulled out a tape recorder and placed it between him and Ray. 'Any objections?' he asked, once the recorder was in place.

'I guess not,' Ray said.

He punched a button, looked at his notes, then began an introduction, for the benefit of the tape. He was an independent insurance examiner, hired by Aviation Underwriters, to investigate a claim filed by Ray Atlee and three other owners for damages to a 1994 Beech Bonanza on June 2. According to the state arson examiner, the airplane was deliberately burned.

Initially, he needed Ray's flying history. Ray had his logbook and Ratterfield pored through it, finding nothing remotely interesting. 'No instrument rating,' he said at one point.

'I'm working on it,' Ray replied.

'Fourteen hours in the Bonanza?'

'Yep.'

He then moved to the consortium of owners, and asked questions about the deal that brought it together. He'd already interviewed the other owners, and they had produced the contracts and documentation. Ray acknowledged the paperwork.

Changing gears, Ratterfield asked, 'Where were you on June the first?'

'Biloxi, Mississippi,' Ray answered, certain that Ratterfield had no idea where that was.

'How long had you been there?'

'A few days.'

'May I ask why you were there?'

'Sure,' Ray said, then launched into an abbreviated version of his recent visits home. His official reason for going to the coast was to visit friends, old buddies from his days at Tulane.

'I'm sure there are people who can verify that you were there on June the first,' Ratterfield said.

'Several people. Plus I have hotel receipts.'

He seemed convinced that Ray had been in

Mississippi. 'The other owners were all at home when the plane burned,' he said, flipping a page to a list of typed notes. 'All have alibis. If we're assuming it's arson, then we have to first find a motive, then whoever torched it. Any ideas?'

'I have no idea who did this,' Ray said quickly, and with conviction.

'How about motive?'

'We had just bought the plane. Why would any of us want to destroy it?'

'To collect the insurance, maybe. Happens occasionally. Perhaps one partner decided he was in over his head. The note is not small – almost two hundred grand over six years, close to nine hundred bucks a month per partner.'

'We knew that two weeks earlier when we signed on,' Ray said.

They shadowboxed for a while around the delicate issue of Ray's personal finances – salary, expenses, obligations. When Ratterfield seemed convinced that Ray could swing his end of the deal, he changed subjects. 'This fire in Mississippi,' he said, scanning a report of some type. 'Tell me about it.'

'What do you want to know?'

'Are you under investigation for arson down there?'

'No.'

'Are you sure?'

'Yes, I'm sure. You can call my attorney if you'd like.'

374

'I already have. And your apartment has been burglarized twice in the past six weeks?'

'Nothing was taken. Both were just break-ins.'

'You're having an exciting summer.'

'Is that a question?'

'Sounds like someone's after you.'

'Again, is that a question?'

It was the only flare-up of the interview, and both Ray and Ratterfield took a breath.

'Any other arson investigations in your past?'

Ray smiled and said, 'No.'

When Ratterfield flipped another page, and there was nothing typed on it, he lost interest in a hurry and went through the motions of wrapping things up. 'I'm sure our attorneys will be in touch,' he said as he turned off the recorder.

'I can't wait,' Ray said.

Ratterfield collected his jacket and his brief-case and made his exit.

After he left, Carl said, 'I think you know more than you're telling.'

'Maybe,' Ray said. 'But I had nothing to do with the arson here, or the arson there.'

'I've heard enough.'

Chapter 39

For almost a week, a string of turbulent summer fronts kept the ceilings low and the winds too dangerous for small planes. When the extended forecasts showed nothing but calm dry air for everywhere but South Texas, Ray left Charlottesville in a Cessna and began the longest cross-country of his brief flying career. Avoiding busy airspace and looking for easy landmarks below, he flew west across the Shenandoah Valley into West Virginia and into Kentucky, where he picked up fuel at a four-thousand-foot strip not far from Lexington. The Cessna could stay aloft for about three and a half hours before the indicator dipped below a quarter of a tank. He landed again in Terre Haute, crossed the Mississippi River at Hannibal, and stopped for the evening in Kirksville, Missouri, where he checked into a motel.

It was his first motel since the odyssey with the cash, and it was precisely because of the cash that he was back in a motel. He was also in

Missouri, and as he flipped through muted channels in his room, he remembered Patton French's story of stumbling upon Ryax at a tort seminar in St. Louis. An old lawyer from a small town in the Ozarks had a son who taught at the university in Columbia, and the son knew the drug was bad. And because of Patton French and his insatiable greed and corruption, he, Ray Atlee, was now in another motel in a town where he knew absolutely no one.

A front was developing over Utah. Ray lifted off just after sunrise and climbed to above five thousand feet. He trimmed his controls and opened a large cup of steaming black coffee. He flew more north than west for the first leg and was soon over the cornfields of Iowa.

Alone a mile above the earth, in the cool quiet air of the early morning, and with not a single pilot chattering on the airwaves, Ray tried to focus on the task before him. It was easier though, to loaf, to enjoy the solitude and the views, and the coffee, and the solitary act of leaving the world down there. And it was quite pleasant to put off thoughts of his brother.

After a stop in Sioux Falls, he turned west again and followed Interstate 90 across the entire state of South Dakota before skirting the restricted space around Mount Rushmore. He landed in Rapid City, rented a car, and took a long drive through Badlands National Park.

Morningstar Ranch was somewhere in the hills south of Kalispell, though its Web site was purposefully vague. Oscar Meave had tried but had been unsuccessful in pinpointing its exact location. At the end of the third day of his journey, Ray landed after dark in Kalispell. He rented a car, found dinner then a motel, and spent hours with aerial and road maps.

It took another day of low-altitude flying around Kalispell and the towns of Woods Bay, Polison, Bigfork, and Elmo. He crossed Flathead Lake a half-dozen times and was ready to surrender the air war and send in the ground troops when he caught a glimpse of a compound of some sort near the town of Somers on the north side of the lake. From fifteen hundred feet, he circled the place until he saw a substantial fence of green chain link almost hidden in the woods and practically invisible from the air. There were small buildings that appeared to be housing units, a larger one for administration perhaps, a pool, tennis courts, a barn with horses grazing nearby. He circled long enough for a few folks within the complex to stop whatever they were doing and look up with shielded eyes.

Finding it on the ground was as challenging as from the air, but by noon the next day Ray was parked outside the unmarked gate, glaring at an armed guard who was glaring back at him. After a few tense questions, the guard finally admitted that, yes, he had in fact found the place he was looking for. 'We don't allow visitors,' he said smugly.

Ray created a tale of a family in crisis and stressed the urgency of finding his brother. The procedure, as the guard grudgingly laid out, was to leave a name and a phone number, and there was a slight chance someone from within would contact him. The next day, he was trout fishing on the Flathead River when his cell phone rang. An unfriendly voice belonging to an Allison with Morningstar asked for Ray Atlee.

Who was she expecting?

He confessed to being Ray Atlee, and she proceeded to ask what was it he wanted from their facility. 'I have a brother there,' he said as politely as possible. 'His name is Forrest Atlee, and I'd like to see him.'

'What makes you think he's here?' she demanded.

'He's there. You know he's there. I know he's there, so can we please stop the games?'

'I'll look into it, but don't expect a return call.' She hung up before he could say anything. The next unfriendly voice belonged to Darrel, an administrator of something or other. It came late in the afternoon while Ray was hiking a trail in the Swan Range near the Hungry Horse Reservoir. Darrel was as abrupt as Allison. 'Half an hour only. Thirty minutes,' he informed Ray. 'At ten in the morning.'

A maximum security prison would have been more agreeable. The same guard frisked him at the gate and inspected his car. 'Follow him,' the

379

guard said. Another guard in a golf cart was waiting on the narrow drive, and Ray followed him to a small parking lot near the front building. When he got out of his car Allison was waiting, unarmed. She was tall and rather masculine, and when she offered the obligatory handshake Ray had never felt so physically overmatched. She marched him inside, where cameras monitored every move with no effort at concealment. She led him to a windowless room and passed him off to a snarling officer of an unknown variety who, with the deft touch of a baggage handler, poked and prodded every bend and crevice except the groin, where, for one awful moment, Ray thought he might just take a jab there too.

'I'm just seeing my brother,' Ray finally protested, and in doing so came close to getting backhanded.

When he was thoroughly searched and sanitized, Allison gathered him up again and led him down a short hallway to a stark square room that felt as though it should have had padded walls. The only door to it had the only window, and, pointing to it, Allison said gravely, 'We will be watching.'

'Watching what?' Ray asked.

She scowled at him and seemed ready to knock him to the floor.

There was a square table in the center of the room, with two chairs on opposite sides. 'Sit here,' she demanded, and Ray took his designated seat. For ten minutes he looked at the walls, his back to the door.

Finally, it opened, and Forrest entered alone, unchained, no handcuffs, no burly guards prodding him along. Without a word he sat across from Ray and folded his hands together on the table as if it was time to meditate. The hair was gone. A buzz cut had removed everything but a thin stand of no more than an eighth of an inch, and above the ears the shearing had gone to the scalp. He was clean-shaven and looked twenty pounds lighter. His baggy shirt was a dark olive button-down with a small collar and two large pockets, almost military-like. It prompted Ray to offer the first words: 'This place is a boot camp.'

'It's tough,' Forrest replied very slowly and softly.

'Do they brainwash you?'

'That's exactly what they do.'

Ray was there because of money, and he decided to confront it head-on. 'So what do you get for seven hundred bucks a day?' he began.

'A new life.'

Ray nodded his approval at the answer. Forrest was staring at him, no blinking, no expression, just gazing almost forlornly at his brother as if he were a stranger.

'And you're here for twelve months?'

'At least.'

'That's a quarter of a million dollars.'

He gave a little shrug, as if money was not a

problem, as if he just might stay for three years, or five.

'Are you sedated?' Ray asked, trying to provoke him.

'No.'

'You act as if you're sedated.'

'I'm not. They don't use drugs here. Can't imagine why not, can you?' His voice picked up a little steam.

Ray was mindful of the ticking clock. Allison would be back at precisely the thirtieth minute to break up things and escort Ray out of the building and out of the compound forever. He needed much more time to cover their issues, but efficiency was required here. Get to the point, he told himself. See how much he's going to admit.

'I took the old man's last will,' Ray said. 'And I took the summons he sent, the one calling us home on May the seventh, and I studied his signatures on both. I think they're forgeries.'

'Good for you.'

'Don't know who did the forging, but I suspect it was you.'

'Sue me.'

'No denial?'

'What difference does it make?'

Ray repeated those words, half-aloud and in disgust as if repeating them made him angry. A long pause while the clock ticked. 'I received my summons on a Thursday. It was postmarked in Clanton on Monday, the same day you drove him to the Taft Clinic in Tupelo to get a morphine pack. Question – how did you manage to type the summons on his old Underwood manual?'

'I don't have to answer your questions.'

'Sure you do. You put together this fraud, Forrest. The least you can do is tell me how it happened. You've won. The old man's dead. The house is gone. You have the money. No one's chasing you but me, and I'll be gone soon. Tell me how it happened.'

'He already had a morphine pack.'

'Okay, so you took him to get another one, or a refill, whatever. That's not the question.'

'But it's important.'

'Why?'

'Because he was stoned.' There was a slight break in the brainwashed facade as he took his hands off the table and glanced away.

'So he was suffering,' Ray said, trying to provoke some emotions here.

'Yes,' Forrest said without a trace of emotion.

'And if you kept the morphine cranked up, then you had the house to yourself?'

'Something like that.'

'When did you first go back there?'

'I'm not too good with dates. Never have been.'

'Don't play stupid with me, Forrest. He died on a Sunday.'

'I went there on a Saturday.'

'So eight days before he died?'

'Yes, I guess.'

'And why did you go back?'

He folded his arms across his chest and lowered his chin and his eyes. And his voice. 'He called me,' he began, 'and asked me to come see him. I went the next day. I couldn't believe how old and sick he was, and how lonely.' A deep breath, a glance up at his brother. 'The pain was terrible. Even with the painkillers, he was in bad shape. We sat on the porch and talked about the war and how things would've been different if Jackson hadn't been killed at Chancellorsville, the same old battles he's been refighting forever. He shifted constantly, trying to fight off the pain. At times it took his breath away. But he just wanted to talk. We never buried the hatchet or tried to make things right. We didn't feel the need to. The fact that I was there was all he wanted. I slept on the sofa in his study, and during the night I woke up to hear him screaming. He was on the floor of his room, his knees up to his chin, shivering from the pain. I got him back in his bed, helped him hit the morphine, finally got him still. It was about three in the morning. I was wild-eyed. I started roaming.'

The narrative fizzled, but the clock didn't.

'And that's when you found the money,' Ray said.

'What money?'

'The money that's paying seven hundred dollars a day here.'

'Oh, that money.'

'That money.'

'Yeah, that's when I found it, same place as you. Twenty-seven boxes. The first one had a hundred thousand bucks in it, so I did some calculations. I had no idea what to do. I just sat there for hours, staring at the boxes all stacked innocently in the cabinets. I thought he might get out of bed, walk down the hall, and catch me looking at all his little boxes, and I was hoping he would. Then he could explain things.' He put his hands back on the table and stared at Ray again. 'By sunrise, though, I thought I had a plan. I decided I'd let you handle the money. You're the firstborn, the favorite son, the big brother, the golden boy, the honor student, the law professor, the executor, the one he trusted the most. I'll just watch Ray, I said to myself, see what he does with the money, because whatever he does must be right. So I closed the cabinets, slid the sofa over, and tried to act as though I'd never found it. I came close to asking the old man about it, but I figured that if he wanted me to know, then he would tell me.'

'When did you type my summons?'

'Later that day. He was passed out under the pecan trees in the backyard, in his hammock. He was feeling a lot better, but by then he was addicted to the morphine. He didn't remember much of that last week.'

'And Monday you took him to Tupelo?'

'Yes. He'd been driving himself, but since I was around he asked me to take him over.'

'And you hid in the trees outside the clinic so no one would see you.'

'That's pretty good. What else do you know?'

'Nothing. All I have is questions. You called me the night I got the summons in the mail, said you had received one too. You asked me if I was going to call the old man. I said no. What would've happened if I had called him?'

'Phones weren't working.'

'Why not?'

'The phone line runs into the basement. There's a loose connecting switch down there.'

Ray nodded as another little mystery was solved.

'Plus, he didn't answer it half the time,' Forrest added.

'When did you redo his will?'

'The day before he died. I found the old one, didn't like it much, so I thought I'd do the right thing and equally divide his estate between the two of us. What a ridiculous idea – an equal split. What a fool I was. I just didn't understand the law in these situations. I thought that since we are the only heirs, that we should divide everything equally. I wasn't aware that lawyers are trained to keep whatever they find, to steal from their brothers, to hide assets that they are sworn to protect, to ignore their oaths. No one told me this. I was trying to be fair. How stupid.'

'When did he die?'

'Two hours before you got there.'

'Did you kill him?'

386

A snort, a sneer. No response.

'Did you kill him?' Ray asked again.

'No, cancer did.'

'Let me get this straight,' Ray said, leaning forward, the cross-examiner moving in for a strike. 'You hung around for eight days, and the entire time he was stoned. Then he conveniently dies two hours before I get there.'

'That's right.'

'You're lying.'

'I assisted him with the morphine, okay? Feel better? He was crying because of the pain. He couldn't walk, eat, drink, sleep, urinate, defecate, or sit up in a chair. You were not there, okay? I was. He got all dressed up for you. I shaved his face. I helped him to the sofa. He was too weak to press the button on the morphine pack. I pressed it for him. He went to sleep. I left the house. You came home, you found him, you found the money, then you began your lying.'

'Do you know where it came from?'

'No. Somewhere on the coast, I presume. I don't really care.'

'Who burned my airplane?'

'That's a criminal act, so I know nothing.'

'Is it the same person who followed me for a month?'

'Yes, two of them, guys I know from prison, old friends. They're very good, and you were very easy. They put a bug under the fender of your cute little car. They tracked you with a GPS. Every move. Piece of cake.'

'Why did you burn the house?'

'I deny any wrongdoing.'

'For the insurance? Or perhaps to completely shut me out of the estate?'

Forrest was shaking his head, denying everything. The door opened and Allison stuck her long, angular face in. 'Everything okay in here?' she demanded.

Fine, yes, we're swell.

'Seven more minutes,' she said, then closed it. They sat there forever, both staring blankly at different spots on the floor. Not a sound from the outside.

'I only wanted half, Ray,' Forrest finally said.

'Take half now.'

'Now's too late. Now I know what I'm supposed to do with the money. You showed me.'

'I was afraid to give you the money, Forrest.'

'Afraid of what?'

'Afraid you'd kill yourself with it.'

'Well, here I am,' Forrest said, waving his right arm at the room, at the ranch, at the entire state of Montana. 'This is what I'm doing with the money. Not exactly killing myself. Not quite as crazy as everybody thought.'

'I was wrong.'

'Oh, that means so much. Wrong because you got caught? Wrong because I'm not such an idiot after all? Or wrong because you want half of the money?'

'All of the above.'

'I'm afraid to share it, Ray, same as you were.

Afraid the money will go to your head. Afraid you'll blow it all on airplanes and casinos. Afraid you'll become an even bigger asshole than you are. I have to protect you here, Ray.'

Ray kept his cool. He couldn't win a fistfight with his brother, and even if he could, what would he gain by it? He'd love to take a bat and beat him around the head, but why bother? If he shot him he wouldn't find the money.

'So what's next for you?' he asked with as much unconcern as he could show.

'Oh, I don't know. Nothing definite. When you're in rehab, you dream a lot, then when you get out all the dreams seem silly. I'll never go back to Memphis, though, too many old friends. And I'll never go back to Clanton. I'll find a new home somewhere. What about you? What will you do now that you've blown your big chance?'

'I had a life, Forrest, and I still do.'

'That's right. You make a hundred and sixty thousand bucks a year, I checked it online, and I doubt if you work real hard. No family, not much overhead, plenty of money to do whatever you want. You got it made. Greed is a strange animal, isn't it, Ray? You found three million bucks and decided you needed all of it. Not one dime for your screwed-up little brother. Not one red cent for me. You took the money, and you tried to run away with it.'

'I wasn't sure what to do with the money. Same as you.'

'But you took it, all of it. And you lied to me about it.'

'That's not true. I was holding the money.'

'And you were spending it – casinos, airplanes.'

'No, dammit! I don't gamble and I've been renting airplanes for three years. I was holding the money, Forrest, trying to figure it out. Hell, it was barely five weeks ago.'

The words were louder and bouncing off the walls. Allison took a look in, ready to break up the meeting if her patient was getting stressed.

'Give me a break here,' Ray said. 'You didn't know what to do with the money, neither did I. As soon as I found it, someone, and I guess that someone was either you or your buddies, started scaring the hell out of me. You can't blame me for running with the money.'

'You lied to me.'

'And you lied to me. You said you hadn't talked to the old man, that you hadn't set foot in the house in nine years. All lies, Forrest. All part of a hoax. Why did you do it? Why didn't you just tell me about the money?'

'Why didn't you tell me?'

'Maybe I was going to, okay? I'm not sure what I had planned. It's kinda hard to think clearly when you find your father dead, then you find three million bucks in cash, then you realize somebody else knows about the money and will gladly kill you for it. These things don't happen every day, so forgive me if I'm a little inexperienced.'

The room went silent. Forrest tapped his fingertips together and watched the ceiling. Ray had said all he planned to say. Allison rattled the doorknob, but did not enter.

Forrest leaned forward and said, 'Those two fires – the house and the airplane – you got any new suspects?'

Ray shook his head no. 'I won't tell a soul,' he said.

Another pause as time expired. Forrest slowly stood and looked down at Ray. 'Give me a year. When I get out of here, then we'll talk.'

The door opened, and as Forrest walked by, he let his hand graze Ray's shoulder, just a light touch, not an affectionate pat by any means, but a touch nonetheless. 'See you in a year, Bro,' he said, then he was gone.

The Broker

John Grisham

In his final hours in the Oval Office the outgoing President grants a full pardon to Joel Backman, a notorious Washington power broker who has spent the last six years hidden away in a federal prison. It's a controversial move, but what no one else knows is that the presidential pardon comes as a result of enormous pressure from the CIA. They claim that Backman may have obtained secrets that compromise the world's most sophisticated satellite surveillance system.

Backman is quietly smuggled out of the country in a military cargo plane; he is given a new name, a new identity, and a new home in Italy. Eventually, once he has settled into his new life, the CIA will leak his whereabouts to the Israelis, the Russians, the Chinese and the Saudis. Then the CIA will do what it does best: sit back and watch. The question is not whether Backman will survive – there's no chance of that. The question the CIA needs answered is: who will kill him?

'You have to know what happens next . . . Grisham hasn't lost his touch' *Daily Mail*

'A killer combination of sheer story-telling nous and no-nonsense prose' *Independent*

'Nail-biting' *Sun*

arrow books

Ford County

John Grisham

Take a journey into Ford County with the master thriller writer.

Worldwide No.1 bestseller John Grisham takes you into the heart of America's Deep South with a collection of stories connected by the life and crimes of Ford County: a place of harsh beauty where broken dreams and final wishes converge.

From a hard-drinking, downtrodden divorce lawyer looking for pay-dirt, to a manipulative death row inmate with one last plea, *Ford County* features a vivid cast of attorneys, crooks, hustlers, and convicts. Through their stories he paints a unique picture of lives lived and lost in Mississippi.

Completely gripping, frequently moving and always entertaining, *Ford County* brims with the same page-turning quality and heart-stopping drama of his previous bestsellers, and is proof once more why John Grisham is our most popular storyteller.

arrow books

Bleachers

John Grisham

An unforgettable novel about fleeting youth, legends and heroes.

High school All-American Neely Crenshaw was probably the best quarterback ever to play for the legendary Messina Spartans. Fifteen years have gone by since those glory days, and Neely has come home to Messina to bury Coach Eddie Rake, the man who molded the Spartans into an unbeatable football dynasty.

As Coach Rake's 'boys' sit in the bleachers waiting for the dimming field lights to signal his passing, they replay the old glories, and try to decide once and for all whether they love Eddie Rake - or hate him. For Neely Crenshaw, still struggling to come to terms with his explosive relationship with the Coach, his dreams of a great career in the NFL, and the choices he made as a young man, the stakes could not be higher.

'Grisham touches the soul and scores a winning touchdown with his sixteenth novel' *Evening Standard*

'I defy even the hardest jock not to shed a tear' *The Mirror*

'John Grisham is a copper-bottomed promise of reliable storytelling' *Independent*

arrow books